The Inner Interpretation of the Holy Scriptures

Efstratios Papanagiotou

ISBN: 978-0-9859074-9-5

"The light of the soul consists in constant meditation upon the scriptures."

(Isaac of Nineveh, *Mystic Treatises*, LIII, p. 254)

Dedication

This English translation is dedicated to Theodore J. Nottingham for all his precious and heartfelt support.

The Bible verses which are used in this work are for the most part from the King James Version (KJV) but where it seems necessary, according to the ancient Greek text, other Bible versions are used such as the Young's Literal Translation (YLT), the English Majority Text Version (EMTV), the Douay-Rheims Bible (DRC) and the World English Bible (WEB).

Contents

Foreword

Lost Teachings of Ancient Christianity
By Theodore J. Nottingham

Some of the most powerful and applicable spiritual teachings of Christianity remain unknown to the general population, even after two millenia. These teachings were preserved in monasteries and were often instructions to monks on inner warfare, internal self-awareness, on ascetical efforts, and efforts of spiritual discipline for their development and awakening to spiritual reality.

These teachings were never meant to be for the few or for specially called out people, or for people with a particular vocation. These teachings are for all people, and this science of spiritual development is one that is available to humanity, not merely to those who have special access to this material. The split between the East and the West in 1054, that is, between the Orthodox and Catholic churches, in many ways cut those of us in the West off from these profound wisdom treasures which are still as valid today as they were in the 4th, 6th and 10th centuries.

Let's take a look at one of these marvelous gifts to humanity that have come down, so hidden, though they were not meant to be. One of them is known as the *Watch of the Heart*. The Desert Fathers of Christianity used this approach as a central method to help people unify themselves around the consciousness of the Divine. The Watch of The Heart translates as self-observation, that is, observation of what is actually taking place within one's psychological and emotional life. Instead of taking for granted every thought and emotion that comes to us and calling it "I", letting it take over in the present moment and cause all sorts of random havoc, we become more objectively aware of this activity within our minds and emotions through a process of inner separation. For instance, if thoughts enter that have negative and violent qualities, we consciously resist them rather than take them as a manifestation of our identity.

There is a graphic and rather crude expression of this methodology to be found in ancient writings which is as follows: When we see the snake coming in through the hole under the door -- when the thought is about to enter your heart and take you over, and cause you to act out --you must cut off the head of the snake. This forceful teaching makes it very clearly that if we allow any emotion or thought to come in unguarded and enter our minds and hearts, the result is that we ascent to it, we agree with it, accept it, receive it—only to become captives of it. So, when the suggestion which initially appears to us is assented to, we become captive to it and we act out its wrongful expression. The Desert Fathers perceived that what happens is a universal phenomena: something comes into our mind, we mull it over, we let it enter into our heart, we bond with it, and then we become the thought or emotion.

Most of you know that we often hear a piece of music in our heads out of nowhere, and we cannot even trace where it came from -- it is just stuck there. The same is true with many thoughts and emotions. Sometimes we pick them up from the environment. Think of how you feel after watching a violent horror movie. Those negative elements of fear, violence, tension or anguish fill us, and we need to be cleansed from them. So this teaching is very much a contemporary recognition of the human condition. Jesus said it loud and clear: we must cleanse the inside of the cup, meaning our inner life, our psychological life, our spiritual life. We cannot go around with heavy, negative thoughts and think that we are going to progress anywhere in the spiritual life, or please God in any way. We certainly cannot call ourselves 'religious people' when we live in these lower states of consciousness, acting out in any old way from the darkest parts of ourselves. This psychological work, from the Christian perspective is spiritual warfare, that is, the battle to lift ourselves out of anything that drags us down. In many ways, the world

We certainly cannot call ourselves 'religious people' when we live in these lower states of consciousness, acting out in any old way from the darkest parts of ourselves. This psychological work, from the Christian perspective is spiritual warfare, that is, the battle to lift ourselves out of anything that drags us down. In many ways, the world around us, our culture for example, seems to actively and aggressively seek to drag us into the lowest centers of our being. It is up to each of us to use our free will not to go that way, but to go another way, to take the Royal Road as it has been called and go the way of love instead of the way of judgment, which only leads to violence. We are not speaking merely of morality; we are talking about the purification of the heart. Purification is a key spiritual concept that we find down through the ages, and it begins with the simple practice of inner attention, of developing some kind of self-awareness and self-control that allows us to not be victimized continuously by whatever is going on around us.

Wouldn't it be wonderful if you could control yourself in such a way that throughout the day you remained consistent in your state of mind no matter what circumstances you find yourself in? For example, something as simple as having to wait in line at a grocery store and causing one to become impatient, stimulating the adrenal glands and all that which generates a state of mind that is far removed from Spirit. This is a daily work effort, and the great genius of the early teachers of Christianity was that they combined this moment-to-moment inner attention with prayer. Attention and prayer became one, so that in every moment we are conscious of the presence of God. We are in tune and in touch, invoking and enabling Spirit to work in our lives. This is, as Jesus said, a pearl of great price and truly a legacy for all people who seek that higher life which gives meaning and purpose to all that we are and to all that we do, and which enables us to consciously bring the invisible into the visible realm of reality, to become part of God's mission of loving the world as our only true purpose.

May you be self-aware and attentive in discerning and freeing yourself from anything that would hold you captive and pull you down into the darkness of any negative thought or emotion. There is help. You can find it if you honestly and with right motivation seek to live out this discipline. Through the practice of uncritical self-observation, this watching of the heart, you will find your way to The Way, to the Royal Road, to the Way of Christ, the way of self-surrender, the way of consciousness of God, and become aware of the presence of God in every moment. May you find this great gift to humanity, this revelation of truth and wisdom.

Prologue

Pursue the Love

"The Love is long-suffering, it is kind, the Love doth not envy,
the Love doth not vaunt itself, is not puffed up, doth not act
unseemly,
doth not seek its own things, is not provoked, doth not impute
evil,
rejoiceth not over the unrighteousness, and rejoiceth with the
truth;
all things it beareth, all it believeth,
all it hopeth, all it endureth.
The Love doth never fail"
(1 Corinthians 13:4-8, YLT).

The *beginning* is Love, the *way* is Love and the *end* is Love. Nevertheless, Her essential meaning is keep slipping us away; many interpretations have been given on what does really Love mean, even crimes have been committed in Her name. So in this work we shall pursue the real Love, according to the words of St Paul, *"Pursue the Love"* (1 Corinthians 14:1, YLT).

Yet, it is true that *real* Love surpasses in reality every human capacity of understanding, since *"God is Love"* (1 John 4:16). Still though, we will try with our human strength and God's Grace, to unfold the deeper meanings of the Gospel of Love; to understand the often unintelligible symbolisms which constitute the Testament of Love; and so tread Her path in order to experience the meaning of life, since Love is both the means and the End.

FIRST PART

The Mutations of Christianity

Introduction

The Triadic Perspective

In order to formulate certain significant ideas, we will use a specific terminology which is based to the known triad: spirit, soul and body (matter). This triad could be also expressed with the terms: Divine, human and subhuman (or animal) level. There is God-man or Man (Jesus Christ, Son of God), man (Adam-Eve, son of man) and "man", the subhuman (the anti-christ, the son of the devil or the son of perdition). In this point, the identification of the material level with the devil's level might seem strange, that is why a further clarification in needed.

Matter itself has nothing *evil* at all, but when it claims a higher place than the one it belongs to, then it *slanders*, it distorts the right order of things and so it consists of a delusion (*slandering*); a pretense; a fraud. That is why in this work we will use our familiar quotation marks ("") as a part of our terminology in order to reveal its disguise.

So the man who has not reached his Divine destination and so he is not a Man, but he has fallen from his rightful human level to the subhuman (animal-material) level, he will be rightfully characterized as a "man". Yet, we need to be very careful because here lurks the danger of an outer comparison between us which other than being invalid and meaningless, is also *perilous*. We should know that with a little attention which will be directed inside us and not outside us, we will easily discern that we ourselves contain these three levels: the Divine, the human and the subhuman (devilish), and we are constantly moving from one to the other. In that way we will understand that whenever we use the terms Man, man and "man" they concern first and foremost *ourselves* and not the others.

So let us repeat: Man is the God-Man (Jesus Christ-Son of God) and this is the level of our spirit, of our Real Self, of our Divine Self. In this particular level of consciousness, our spiritual organs of perception are awakened and they can perceive the corresponding spiritual realities. We are Conscious to the things of the Spirit, to Unity, to Love.

Next: man means man (the son of man). This term signifies the level of soul in which our psychological organs of perception are awakened and perceive the corresponding psychological realities. Here we are also faced with a particular level of consciousness. We are conscious to the human realities but also to division: to good and evil, to truth and falsehood, to love and hate.

And finally, "man" is the man (the son of *perdition*) who has fallen from the human (psychological) level to the animal (material) level. In this level of "consciousness" (or better, *lack* of consciousness), only our physical organs of perception are awakened which perceive only the corresponding material realities, and then, as strange as it seems, we cannot feel anything from what belongs to our human, natural level, because the corresponding organs of perception are either asleep or deadened.

For example, a torturer can torment another being only to the degree that his spirit and soul are asleep or deadened and cannot feel *anything*. That is why he can provoke pain to another being, since he cannot feel it in *any* way. He is *unable* to. And that is because his physical organs of perception *cannot* transmit him any relevant stimulus. He is deeply asleep or dead within him to the physical, psychological or spiritual world of the beings around him. He doesn't know, he doesn't *feel* what he is doing, "*Forgive them; for they know not what they do*" (Luke 23:34), and *thus* he can perform any hideous and inhuman action. It is self-evident of course, that this kind of man can only be characterized as a "man" (or devil).

This triadic perspective can be applied to almost every notion and we will be based on it in all this work. So there can be: Love, love and "love"; Life, life and "life"; Church, church and "church"; Orthodoxy, orthodoxy and "orthodoxy"; Christianity, christianity and "christianity". And also: Saints, saints and "saints", Theologians, theologians and "theologians"; Prophets, prophets and "prophets", Teachers, teachers and "teachers"; Good, good and "good"; Truth, truth and "truth".

The third level, the one in the quotation marks, can usually be rendered also with an opposite or composite word which declares its reality. That is, the "prophet" is the false-prophet, the "teacher" is the false-teacher and "good" means evil, "truth" means lie and "love" means hate.

In this point we should be reminded that the third level represents the material level which has nothing evil in itself. The evil, that is, *distortion*, begins when the material level claims inside us (and outside us) the highest place, the place of God.

So a materialist "christian" is very dangerous because through his spiritual and psychological lethargy (or necrosis) and through his materialistic perception, he distorts all the psychological and spiritual meanings of Christ's Teaching and turns them into their opposite; thus he ends up killing and torturing in the name of Love (that is, of "love", of hate). This kind of "man" cannot of course be called neither Christian nor christian, but only "christian" or more appropriately false-christian.

In the same sense, for example, there are Saints, saints and "saints".

The Saints are mostly unknown (to us) people who were freed from the darkness of their egoism and shined in the Light of their Real, Divine Self.

The saints are partly purified, really good people who exerted a positive and luminous influence in the world around them and were usually acknowledged by their fellow-men as truly remarkable men.

The "saints" are intolerant "men" in whom the degree of their "sainthood" is proportional to the degree of their fanaticism. The more fanatics they are, the more "saints" are self-presented.

Unfortunately many such fanatic "men" have been recorded in the church history as "saints" creating thus an air of disbelief towards both the saints and the Saints. It is obvious of course that the Saints are rare, whilst it's not easy to know whether the saints are more than the "saints" or the reverse.

But again let us not forget that we *all* contain *all* these three levels (Divine-human-devilish) and we express them variously...

So in the same way, whenever we are referring to the notion of Christianity, which is the main notion that we will be dealing with, the following distinction will be maintained:

With a capital C – Christianity – we will mean the authentic Teaching of Christ with its Divine origin.

With a small c – christianity – we will mean the Teaching of Christ as it was understood by its human interpreters and representatives, having therefore a human fatherhood as well which inevitably turns the great Christianity into a smaller christianity.

And the third distinction is the one which puts "christianity" in its quotation-bonds and is related to the distorted version of christianity (first Christianity gets inevitably smaller as it is understood by men and then it is distorted as it is misunderstood by "men").

In a few words, we have Christianity which is from God, christianity which is from men and "christianity" which is from "men" or from the devil, if you prefer.

The history of Christianity (from God) in the outer level begun and ended with the life of Jesus Christ and in the inner level is preserved up today in the few hearts of those who put (choose) God above themselves.

The history of christianity (from men) begun after the life of Christ. Some of its few but strong remnants managed to survive through many hardships and trials up today, since for the most part it has been supplanted by the history of "christianity" (from the devil) which led a parallel life to christianity, managing from time to time to brush it aside more or less, overtaking *proudly* its place.

In reality, we can only study the history of christianity and "christianity". The History of Christianity is in essence invisible, from our human eyes at least.

The history of christianity has been studied extensively and the conclusions differ to a great extent, which is reasonable and inevitable since they are based to our subjective human perspectives.

Yet, in relation to the history of "christianity" we can easily ascertain with a brief, *impartial* look that "christianity" *demonized* everything: man, love, music, arts, science, nature, other religions, the *others* in general and even life herself. Anything that Christianity came to sanctify and elevate, "christianity" tarnished and belittled it, or rather shattered it.

That is why in this first part our main concern will be to study the basic mutations to which christianity was subjected to with the result of being enslaved to its quotation-bonds as "christianity".

Survival

*"Render unto Caesar the things which are Caesar's;
and unto God the things that are God's"* (Matthew
22:21).

At 313 AD Imperator Caesar Flavius Valerius Constantinus Augustus (the full name of Constantine I when he became monocrat at 324 AD) along with Licinius (another contender of the imperial throne) issued with the Edict of Milan the *tolerance of all religions*, continuing in that way the politics of the emperor Galerius, a harsh persecutor of christianity, whom before he died (311 AD) issued an edict of tolerance of the christian religion in order to ensure the much desired and of vital significance peace (*Pax Romana*) of the roman empire.

The Edict of Milan secured the safe existence of the new religion of christianity and offered it also the opportunity to acquire some unprecedented up to then benefits from the new emperor Constantine, something which led it gradually to claim or just accept the place of the official state religion of the roman empire which was offered to it by a next emperor (caesar), Theodosius I, at 380 BC.

Temptations always prepare fitly the ground before they attempt their decisive effort of our enslavement. They begin (usually in a moment of weakness or *need*) with a *provocation* which exhibits their lures and they are strengthened as we *assent* to their study, resulting in claiming a "rightful" place in our heart, until their final attempt of captivity to which we usually *surrender* unconditionally, perhaps even with a sense of relief (after so much resistance to them).

So it was in the case of christianity as well. After *three centuries of persecutions* and hardships, the "perfect" temptation appeared in the most fitting moment: the temptation of all the powers and the kingdoms of the world, *"The devil taketh him up into an exceeding high mountain, and sheweth him all the kingdoms of the world, and the glory of them; And saith unto him,*

"All these things will I give thee, if thou wilt fall down and worship me" (Matthew 4:8-9). After 300 years of cruel persecutions, it was too easy for christianity to give in to the temptation, basically for two reasons: on the one hand because it would wonder whether it would be able to keep surviving through all these persecutions and on the other hand because it would probably thought that if it were established as the official religion of the roman state, it would be able to spread in the whole world, according to the word of Christ, *"And this gospel of the kingdom shall be preached in all the world"* (Matthew 24:14). Yet, Christ had indicated explicitly and categorically the path of *persecutions*, *"Blessed are they which are persecuted for righteousness' sake: for theirs is the kingdom of heaven. Blessed are ye, when men shall revile you, and persecute you, and shall say all manner of evil against you falsely, for my sake. Rejoice, and be exceeding glad: for great is your reward in heaven: for so persecuted they the prophets which were before you"* (Matthew 5:10-12), and *not* the path of caesar (emperor), of the world, *"If the world hate you, ye know that it hated me before it hated you. If ye were of the world, the world would love his own: but because ye are not of the world, but I have chosen you out of the world, therefore the world hateth you"* (John 15:18-19).

Several scholars have asserted that the emperor Constantine acknowledged the value of christianity and distinguished it from the other religions, offering it its first benefits, for the sake of the empire. But this view seems extremely implausible (and even if it's true, the conclusion is still the same) because the *world* (which the roman empire represented), that is, the *earthly perspective*, is destined to "hate" the things of God, that is, the *heavenly perspective*, *"because the carnal mind is enmity against God"* (Romans 8:7), simply because it *doesn't understand* it. The only way to accept it, is to *lower* it down to its level, as was the case.

Instead of the roman empire ascending to the level of christianity, christianity descended to the level, to the "height" of the roman empire. And since then its slow but steady mutation begun.

That is why Jesus Christ distinguished strictly these two levels by saying to render unto the emperor the things of the emperor, that is, to render the things of the world to the world, and the things of God to God, *"Render unto Caesar the things which are*

Caesar's; and unto God the things that are God's" (Matthew 22:21).

Jesus had already being through the temptation of following an earthly path of power and declaring *through it* the Kingdom of Heaven. But He knew that the mixture of levels, and basically the one who wants the higher to descend to the level of the lower, can only bring forth dangerous mutations.

For example, the way of the world, of the earth, includes propaganda, imposition and domination. The way of God, of Heaven, includes ev-angelism, that is, the annunciation of the good news, love and humbleness. If we combine these two paths, the result will be trying to *impose* Love, which is unfeasible and by definition contradictory, and leads inevitably to Her distortion.

That is what happened to christianity. It succumb out of fear (the first mistake) of extinction and out of the desire (the second mistake) to be spread, to the temptation of following an earthly path (the third mistake) and thus receive all the powers and kingdoms of this world.

It became the official state religion of the roman empire, or more correctly, it was imposed as the official religion with the threat of death for those who continued their ancient religious practices and watched complicitly the violation of the very edict (of Milan) which ensured it a breath of life, from the emperor Theodosius I, whom outlawed the ancient religions, opening thus the way for the persecutions of the *heathens* and the destruction of their libraries, monuments and temples.

This temptation to which christianity succumbed, perhaps justifiably, had of course its unavoidable consequence: the mutation of christianity into "christianity" and its captivity in its quotation-bonds from which it still hasn't managed to escape, for the temptation in which it succumbed before 1.700 years, is still enticing it with the exactly same allurements.

The question: "What would have happened to christianity if it had chosen the strait gate and the narrow way (of the persecutions), instead of the wide gate and the broad way of loss?" is still extremely opportune and in a certain way painful since its answer is tragically obvious.

So, for christianity to survive, it had to keep being crucified perpetually? Unfortunately, yes! Since this was the path that its

Founder walked and indicated. And He was very clear in His words: *"Whosoever will save his life shall lose it: and whosoever will lose his life for my sake shall find it"* (Matthew 16:25).

After three centuries of persecutions, christianity became afraid for its soul and wanted to save it and so lost it. But it can always repent and deny its "self" in order to come to its Self and thus return to its Father.

> *"And having come to himself, he said, "How many hirelings of my father have a superabundance of bread, and I here with hunger am perishing, having risen, I will go on unto my father, and will say to him, Father, I did sin to the heaven, and before thee, and no more am I worthy to be called thy son; make me as one of thy hirelings". And having risen, he went unto his own father"* (Luke 15:17-20).

It can always reject its quotation-bonds and stop being "christianity". But in order to be re-born it must first be crucified; and keep being crucified again and again and again. For only in that way it will be able to keep being re-born.

Treasures upon the Earth

"Lay not up for yourselves treasures upon earth, where moth and rust doth corrupt, and where thieves break through and steal: But lay up for yourselves treasures in heaven, where neither moth nor rust doth corrupt, and where thieves do not break through nor steal: For where your treasure is, there will your heart be also" (Matthew 6:19-21)

In order for "christianity" to be able to reject its quotation-bonds that keep it captivate and become again christianity, with the aim to be, at least, a conveyor of Christianity, it must simple deny its "self". It should become again "poor in spirit" both metaphorically and literally.

It should become again humble in heart as well as in appearance. A resounding example of the mutation of christianity are the clothes of "christianity". The words of Jesus, *"But he that is greatest among you shall be your servant"* (Matthew 23:11), indicate that christianity was destined to constitute a religious *service* and not a religious *authority*, *"Ye know that the princes of the Gentiles exercise dominion over them, and they that are great exercise authority upon them. But it shall not be so among you: but whosoever will be great among you, let him be your minister; And whosoever will be chief among you, let him be your servant: Even as the Son of man came not to be ministered unto, but to minister, and to give his life a ransom for many"* (Matthew 20:25-28). But when it was imposed as the official state religion, it got enchanted by the power of authority and in time got jealous also of the clothes of the imperial dominion. Gradually it shed the simple and plain vestments with which it was dressed and started to accept bishop miters, vestments inlaid with gold, and other similar bonds. It preferred to imitate the vainglory of the emperors, who ensured its "survival" after all, than keep imitating the humbleness of its Founder, who was indicating its constant crucifixion. And since it could no longer imitate the crucifixion of its Lord, it began *pretending* it! In the place of the crown of thorns which was put on Christ, it wore the bishop miter which has its origin in the imperial crown, and claimed that its luxurious religious crown symbolizes the crown of thorns (!) of Christ, reaching thus to the ultimate limits of mutation!

But the path of *metanoia* (repentance) is always open. And in this case a first and extremely simple, that is why so difficult, step in this conversion, is for "christianity" to reject first of all its outer bonds, that is, its *outer* wealth.

It should distribute it to the poor and never desire it again, so it can be restored to its initial place but also so it can *do good*. It must become merciful so it can obtain mercy, "*Blessed are the merciful: for they shall obtain mercy*" (Matthew 5:7). It must stop playing the role of the rich man in the parable (cf. Luke 16:19-31) and play again the role of the poor Lazarus for which it was destined all along.

But it shouldn't come as a surprise if "christianity" upon hearing these words goes away sorrowful, as did this other rich man who wanted a place in the Kingdom of Heaven (cf. Matthew 19:22), for it has also great *possessions* both in material and psychological (that is, in its idea for itself) wealth. And we all know that golden cages are on the one hand limitative since *they are* cages but on the other hand they are gold.

Indeed, this idea of "christianity" giving back its *foreign* material wealth for the hungry to be fed and the underprivileged to be shown mercy is so beautiful and simple, and thus magnificent, which unfortunately seems very romantic or even worse, utopian.

On the other hand, the cunning (evil) thought may appear, "But the church always did and does philanthropic work". Unfortunately this work is nothing else but the feeble efforts of christianity which struggles to preserve whatever it can from its freedom; and these efforts are exploited by "christianity" so it can gather even more material treasures upon the earth, forging thus even stronger bonds for what is left of christianity.

We could imagine "christianity" as the illegitimate brother of christianity, which after having usurped the rightful place of his brother, seats glaringly as a king in his stolen throne and gives some crumbs from his gathered wealth to his wretched brother whom he keeps imprisoned. Now, his brother, the genuine heir, offers whatever he cans from the crumbs he saves but very often is so destitute himself that he ends up asking the others' mite so he can be sustained.

This is the situation in which christianity has been reduced to because of "christianity", its illegitimate brother, which has forced it to live under the shadow of these tormenting quotation-bonds.

It's necessary for "christianity" to be contrite and mourn so it can be comforted, it must deprived so it can receive, it must become humble and poor again, abandon the broad way of loss, in order to pass through the strait gate and walk the narrow way which leads to Life.

It's true that by surrendering its religious authority, that is, by cutting its bond with the secular authority, a bond (or bonds) which is based entirely on *material wealth*, "christianity" would be in imminent danger of vanishing. And this would be its salvation. The secular authority would crucify it immediately but it would be resurrected in the hearts of men and it would gain again hundreds of martyrs. Yet, the path of Truth, of Freedom, consists always of a challenge.

Indeed, what challenge would it be for "christianity" to give away its material wealth to the poor so it can benefit them, acting according to the spirit of alms (mercifulness) that it always advocates, sacrificing thus the earthly and ephemeral goods for the heavenly and eternal Goods!

What a challenge! After so many centuries of gathering treasures upon the earth, renounce them in order to begin gathering (or receiving) again humbly, treasures in Heaven!

"In leaving then these visible goods of the world we forsake not our own wealth, but that which is not ours, although we boast of it as either gained by our own exertions or inherited by us from our forefathers. For as I said nothing is our own, save this only which we possess with our heart, and which cleaves to our soul, and therefore cannot be taken away from us by any one. But Christ speaks in terms of censure of those visible riches, to those who clutch them as if they were their own, and refuse to share them with those in want. *"If ye have not been faithful in what is another's, who will give to you what is your own?"* (Luke 16:12).

(John Cassian, *Conferences*, 3, Chapter 10, pp. 324-325)

What a challenge! After so many centuries of prodigality to return back to the house of its Father (of Jesus Christ) in order to be released from its captivity and become again pure, free christianity and so remember again the Spirit of Christianity which begotten it, the Spirit of Love!

"Holy" Wars

"Love your enemies, bless them that curse you, do good to them that hate you, and pray for them which despitefully use you, and persecute you" (Matthew 5:44).

The symbol of the world, of mammon (the "god" of material wealth) is the coin, money. The symbol of Love, of God is the Cross (self-sacrifice). This is rendered with extremely clarity in the incident where Pharisees try to entangle Jesus:

"Tell us therefore, What thinkest thou? Is it lawful to give tribute unto Caesar, or not? But Jesus perceived their wickedness, and said, Why tempt ye me, ye hypocrites? Shew me the tribute money. And they brought unto him a penny. And he saith unto them, Whose is this image and superscription? They say unto him, Caesar's. Then saith he unto them, Render therefore unto Caesar the things which are Caesar's; and unto God the things that are God's. When they had heard these words , they marveled" (Matthew 22:17-22).

Why the Pharisees did marvel when they heard this?
They marveled because they understood what it wasn't understood three centuries later when Caesar Constantine introduced in his coins the symbol of the Cross (in a gold coin of

324 BC Constantine is shown to hold a spear and a cross...) a practice that was also followed by subsequent emperors. And so the symbol of God was connected indissolubly with the symbol of mammon; yet, "*No servant can serve two masters: for either he will hate the one, and love the other; or else he will hold to the one, and despise the other. Ye cannot serve God and mammon*" (Luke 16:13). And later on of course, Christ Himself was craved on the coins!

Yet, besides this trap in which christianity fell by forgetting the clear instructions of Christ, it fell also in a much worse trap when it allowed for the Symbol of Life to be connected with the practice of death. Before the Cross adorned the coins, it adorned the banners of war and the symbol of Jesus Christ, the Christogram (XP), the soldiers' shields!

That is why another necessary and of decisive significance step for christianity is to renounce altogether and forever its "right" to war. Many crimes and "holy" wars were committed by "christianity" for which christianity must again answer for, because they were again performed with its toleration. It should ask forgiveness on behalf of its illegitimate brother (which remains of course unrepentant) and trace a new course, the one which was indicated by the painful example of its Father. And not the one which has indicated by the first crusader emperor (Constantine) who used the ultimate symbol of self-sacrifice, the Cross, as a symbol of war!

There is only *one* holy war and that is the *inner* one; the war which is aimed against our superficial, acquired, false "self". There is not and there cannot be any other holy war.

God never gave His blessing, nor He will ever give it, to any kind of outer war. And this is most clearly shown by Jesus Christ when he cured one of those men that arrested Him and at the same time *reprimanded His own disciple* for his "just" defending action:

> "*When they which were about him saw what would follow, they said unto him, Lord, shall we smite with the sword? And one of them smote the servant of the high priest, and cut off his right ear. And Jesus answered and said, Suffer ye thus far. And he touched his ear, and healed him*" (Luke 22:49-51).

25

Jesus didn't turn against His persecutors as He could easily have done, as he declared with extreme confidence: *"Put up again thy sword into his place: for all they that take the sword shall perish with the sword. Thinkest thou that I cannot now pray to my Father, and he shall presently give me more than twelve legions of angels? But how then shall the scriptures be fulfilled, that thus it must be?"* (Matthew 26:52-54).

What He came to do was the work of His Father (cf. John 5:30, 10:37-38) and the work of His Father was *self-sacrifice* which leads through *forgiveness* to *Unity*. His work, in one word, was Love; that is, the abolition or transcendence of vindictiveness, hatred, hostility, human "justice" which claims "an eye for an eye".

So Love never blessed, *nor is able* to bless, any kind of crusade, conflict, war, either offensive or defensive. She can forgive crimes and murders but she cannot ever bless any kind of violent act. Love only embraces, purges, heals and *Unites*.

Disunity

Unanimity (homophony) belongs to the perception of Unity (Love) and constitutes a fruit of the Tree of Life. On the contrary, disunity (diaphony) belongs to the perception of multiplicity (duality) and constitutes a fruit of the tree of knowledge of good and evil.

Despite the fact that Christianity constitutes the Teaching of Unity, in its human level (christianity) it couldn't avoid the disputes. But whilst christianity assimilated the disagreements and claimed the unanimity, "christianity" on the other hand, was by nature disputatious and *legislated* the division (disunity) with its "holy" canons (rules).

In Reality there is only one Canon (Rule), one Law which could be expressed as: "Listen to the voice of Your Conscience". That is, listen to the voice of God inside you, to the voice of Love and act accordingly. In other words, this Law can be expressed also as: *"Thy Will be Done"*. Or as, *"Thou shalt love the Lord thy God with all thy heart, and with all thy soul, and with all thy mind. This is the first and great commandment. And the second is like unto it, Thou shalt love thy neighbour as thyself"* (Matthew 22:37-39).

In this inner, Divine level, Man has no need of outer indications, threats and punishments, for he constitutes a manifestation of the One Law, of Love. But when he falls from this level, then appears the need of rules, instructions and commandments. The more he falls, the more increase the rules.

This happens because in the fallen level he has more options than the *One Option* (the Will of Love). In this level, man acquires the knowledge of good and evil and must learn to discern in between them. So he has the possibility of good and wrong. And of course this duality results in disagreements.

In the beginnings of christianity, one of its biggest threats of survival were the disagreements and the following disunity. For disunity was completely contradictory to its message.

Disagreements existed of course in between the Apostles as well but they took care in solving them immediately based on the perception of Unity (Love). With reasoning and *dialogue* they tried to bring forth the necessary *understanding* which would lead in the unforced acceptance of a view or idea and to the indispensable unanimity.

> *"And the apostles and brethren that were in Judaea heard that the Gentiles had also received the word of God. And when Peter was come up to Jerusalem, they that were of the circumcision contended with him, "Saying, Thou wentest in to men uncircumcised, and didst eat with them." But Peter rehearsed the matter from the beginning, and expounded it by order unto them [...] When they heard these things, they held their peace, and glorified God, saying, Then hath God also to the Gentiles granted repentance unto life"* (Acts 11:1-18).

This practice was distorted in the subsequent years and the *indispensable* unanimity was perceived as *imperative* (enforce) agreement. Whoever disagreed was excommunicated and persecuted. And as the effort to impose the *correct* perception was growing, from whoever claimed it, the more disagreements and disputes were sprouting.

The result was the need of even more canons (rules) which made sure to fix even the slightest detail of the "correct" life. So more and more "holy" rules were enacted which ended up in full contradiction of their initial intention, making the words of Jesus opportune once again:

> *"Ye have made the commandment of God of none effect by your tradition. Ye hypocrites, well did Esaias prophesy of you, saying, "This people draweth nigh unto me with their mouth, and honoureth me with their lips; but their heart is far from me. But in vain they do worship me, teaching for doctrines the commandments of men"* (Matthew 15:6-9).

These rules, instead of setting the boundaries for man in order to lead him to the *inner* perception of the One Rule, they bind him so tight ending up in smothering his ability to listen internally the Voice of Love, "*Why tempt ye God, to put a yoke upon the neck of the disciples, which neither our fathers nor we were able to bear?*" (Acts 15:10). And when the Voice of Love is smothered inside us, then the voice of our egoism runs wild and excommunicates, curses and condemns the *different voices* with fury and rage, having at the same time the absolute certainty that it performs a holy duty.

"I am weary of the struggle with envy and with the *holy* bishops, who destroyed all chance of union on public-spirited grounds, and sacrificed *the cause of the faith to their private squabbles.*"

"For my part, if I am to write the truth, my inclination is to avoid all assemblies of bishops, because I have never seen any Council come to a good end, nor turn out to be a solution of evils. On the contrary, it usually increases them. You always find there love of contention and love of power (I hope you will not think me a bore, for writing like this), which beggar description; and, while sitting in judgment on others, a man might well be convicted of ill-doing himself long before he should put down the ill-doings of his opponents. So I retired into myself; and came to the conclusion that the only security for one's soul lies in keeping quiet."

(Gregory of Nazianzus, *Epistle 87 to Philagrius* & *Epistle 130 to Procopius*)

Now, let us repeat that from the moment man falls from his Divine level, he needs rules and commandments in order to walk safely in his holy, inner path which will lead him to his Lost Paradise. Yet, since all these rules constitute only a means to an end, they should gradually be lessened and condensed to the One Commandment, to Love, and not multiply. And it's self-evident that they must not be imposed. For this comes in absolute contradiction to the Law of Love. They must be voluntarily accepted through their (gradually increased) understanding. And the same goes for the acceptance of the correct-right (orthos) dogmas. *Orthodoxy* [*correct perception*, since *Orthodoxy* in Greek means "right, correct, true" (orthos) "opinion, perception, belief" (doxa)], cannot be imposed because in that way is self-refuted. An *Orthodox* cannot be intolerant; for thus he negates Love. And when we negate Love, we negate Christianity and consequently we get outside of the borders of *Orthodoxy* (*right perception and belief*).

> "One who in modern times refrains from surreptitiously introducing a dogma into the Church of God is not thereby orthodox, but an orthodox is someone who has achieved a mode of life consistent with right doctrine."

> (St. Symeon the New Theologian, *On Confession*, Epistle I, *The Epistles of St Symeon the New Theologian*, p. 55)

The Apostles emphasized constantly the need of unanimity and *endeavored* in every way to promote it because they deeply knew that one of the biggest dangers of the Teaching's survival was the disputes and *divisions*.

> "*I therefore, the prisoner of the Lord, beseech you that ye walk worthy of the vocation wherewith ye are called, with all lowliness and meekness, with longsuffering, forbearing one another in love; endeavoring to keep the unity of the Spirit in the bond of peace. There is one body, and one Spirit*" (Ephesians 4:1-4).

But their painful and moving effort was misinterpreted and in the subsequent years the notion of heresy took immense proportions and was considered by many as the worst sin. And that is because they misunderstood the *effort* for unanimity, and instead of *striving* through their own *example* (cf. 2 Corinthians 11:1-7, 1 Corinthians 9:1-27, 1 Thessalonians 2:1-12) to lead the dissidents in understanding, they gave themselves in the persecution of the so-called heresies.

Heresies

The so-called *heretics* have been mocked, persecuted and condemned perhaps more roughly than any other victimized human group. And of course "christianity" didn't escape from the application of this rule, having completely forgotten that Christianity itself was initially considered as a dangerous and sacrilegious Judaic heresy (cf. Acts 24:5).

The word *heresy*, in ancient Greek meant *choosing* – that is, free choice. So heretic is the one who doesn't accept the standard perspectives and views and makes use of his right to choose his own view.

It's true that our view determines our life. We tread the paths we see opening before us; we cannot walk on paths we do not see or perceive. And if our view is incorrect, then certainly our course will be dangerous.

On the basis of this idea, heresies—that is, the freedom to choose—and mostly the heresiarchs—the founders of the different views—were fought mercilessly. The foundation of this polemic was, as it becomes obvious, the supposed salvation of our fellow-men from the incorrect perspectives that could lead them in their destruction.

Yet, in this point there is a fundamental misunderstanding. We cannot force another man—nor there is any meaning to it—to adopt a view he doesn't perceive. That means, we cannot force him to walk on a path he doesn't see, simply because he *doesn't* see it! The only thing we can do is to drag him on it! With the result to injure him and lead him to a worse state than the one we tried to save him from.

And that is what happened historically with the persecutors of the heretics which in order to save the heresiarchs themselves or their (possible) followers from destruction they preferred to destroy them themselves!

Thousands of men suffered martyrdom from the "correct belief", heathens, pagans, idolaters, heretics, and their martyrs not only weren't considered as holy men but often they were considered as deserving their fate!

As it has been said very accurately before christianity was connected with the imperial authority, it was dangerous to be a Christian, after the connection of "christianity" with the secular authority, it was dangerous not to be a "christian"!

Yet, as real as the danger of the wrong view might be, it remains an inalienable right of every man. The word heresy itself, when it indicates the freedom of choice, it includes the possibility of wrong choice along with its possible unpleasant consequences. And this freedom of choice is endowed by God Himself; but "men" cannot perceive the greatness of Love and in their smallness they take away, as other "gods", the gifts of God and decide that it is better for a man to die (to be burned, to be crucified) than to make use, even wrongly, of his God-given right to choice.

Now, in our time we are not so "barbarians" to burn people on stake but we preserve our "inalienable right" in exerting *psychological violence* through excommunications and threats of eternal punishment in case some of our fellow-men fall in the sin of heresy, that is, in the choice of a different perspective or view, which we consider wrong.

And here lies one of our greatest weaknesses: our inability to accept the different views. What we see, that only exists; and therefore that is the only *correct* thing. And since our perception is correct, the different one can only be wrong. And if it is wrong it will surely be evil and harmful. That is why historically the conflicts and disputes between the various theological perceptions were cruel and unrelenting.

Many so-called heretics were accused for debauchery, blasphemy and sacrilege. Yet, in reality it's almost impossible to determine the truth of the claims of the various contending groups since the hideous actions that were attributed to each heretic group, were basically launched towards all directions. The first christians were accused and persecuted for the same atrocious actions that were later attributed to the various dissentient heretics.

The demonization of the other's view was and is a typical practice of the closed heart and is called, in one word, *intolerance*. But the views of humanity differ in an immense degree and if there is no tolerance to the different perceptions, then we will only be in a constant, relentless conflict. The views on the same subject might differ truly in the utmost degree. For example, the views around Jesus Christ ranged and range from seeing Him as a dangerous demagogue up to God Himself.

Even though it's true that our mentality and outlook determines in a great extent our lives, our heart's inclination and opening is what eventually decides on the result of our course. And this can be easily shown by a simple example: Who is closer to Truth, to Love: A man who doesn't believe in God but tries to be as much righteous as he can or a "man" who burns in stake his fellow-men in the name of God?

Now, the disputes and conflicts which took place (and continue to take place) in the borders of christianity were related to all of its aspects. There were disputes about the nature of Christ, the nature of God and also of the Holy Spirit; disputes about the church mysteries and practices; disputes about the Virgin Mary; disputes about the nature of man and his salvation; about the nature of the soul, as well as about her origin and destination.

To some of these different perceptions around these matters, were given names as, Gnosticism, Arianism, Nestorianism, Montanism, Sabellianism, Monarchianism, Monophysitism, Monothelitism, and others. All these words signify nothing more than different views on the same pursuits. Views (paths) that indeed might lead to the mountain's top or to the precipice; but if our mentality defines us *where* we can head, our heart defines us *how* shall we head there, which is equally, if not more, important.

That means that if we choose (mistakenly) to follow a path that leads to the precipice, our heart can save us at any time from falling, if her inclination is correct. If we choose to follow a right path which can lead to the mountain's top and our heart is closed and cruel, then we will inevitably be misled, from our very first steps, and we will be lost in the pride deviations of our "orthodoxy" (our "correct perception"). Whilst we will crawl to the foot of the mountain, we will think that we have conquered the heavenly heights. And of course, when we fall in this blind intolerance, we are more certain than ever regarding the correctness and the *infallibility* of our view.

Yet, it's obvious that the claim to infallibility, from wherever it comes from, is only a tragic consequence of the human pride. Even if we assert that our view is a revelation of God and that is where we base its infallibility, if we have even the slightest self-knowledge we will know that the revelations of God are realized always *according* to our level and so they can never be absolute and consequently infallible. What may be revealed to us today (either personally or collectively) might not be the same with what shall be revealed to us tomorrow, when we will be able to assimilate a more *solid food* (cf. Hebrews 5:12). And so our present revelation might seem inadequate or even wrong in front of the future revelation.

Once was revealed to man (according to his level) the law of "*an eye for an eye*" (cf. Leviticus 24:19-20) which was later replaced by the new commandment, "*Love your enemies*" (cf. Matthew 5:38-44). And those who claimed the infallibility of the first revelation crucified the new Lawgiver which brought a new revelation, a new perspective.

Usually we are not ready for the new revelation, and so it's reasonable to misunderstand it and bring it to our present level. For example, the narration about Ananias and Sapphira in the Acts of the New Testament (cf. Acts 5:1-11) who fell down and died upon hearing the reprimanding words of Peter is understood as an act of divine justice. The inner interpretation of this narration which indicates an inner death, an inner spiritual fall (which concerns us all directly) seems to us ungrounded and imaginary. It is much easier for us to accept the notion of the harsh and rigorous "divine" punishment than the notion of the pedagogic mercy of Divine forgiveness.

That is why for the various misunderstandings and distortions of the Christian Teaching, we cannot accuse anyone other than our own selves. The only reason for the mutation of Christianity to "christianity" is our level of understanding. And those teachers of christianity who were enlightened enough to perceive this, adjusted out of necessity its teachings to the level of the people they taught. And often they spoke openly about this adjustment which was based on the example of Jesus Christ Himself:

> "*And the disciples came, and said unto him, "Why speakest thou unto them in parables?" He answered and said unto them, "Because it is given unto you to know the*

mysteries of the kingdom of heaven, but to them it is not given. For whosoever hath, to him shall be given, and he shall have more abundance: but whosoever hath not, from him shall be taken away even that he hath. Therefore speak I to them in parables: because they seeing see not; and hearing they hear not, neither do they understand. And in them is fulfilled the prophecy of Esaias, which saith, "By hearing ye shall hear, and shall not understand; and seeing ye shall see, and shall not perceive: For this people's heart is waxed gross, and their ears are dull of hearing, and their eyes they have closed" (Matthew 13:10-15).

The only misfortune was that these teachers perhaps anticipated that the overall (inner) level of humanity would be increased sooner than it did, and that the teachings which were adjusted to her low level would soon give their place to the higher Teachings. Perhaps they couldn't foresee that the adjusted teachings would eventually be perpetuated and would claim in their turn the known infallibility. And even if they foresaw it, perhaps they couldn't prevent it.

In the beginnings of christianity, humanity was not prepared enough for the Gospel of Love which very soon was lowered to the declaration of fear and threat; for that was the level of humanity. And in order to understand even a tiny part of the Teaching of Christ, she had to reduce it to her level. That is why the Good (Joyful) News (Ev-angelia) of Christ were forced to be transmitted through intimidation and threats!

Threats

There are three kinds of call for man. One is through fear, the other through hope and the third through Love. The fear of hell (of pain) generates *need*; the hope of paradise (of pleasure) generates *desire*; and the Love of Good generates *self-sacrifice*.

In christianity these three inner levels are called "slave of God", "wage laborer of God" (or "hireling", "hired servant") and "son of God". The slave of God is the one who fulfills the commandments out of fear of punishment. The wage laborer is the one who fulfills them out of hope of reward. And the son is the one who fulfills God's Will out of the Love of Good.

> "There are three states, as St. Basil says, by which we can please God. Either by fearing Hell and therefore pleasing Him, in which case we are in the state of slave. Or, by fulfilling the commandments or benefiting by seeking the profits that we will receive as reward. In which case, we are in the state of wage labourers. Or, by pleasing God through the love of good and in that case we are in the state of the sons of God."
>
> (Abba Dorotheos, *Practical Teaching on the Christian Life*, Lesson 4, Pgh 48, pp. 109-110)

In these three levels belong the corresponding teachings. For example, in the first level corresponds the teaching of eternal hell, in the second the teaching of eternal paradise and in the third the teaching of the final restoration (apokatastasis) of all.

We experience these three levels both individually, as persons, and collectively, as humanity. Yet, it is well known that humanity as a whole stands always lower than the height that her individual cells reach.

That is why christianity addresses to the whole, to the mass and is adjusted to its level. Whilst Christianity addresses to the few who are *vitally* interested in Its Teachings and *for this reason* they can understand deeper and be more enlightened.

So Jesus taught in a different way His few closed disciples and in a different way the multitude (crowds). When He was attempting to reveal to the multitude the truths which had elevated the understanding of His disciples, they were getting immediately hostile and wanted to stone Him. For in our low level, whatever we do not understand, we are afraid of it, and whatever we are afraid of, we fight it. We want to destroy it in order to be protected by it since we feel that it threatens our existence, both the physical and the psychical.

So Christianity is forced to reduce its level, and we could say that it *alters* it temporarily so that it can make it popular, that is, accessible to the mass' understanding. It is forced to talk about heaven and hell as places of existence and not as states of consciousness. It has to talk about reward and punishment and it has to promise crowns in order to attract men and thus remove them from the precipices or else it has to use threats.

In that way christianity is placed on the level of teaching that parents must adopt towards their children. Parents are obliged to set constantly boundaries, using rewards and punishments, prohibitions and perhaps even "threats", until their children's understanding will increase and they will be able to perceive by themselves the deeper truths of life. Parents might be obliged to pretend to be harsh, angry, but they know that *they cannot*, even if they wanted, to hurt in any way their children because their love for them *doesn't allow it*! But the children *ignore* this *reality* and might even think the opposite: that their parents are capable of anything!

Now, parents are also obliged to adjust their understanding to their children's level and present it even in a simplistic form so they will be able to assimilate it. They do not underestimate their children in any way but they know that the more their children grow by assimilating knowledge the more increases their faculty of understanding. Their stomach, both the physical and the psychological, is still very weak and small and it can accept only a specific kind of food and in specific quantities.

So Christianity doesn't underestimate the mass of humanity but it's obliged to be expressed in a simplistic way in order to be digestible. Yet, it expects and anticipates her growth so she will stop to be fed with liquid food, with milk, which is easier to be assimilated, *"For everyone who partakes only of milk is unacquainted with the word of righteousness, for he is an infant"* (Hebrews 5:13, EMTV) and begin to be fed with solid food, which is heavier and deeper, *"But solid food is for the mature, for those because of their practice have their senses trained for the distinguishing of both good and evil"* (Hebrews 5:14, EMTV).

Jesus Christ is teaching in the same way and all His "threats" aim in the salvation of the hardened mass of humanity. They constitute, as it were, sledge-hammers that aim in breaking the hard shell which encompasses the heart of humanity. They are like swords that want to shed the veils that are covering her ears and eyes.

That is why in the Gospels we see all these three levels of teaching: the threat, the promise and the self-sacrifice. Christ "threatens" the deaf and blind; He gives promises to the repented; and to His beloved ones He teaches the self-sacrifice of Love.

This way of teaching aims at the same time in three things: To save humanity as a whole from her dangerous tumble; to sustain her in a relatively health state (either in majority or in minority); and to enlighten certain individual cells which sooner or later will carry along with them her rest cells towards their upward course to the Light.

These individual cells are the known *chosen* ones, *"For many are called, but few are chosen"* (Matthew 22:14) to which belong whoever *chooses* to. For these three kinds of call are bidirectional and exist as possibilities in all of us, as well as in humanity.

Unfortunately though, humanity has remained for a very long time in the first level. It's true of course that the personal time of man is different than the collective time of humanity. Humanity is certainly moving much slower than her individual cells. But when Jesus Christ appeared, humanity had already aged in the first level and 2.000 years later she doesn't seem to have made any significant progress.

Perhaps she is no longer motivated so much by fear but more by hope. Perhaps she has learned from her sufferings and has been enough disappointed from her "self" to begin coming to her Self (cf. Luke 15:17-20). Nevertheless, it's now obvious to all her cells that her time of return must by accelerated because she has already delayed too long and the consequences of her delay seem irreversible. She must start being fed with more solid food because the liquid food is good only for a certain period, afterwards appear signs of undernourishment.

Humanity starves spiritually because she is underfed too long now. Even though she has been given the Gospel of Love which could feed her generously, "I *am come that they might have life, and that they might have it more abundantly*" (John 10:10), she only assimilated only its two initial levels and even those were pretty "mutated". It's time now that she realizes deeply her need, so she can return to her Father's house in order to receive the food which was destined for her, the *Gospel of Love*.

The Gospel of Love

The external history of humanity is the history of mammon, that is, of the "god" of material wealth, the "god" of this "world". And the lesson we can derive from it is clear: As long as we will believe in matter, we will be possessed by a sense of separation, hostility, conflict, violence and unavoidable war. For in the level of matter we seem separated and so we are divided. And where there is division, discord reigns. Where there is unity, concord reigns. But we can perceive our unity only psychologically and spiritually; only through a higher, heavenly perspective. Through the perspective of matter, of the earth, we are obliged to see only division and separation, which leads us inevitably in the recording of endless volumes of external history of evil, that is, of violence, crime and bloodshed; an endless offering to the altar of mammon, to the "god" of avarice, ambition and voluptuousness.

All this however doesn't mean that matter is evil in itself or that it is a carrier of evil. Evil, that is, wrong and reversed, is our relationship with it. As long as the lower will dominate the higher, that is, as long as matter will dominate the spirit, we will record the endless history of humanity's war with its short rests of "peace".

If humanity ever reaches to *meta-noia*, that is, if she comes back to the right balance and spirit leads matter, then the external history of violence will lose is tremendous "interest" and our interest will be displaced to our internal history, which constitutes

42

an invisible course of learning having as a perpetual aim the experience of Love.

Jesus Christ came to open our eyes and ears exactly to this truly *joyful* message of Unity, of Love. He didn't come to bring another threat, and in particular the worst threat that ever existed for humanity, "If you do not follow me, if you do not believe in me, nothing will save you, you will burn *eternally* in hell". This is not a joyful message, this is the most unpleasant and dark thing that can be said to any living being. But that is the way we hear, due to our level, the Gospel of Jesus:

> *"Lord, wilt thou that we command fire to come down from heaven, and consume them, even as Elias did?" But he turned, and rebuked them, and said, "Ye know not what manner of spirit ye are of. For the Son of man is not come to destroy men's lives, but to save them."* (Luke 9:54-56)

His words don't contain neither open nor hidden threats because despite the fact that Love cannot by definition threaten, how can you possible threaten someone that he will suffer the evil he *already* lives?

If you go to someone who is unhappy and tell him, "If you follow me, you will be happy" your words do not contain any threat but only a joyful prospect. If this man was already happy and you told him, "If you don't follow me, you will be unhappy" then it's obvious that you would coercing him.

Humanity has been unimaginably violent for so many centuries and when she is tired of killing one another and lessens just a little her violence, she believes she prospers. And of course, her egoism and pride prevent her from *acknowledging* and *admitting* her immense misery and also her responsibility for it. Trapped in her "self" she perpetuates her evil and deprives herself from the gift she is being given. What worst can there be other than that? With her actions she negates her very Existence.

So Jesus Christ comes and tells us: Do not despair, there is *another* possibility, *right here* and *right now*, within you (cf. Luke 17:20-21). Within you there is an endless Source of Happiness, Beauty, Peace, Perfection, Love. The only thing you need to find It, is to renounce whatever you knew up to now; all the ugliness, the egocentrism, the pride; whatever you believed you *were*. The only thing you need is to deny your false self, your delusion, your erroneous perception, nothing else.

But we do not understand this message. That is, we do not understand that it's addressed to *us*. In the best case we think it's addressed to the *others*, that we don't need it. So we hasten to warn the "others", the "evil ones", saying, "You heard Him, repent or perish... in eternal torments."

And we keep on destroying one another, directing our wrath with extreme fury to the sinners, the heretics, the blasphemous, the sacrilegious, to the *other* religions. And we honor the bloodstained persecutors which undertake the annihilation of the profane. We consider them heroes, defenders of the true faith; we believe that God blesses them. They ask God's blessing for their "God-pleasing" work and we pray for them to be victorious in their violent wars. We praise the forbearance and magnanimity of "christian" emperors and generals who after exterminating thousands *enemies*, they spared the "life" of their captives *simply* by enslaving them.

Yet, it's requisite to understand that these "heroic" leaders were never exclusively responsible for their various bloodsheds, as much convenient as it is for our superficial eyes to credit them with the responsibility (or the glory...). They simply played the *unfortunate role* that *humanity herself* had given them. A role that is apart from the Divine Truths of Jesus Christ, as *heaven* is from the *bottoms of earth*, "*Love your* enemies*, bless those who curse you, do good to those who hate you, and pray for those who mistreat you and persecute you*" (Matthew 5:44).

Unfortunately though, all peoples, through an ego-centric perception, have admired (and admire), and even worse, have *sanctified* (and *canonized*) in their "conscience", men who happened to play extremely tragic roles regarding which we should shiver only by thinking them. They played roles through which they contribute to the annihilation of thousands of human lives. But instead of mourning and praying to be forgiven as humanity for our atrocious acts; to be forgiven for our criminal egoism which has been a source of misery and *evil* in all these centuries; we continue with a "light" heart and a "clean" but mostly proud "conscience" to admire and teach our children the "God pleasing" achievements of our intolerance.

We still haven't realized as humanity—and even more as "christians"—that every war is *domestic* (*emfylios* in Greek, which means between the same race) since we are all members of the *same human race*.

"All wars are civil wars because all men are brothers."
(François Fénelon, 1651-1715)

We haven't yet realized that every man is our brother and sister, not ideologically, not emotionally, but ontologically and spiritually. Our whole being is interconnected with every other human being.

Human beings are cells of *One* human body, of *One* Humanity.

So what do we expect that will happen to humanity when her cells are fighting each other utterly unnaturally and irrationally, without any *real* reason, simply because through their materialistic perception they see other cells as "hostile" or "friendly" to themselves without realizing at all the *reality* of the *One Humanity*?

Jesus said to His disciples to spread the Gospel of Love to the entire world. What did He mean? To subordinate everyone in the name of Love? To terrify them, "If you do not believe in God, you will burn in hell"? Of course, not. What He told them (so simple and that is why so difficult to understand) was to declare to humanity the Good News (Gospel) that *we are all One*. That if we make room in our heart for the *other* people then we will be able to hold something of the greatness of Divine Love, "*For he that loveth not his brother whom he hath seen, how can he love God whom he hath not seen?*" (1 John 4:20). If we allow to God, to Love, enter our heart, "*God is love; and he that dwelleth in love dwelleth in God, and God in him*" (1 John 4:16), we will realized our unity with everything around us and with all men, "*And the glory which thou gavest me I have given them; that they may be one, even as we are one*" (John 17:21).

Fortunately, despite the amount of distortions that the Divine Message—the Divine Joyful News—might have been subjected to in the "human" level, still remains unalterable and consists of an *eternal* chance for *metanoia*. That is to say, for choosing Beauty, Goodness, Love, since for these Divine Realities we were created for and these Realities came Jesus Christ to *revive* in the soul of humanity.

SECOND PART

Jesus Christ

Introduction

The Role of Jesus Christ

"Fear not, for lo, I bring you good news of great joy, that shall be to all the people, because there was born to you today a Saviour, who is Christ the Lord" (Luke 2:10-11, YLT).

We will never be able to understand the real role of Jesus Christ upon the earth if we do not perceive humanity as *One*, with human beings constituting cells of One Body. In antiquity there was this understanding and humanity was named as a United Whole, as One person, Adam (including of course in this name both its male and female cells).

So the role of Jesus Christ (who has been named, *second Adam*) was related to both humanity as *One Being* and with each human individually, as a unique but interconnected part or cell of it.

That is why His every work and all of His life aimed in influencing the whole of humanity-Adam but also every cell of it, that is, every individually man-Adam, both then and now, and as long as this created being, humanity, will continue to exist.

The view of humanity as One is obviously not easy; because our smallness, as her cells, doesn't allow us such a high and whole perspective. Our physical senses not only don't testify to such a unity but assure us for the opposite. Only our psychological and especially our spiritual organs of perception can inform us about this truly joyful Reality.

And that is why it remains a fact that only through this (psychological and spiritual) view of humanity and of man, we can begin to suspect and understand the role of Jesus Christ upon the earth and *within* humanity.

It is sometimes considered that there is a certain disagreement in the New Testament regarding the question, "Why was Jesus crucified?" But this disagreement is only seeming because the New

Testament is simply presenting the three basic reasons for the coming of Jesus to earth, which if seen isolated might in some way seem contradictory. Yet, in reality they constitute three aspects or three stages of the same Plan.

Jesus Christ came to earth mainly for three reasons:
1) To save "humanity" from its sin (missing of the Mark).
2) To indicate (teach) the path of Love.
3) And to walk Himself the path of Love so He can (re)open it for humanity.

All these three reasons were based on Love: they incarnated Love and through Love were realized, having as a zenith the act of Crucifixion. These three stages found their fulfillment on the Cross and of course to the subsequent Resurrection and Ascension. These three stages correspond to each man's personal journey of transformation and could be defined as *purgation*, *illumination* and *Theosis*.

So in the next three chapters we will examine briefly these three aspects of Jesus Christ's role upon the earth.

The salvation of "humanity"

The first stage is the one of purgation.

When Humanity falls from her height she becomes humanity and gradually mutates into "humanity". Consequently she starts accumulating an extremely negative load (of negation of Good) which brings inevitably its fruits: disorder, confusion, conflict, ugliness and darkness. From this evil, she surely needs to be purged, but not to satisfy the Creator of everything, who forgives and shows mercy to all, but in order to escape herself from its fruits. It is known and constitutes a Divine Law that what we sow, we reap, "*Whatsoever a man soweth, that shall he also reap*" (Galatians 6:7). So if we sow discord, we reap conflict. And if we sow conflict, we reap misery and death. From this sin (missing the Mark) of "humanity" came Jesus Christ to save us.

In spite of whether we accept the myth of Fall (which is interpreted variously) it's obvious to every impartial view that Humanity doesn't stand in Her height. And despite of when exactly did this Fall might happen, it's a still a fact that on Jesus'

time, Humanity had already degenerated into "humanity".
Violence, bloody conflicts and disorder was the rule, something
which applied to all the known "human" history up to then.

So it's truly impossible to imagine the negative load that had
accumulated until the appearance of Jesus on earth. Every murder,
every violent act (physical and psychological), every kind of
negativity; all accumulated in the soul of humanity ready to burst
out leading it to her self-destruction.

Jesus Christ came to take up this load and defuse it through
His Sacrifice. And He undertook this mission not in order to satisfy
a "God" of wrath and violence but due to the compassion of the
God of Love. And the Will of God was to save us from our
blindness, from our missing of the Mark, because we were heading
straight to the cliff, to self-destruction.

The description of His Passion and Crucifixion renders very
plainly and humbly this great self-sacrifice. It presents us
essentially a Being who takes up, as it is said, the sin of the world,
not only physically but mostly psychologically.

The Passion and Crucifixion of Jesus haven't been yet
adequately understood, because for the most part we remain carnal
men and so we perceive everything through our carnal eyes. So in
relation to the self-sacrifice of Jesus, we emphasize His bodily
Passion and Crucifixion. But His physical pain, without being
underestimated in the least, is incomparable before the
psychological pain he took up, especially during His crucifixion.

"We should not think only of the bodily sufferings
which Christ endured at his Passion – the scourging, the
stumbling beneath the weight of the Cross, the nails, the
thirst and heat, the torment of hanging stretched on the
wood. The true meaning of the Passion is found, not in this
only, but much more in his spiritual sufferings – in his
sense of failure, isolation and utter loneliness, in the pain
of love offered but rejected. [...] Full weight must be
given to Christ's words at Gethsemane, "My soul is
exceedingly sorrowful, even unto death" (Matt. 26:38).
Jesus enters at this moment totally into the experience of
spiritual death. He is at this moment identifying himself
with all the despair and mental pain of humanity; and this

identification is far more important to us that his participation in our physical pain."

(Bishop Kallistos Ware, *The Orthodox Way*, pp. 79-80)

From the Gospels descriptions we can perceive that during Jesus' Crucifixion an *immense* amount of *vital energy* was released, *"The earth did quake, and the rocks rent; and* the graves were opened" (Matthew 27:51-52). After Jesus experienced within Him all the accumulated negativity of "humanity", he transform it into a positive energy, through pain, that is, through Understanding and Forgiveness, *"Forgive them; for they know not what they do"* (Luke 23:34). The Forgiveness to which He referred wasn't only related to His Crucifixion but also to all the accumulated negativity of "humanity". It was related to the *missing of the Mark* (sin) of "humanity" which had reversed the values and instead of being a carrier of life and creation, she consisted a carrier of death and destruction.

All that immense negativity which had accumulated and waited to burst out on the unsuspected humanity, was released and transformed into positive energy, giving her a new breath of life and a new chance of resurrection of her deadened spirit, *"The graves were opened; and many bodies of the saints which slept arose, and came out of the graves after his resurrection, and went into the holy city, and appeared unto many"* (Matthew 27:52-53).

This was the real pain of Christ: accepting to feel within Him all the evil of "humanity" and understand it, forgive it and transform it; to take it upon Himself, turn it against Himself, so it won't be turned against humanity. That is why the Crucifixion was necessary, which He finally accepted, after asking (three times) to complete His work without it; for He knew what it meant in its essence. It wasn't just an issue of feeling some temporary physical pain, it was an issue of experiencing all the "human" evil and mostly its consequences. So he directed the fruits of the "human" missing of the Mark (sin) against Him, so they won't be directed against humanity herself and thus destroy her.

"Totally, unreservedly, he identifies himself with all man's anguish and alienation. He assumed it into himself, and by assuming it he healed it. There was no other way he could heal it, except by making it his own."

(Bishop Kallistos Ware, *The Orthodox Way*, p. 80)

In an infinitesimal, comparatively, degree, many of us have perhaps felt a corresponding experience when we intervened in a negative situation and accepted to take up a part of its unpleasant load so the evil won't be inflated leading to even worse situations. So now we can deeper understand the words:

"For God so loved the world, that he gave his only begotten Son, that whosoever believeth in him should not perish, but have everlasting life. For God sent not his Son into the world to condemn the world; but that the world through him might be saved" (John 3:16-17).

The self-sacrifice of Jesus Christ wasn't aiming in appeasing the "divine" wrath, as the hard-hearted "human" perception has thought from time to time, but instead in making known His infinite Mercy; it was an Act of Love.

"The aim of Christ's coming is identical with the aim of the world's existence: the cause of both is the manifestation of God's great love."

(Isaac the Syrian, *Ascetical Writings*, from the Second Part, 3rd treatise,

4th century of Gnostic Chapters, Chapter 79, Vol. 2b, p. 119)

By taking upon Him (voluntarily) the negative burden of humanity, Jesus gave her another unprecedented chance to be led (voluntarily) to her Divine destination. He intervened for her forgiveness, not because God wouldn't forgive her, by exactly because God forgave her. He didn't intervene between God and men but between "men" and the consequences of their misguided actions. The negative load which had accumulated, the evil that had been sown, had to be defused; someone had to reap it. And Christ reaped it with His self-sacrifice which He taught as a Path of Salvation both for humanity as a whole and for man personally.

The Path of Humanity

The second stage is the one of illumination.

Adam (that is, humanity and man) negates (disobeys) the Spirit (God) and dies to his spirit by tasting the fruit of egoism and its will. So he loses the essence and reverses the values. He falls; and sees things reversely. He sees them upside-down. Instead of spirit, soul and body, he becomes body, soul and... dead to spirit. Consequently he misses the Mark, that is, the Meaning of his existence. He sees from outside to inside instead of seeing outside from inside. He raises himself and the creation, and lowers or rejects the Creator; and so he cuts off himself from the Source of Life. He negates the Creator of Life and therefore Real Life, and "lives" in death. Whilst he was created to be a carrier of Creation, he degenerates to a carrier of negation of Creation, that is, to a carrier of destruction.

So Jesus Christ comes as second Adam, constituting the head (or the spirit) of the One Humanity and restores the order. He resurrects the deadened spirit of humanity and shows it the path to its Rebirth; the path of Self-Sacrifice, of Love.

> "If the divine Logos of God the Father became son of man and man so that He might make men gods and the sons of God, let us believe that we shall reach the realm where Christ Himself now is; for He is the head of the whole body (cf. Col. 1:18), and endued with our humanity has gone to the Father as forerunner on our behalf."
>
> (St Maximos the Confessor, *On Theology and the Incarnate Dispensation of the Son of God*, Second Century, Text 25, p. 143, Vol. 2, Philokalia)

The entire Teaching of Christ revolves around the notion of *self-sacrifice* as a necessary element for that state of being which

He calls Love. *Love means Unity* (with God, with our neighbor, with creation) and Unity entails self-sacrifice; that is, *self-surrender*. It entails to be given completely to the object of our Love; not to be lost in it. Love doesn't imply annihilation. For if we lose ourselves in something, then we don't have anything to offer it, because what we really have to give is our Self. So Love (Unity) doesn't mean loss but *Enlargement*. Love brings forth the realization that we are essentially *One* with everything; that there is not really a separation between you and me, yet without losing or confusing our personal identities but constituting parts of the same Whole.

So Christ teaches that in order for man-Adam to be reborn (resurrected) he needs to die (be crucified) to his old man of egoism that disobeyed God who indicated him to be fed from the fruit of Life, of Unity and started being fed by the fruit of death, of multiplicity.

In order for the *original sin (missing of the Mark)* to be effaced (collectively and personally) it needs to be understood. In this understanding was aiming Jesus' Teaching which had not only to be transmitted but also to be *experienced*. It's not enough to know Jesus' Teaching or to "believe" in Him. Nor it is enough to thank Him for His self-sacrifice if we don't give it the value and meaning it deserves. And for this to happen, *we ourselves* ought to walk His Path, both personally and collectively.

The Theosis of Humanity

The third stage is the one of *Theosis*, of union with God.

The story of Bible illustrates the psycho-spiritual history both of humanity as a whole and of man as an individual person. Every man who is born lives from the *beginning* the story of the Bible internally, that is, psychologically and spiritually.

Man could be illustrated with a circle:

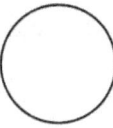

The inner centre of the circle illustrates his heart, his psycho-spiritual centre. And we could say that the periphery of the circle symbolizes his body and his physical senses:

As man is born in the material world, he follows a course which begins from his centre, from his heart, from his Paradise (in his heart he is united with God and remains pure and innocent, *naked*) and without knowing it he reaches to the limits of himself:

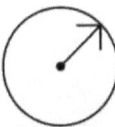

And next he comes *out of himself*:

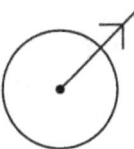

He turns his attention outwards; he worships the external Creation and so loses his Self, his heart, *"For where your treasure is, there will your heart be also"* (Matthew 6:21). This results in being delusive and lost, forgetting thus the Paradise as well as the Path to it.

Yet, when he begins to be disappointed, one way or the other, from the outside, he longs for the return to his initial inner Paradise; he longs for the Lost Innocence. Jesus tells us, *"Verily I say unto you, except ye be converted, and become as little children, ye shall not enter into the kingdom of heaven"* (Matthew 18:3), which means, unless you return to your initial pure Centre.

The path which man follows to go outside is also the path of his return. And this path is connected essentially with the totality of himself, therefore his outward state (since his attention is drawn towards all possible external directions) is more like this:

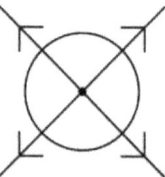

So initially he returns to the periphery of himself through *self-concentration*:

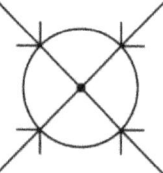

And begins to look for his inner path in order to return to his centre, to his heart and so (through *prayer*) to his initial Union with God, more mature this time, that is, more *conscious*.

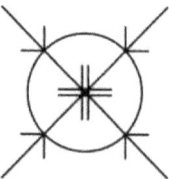

His initial state of purity and innocence constitutes his state before the fall, his Edenic state. His subsequent extro-version constitutes his fallen state. And his return constitutes his Rebirth in his Father's bosoms, his Resurrection and Salvation. By returning to his Centre, he is reborn as a new psycho-spiritual being!

All the aforementioned apply also to humanity.

It's very difficult, almost impossible, to see humanity as *One Being*; as difficult as it is for one of our cells to perceive that we are in all One Man. So we can only conclude through reasoning the existence of a Whole (in which we constitute only an infinitesimal member) but we cannot even speculate to the least what its form might be!

Man is composed of human cells (physical-psychical-spiritual) and so humanity is composed of men-cells. Our cells live and die but our Whole continues to exist. The same is true for humanity. Her cells live and die but the Whole continues to exist and to grow; not necessarily evolve in the positive sense we usually attribute to the word, because it might grow for better or for worse, as it is true for every individual man.

Now, the course either of a man or of humanity is eventually *overall*. That is, man follows eventually the path that one or more of his cells have traced; in the sense that one of our sides indicates a path and if it persuades our other sides as well, they will, sooner or later, follow it. So if the Divine Spark (Jesus) inside us, convinces us to follow it, gradually all our cells-sides will submit to it and will form One Body (psycho-somatic and psycho-spiritual). The same happens with humanity; that is why it's been said that man cannot be saved alone but only as a Church, that is, as *One Body*.

Jesus Christ is that Being, that Divine cell of humanity which returns to her Centre, opening the path of return for all her cells-beings. After Christ follows a pyramid of cells which in the Gospels is symbolized by the following hierarchy: There is the multitude (crowds), then follows the large circle of the seventy disciples, next the small circle of the Twelve Disciples, then we have the three closest Apostles, Peter, James and John, one of which, John, is shown as His beloved disciple and he is the one that is supposed to have written the fourth Gospel which is considered as the deepest and more spiritual one. And John of course is named also *Theologian*, because in his Gospel we read the Logos (Word) about God (Theos).

So we are being taught that man cannot do anything by himself. He needs also the other cell-humans because altogether we constitute inseparable members of the same Whole. Indeed, the more spiritual men-cells of humanity might have a lead, as is the case with one man as well, but eventually all the men-cells are destined to follow this course of return to the Lost Innocence, to Unity.

Jesus Christ wanted to experience the Truth Himself and then transmit it, initially, to few men-cells, so the healthy inoculation of the entire humanity can begin. He came to implant (or revive) in the soul of humanity the seed of Love. He came for humanity to be (re)united both with herself and with God.

> "Indeed, the Savior endured His sufferings so that '*He should*
> *gather together into one the scattered children of God*'
> (John 11: 52)."
> (St Maximos the Confessor, *Four Hundred Texts on Love*, Fourth Century, Text 17, p. 102, Vol. 2, Philokalia)

> "In His love for man God became man so that He might unite human nature to Himself and stop it from acting evilly towards itself, or rather from being at strife and divided against itself, and from having no rest because of the instability of its will and purpose."
> (St Maximos the Confessor, *Various Texts on Theology, the Divine Economy, and Virtue and Vice*, First Century, 47, p. 174, Vol. 2, Philokalia)

> "However, as we have seen, when examining the teaching of St. Maximus on creation, Adam was destined to unite in his own being the different spheres of the cosmos, in order that deification might be conferred upon them, through union with God. If these unions or successive "syntheses" that surmount the natural divisions

are brought about by Christ, it is because Adam failed in his vocation. Christ achieves them successively by following the order which was assigned to the first Adam.

By his birth of the Virgin, He suppressed the division of human nature into male and female. On the cross He unites paradise, the dwelling place of the first men before the fall, with the terrestrial reality where the fallen descendants of the first Adam now dwell; indeed, He says to the good thief, "today thou shalt be with Me in paradise", yet he nevertheless continues to hold converse with His disciples during His sojourn on earth after the resurrection. At His ascension, first of all, He unites the earth to the heavenly spheres, that is to the sensible heaven; then He penetrates into the empyreum, passes through the angelic hierarchies and unites the spiritual heaven, the world of mind, with the sensible world. Finally, like a new cosmic Adam, He presents to the Father the totality of the universe restored to unity in Him, by uniting the created to the uncreated. In this conception of Christ, as the new Adam, who unifies and sanctifies created being, redemption appears as one of the stages in his work, a stage conditioned by sin and the historic reality of the fallen world, in which the incarnation has taken place."

(Vladimir Lossky, *The Mystical Theology of the Eastern Church*, pp. 136-137, St. Vladimir's Seminary Press)

"He recapitulated everything in a divine way in Himself

and showed that the whole creation is one."

(Maximus the Confessor, *On Various Questions of St. Denys and St. Gregory*, Question 103, pp. 431-433, Vol. 14D, Philokalia)

In this point it might be important to examine briefly the known question, "And what was happening before Jesus? Men couldn't be saved?" which relates also to the saying, *"I am the way, the truth, and the life: no man cometh unto the Father, but by me"* (John 14:6) which seems strangely exclusive or at least has been a foundation for many *intolerant misunderstandings* of Jesus' Gospel.

> "That the complete knowledge of the law was implanted in man at his first creation, is clearly proved from this; viz., that we know that before the law, aye, and even before the flood, all holy men observed the commands of the law without having the letter to read."

> (John Cassian, *Conferences*, 8, Chapter 23, p. 385)

As a man can have his personal before Christ and after Christ period (in the sense of his spiritual awakening and metamorphosis) so humanity has her own before Christ and after Christ period. And as it's true for a man that God was there for him and acted dynamically in his life (despite whether he could realize it or not) both in his before and after Christ period, the same goes for humanity, which manifested from her very beginning her inner and spiritual pursuits.

One, at least, common element of all *spiritual* traditions is the following: That there is another invisible world beyond this material visible world that is revealed by our physical senses, with which we can be related.

So all the spiritual traditions are referring essentially to this invisible world and map it. Now, we know that even though the maps of earth are referring to the same object as well, other than that they differ greatly in the destinations they depict, in their way of approach but also in their accuracy. The same is true about the spiritual traditions which map the inconceivably beautiful world of Heaven (of Spirit) yet they also differ in the destinations they depict, in the ways of approaching them and of course in their accuracy.

Christianity is often accused that it constitutes in reality a synthesis of various mythological elements but also of ideas of preceding religions and traditions. So we can trace in it similarities and parallelisms, for example, with the ancient Greek, the Buddhist, the Egyptian traditions and also with others. In this point there is of course a danger which has been called *parallelomania* and indicates the obsession of seeing parallelisms where they don't exist. Nevertheless, it's true that there are a lot of similarities in the description of the Christian drama with other corresponding descriptions of preceding spiritual traditions. These similarities have been interpreted variously, to such an extent that they have been attributed even to the cunningness of the devil itself!

Yet, the deeper interpretation of these parallelisms can be traced in a saying of the Gospels which is often repeated and says that all must be done in a *specific* way in order for the Scriptures to be fulfilled, *"But all this was done, that the Scriptures (of the prophets) might be fulfilled"* (Matthew 26:56).

The saying that, *"the Scriptures might be fulfilled"*, means to be *effected*, to be *realized*, that is, to acquire *Flesh and Bone*. And here they are obviously meant all the real Holy Scriptures and not only the Judaic; all those real Scriptures that depict with mythological narrations and allegories the inner course of man who is resurrected from being a "man" and becomes again a God-Man (or Man).

The essential difference of Jesus Christ from the mythical saviors is that they constitute model-images, whilst Christ appears in *Flesh and Blood* and He Himself walks the Path till the very end!

And we need to be very careful here because the internalization of Jesus' Life which we must experience psychologically and spiritually, has led eventually some people in negating His historical reality. Jesus Christ lived truly as a man (and Man, that is, God-Man) upon the earth, otherwise *it wouldn't be possible* for the spirit of humanity to be revived. His life and drama were historical events which transcend nevertheless the limits of history, that is, space and time, and constitute a live experience of humanity which should be re-experienced internally by each of her cells; without though forgetting its dimension in space-time because then we forget (and thus we question) the redeeming self-sacrifice of Christ.

So the Way existed before Christ as well and it was taught through myths, allegories and religions; and there were always those who walked (internally) upon it. Jesus simply walked it until its ultimate *end* and in its fullness (internal and external) opening completely the way for *all* humanity.

So all the subsequent (but also the preceding) real spiritual teachers, taught, in one way or the other, the Way of Jesus, since this Path includes all the real spiritual paths which constitute reflection-rays of the same Royal Way and lead eventually to the same Centre.

That is why Jesus claims, "I am the Way" indicating the Way He (re)opened in which He constantly calls us to follow Him. And at the same time, when the Apostles tell him: "*Master, we saw one casting out devils in thy name; and we forbad him, because he followeth not with us*" (Luke 9:49), He replies, "*Forbid him not: for he that is not against us is for us*" (Luke 9:50), implying that *acting* in the name of Jesus Christ, is directly related to what His name *indicates*. And His name indicates Love; since He is the Son of Love.

So whoever acts in the name of Love, that is, whoever walks the Path of Unity, whichever path-ray he might follow, he will end up in the same Centre. Thus all the *real* spiritual paths constitute a form-aspect of the Path of Jesus and lead safely to their Mark, since only through the Path of Jesus—that is, all the real spiritual paths—can someone reach to God, to Life.

Jesus walked all the Way from the Absolute Beginning till the Absolute End, but if we decide to follow Him, it doesn't matter so much if we will be able to follow Him absolutely (if that's ever possible…) for wherever we get, if we follow in His footsteps, it's worthy: Jesus tells us, "*In my Father's house are many mansions*" (John 14:2) and so each one can have his own specific destination and *his own perfection* to which he is called. Each one performs a specific role in the *one body* of humanity and so he is called to make use of his own *talents*. He is called to walk his own inner path, for as Jesus indicated, it's not enough to worship Him externally, "*And why call ye me, "Lord, Lord" and do not the things which I say?"* (Luke 6:46) but we are called to *follow* Him by *applying*, internally first and foremost, His Teaching:

> *"Not every one that saith unto me, "Lord, Lord" shall enter into the kingdom of heaven; but he that doeth the will of my Father which is in heaven"* (Matthew 7:21).

THIRD PART

The Inner Interpretation of the Gospel of Love

"Do not approach the words of the mysteries,

contained in the Divine Scriptures,

without prayer and asking God's help,

but say: "Grant me, O Lord, to be open

to receive the power contained in them."

Regard prayer as the key to the true meaning

of what is said in the Divine Scriptures."

(St Isaac of Syria, *Early Fathers from the Philokalia*, p. 271)

Introduction

The interpretation of the Scriptures

"Wherefore on those passages which are brought forward with a clear explanation we also can constantly lay down the meaning and boldly state our own opinions. But those which the Holy Spirit, reserving for our meditation and exercise, has inserted in holy Scripture with veiled meaning, wishing some of them to be gathered from various proofs and conjectures, ought to be step by step and carefully brought together, so that their assertions and proofs may be arranged by the discretion of the man who is arguing or supporting them. For sometimes when a difference of opinion is expressed on one and the same subject, either view may be considered reasonable and be held without injury to the faith either firmly, or doubtfully, i.e., in such a way that neither is full belief nor absolute rejection accorded to it, and the second view need not interfere with the former, if neither of them is found to be opposed to the faith."

(John Cassian, *Conferences*, 8, Chapter 4, p. 377)

It's a fact that the Word of God in one thing and its *interpretation* another.

The Word of God might be specific but Its interpretations are multiform and multidimensional. So it's a sign of *pharisaism*, that is, of arrogant hypocrisy, to claim an interpretation and when it is questioned: "Why do you claim this? How do you know it's true?" to respond: "For that's what the Word of God says". The honest answer should be: "For that's how *I understand* the Word of God".

Christianity is the Word of God; the various christian dogmas are Its human interpretations and these can be God-inspired or not, and when they are, this can be in a greater or lesser degree.

Another fact: Each interpretation claims for itself the correctness, and often the infallibility, but mostly what we call *Divine inspiration* (*Theopneustia*). For Divine inspiration is eventually the ultimate judge of its *ortho-doxy* (correct perception).

Now, if an interpretation appeals to few or many people usually doesn't affect it, for both of these situations turns them on its behalf. If it has few followers, then they are the few chosen ones who have gotten away from the masses. If it has many followers, then it makes known its prevalence (that is, its correctness) through the force of the crowd. The natural consequence of this situation is for each interpretation to perceive the other interpretations as wrong or delusive.

So it's natural to wonder: "And what can be done? Which is interpretation is the correct one? They cannot all be correct when they disagree with each other."

This is a difficult question but with one certain, indirect, answer: Whoever claims the infallibility of his own interpretation, will be isolated easily and quickly by his fellow-men who perceive things differently and thus he will walk the dangerous path of "being right", that is, of "*I know* what is right and all the others are wrong".

"No one from those who interpret the Holy Scripture

should interpret anything as if it could not be interpreted differently."

(Maximus the Confessor, *To Thalassius on Various Questions of the Divine Scripture*, Question 21, Comment 12, p. 133, Vol. 14B, Philokalia)

So in this work there is nothing more that another attempt of interpretation. And so this attempt is subject to the effect of the above facts:

First of all it claims the Divine inspiration, that is, the correctness. But it is not interested in its overall or partial acceptance since it knows that if it wants (to fall in the trap) it can turn both of them for it.

And secondly it tries not to claim the infallibility, being aware that as much Divine inspiration an interpretation might claim, it never ceases to correspond to the human weights and measures. As much Divine inspiration can a human heart hold, such it is given and its works are always proportional.

And let us not forget that the criterion for every interpretation was and is the same: "*If this counsel or this work be of men, it will come to nought: But if it be of God, ye cannot overthrow it; lest haply ye be found even to fight against God*" (Acts 5:38-39).

Three Levels of Interpretation

"The right way, then, to read the Scriptures and extract their meaning, so far as we have been able to discover from examining the oracles themselves, appears to be as follows: Solomon in the Proverbs gives a rule respecting the Divine doctrines of Scripture to this effect: *"Do thou thrice record them with counsel and knowledge that thou mayest answer with words of truth to those who try thee with hard questions"* (Proverbs 22:20-21). A man ought then in three ways to record in his own soul the purposes of the Holy Scriptures; that the simple may be edified by, as it were, the *flesh* of Scripture (for thus we designate the primary sense), the more advanced by its *soul,* and the perfect by the spiritual law, which has a shadow of the good things to come. For the perfect man resembles those of whom the Apostle speaks: *"Howbeit we speak wisdom among the perfect; yet a wisdom not of this world, nor of the rulers of this world, which are coming to nought: but we speak God's wisdom in a mystery, even the wisdom that hath been hidden, which God foreordained before the worlds unto our glory"* (1 Corinthians 2:6-7), from the spiritual law which hath a shadow of the good things to come (Cf. Hebrews 10:1). As man consists of body, soul, and spirit, so too does Scripture which has been granted by God for the salvation of men."

(Origen, Chapter 1.11 from *The Philocalia of Origen*, the anthology of texts which was compiled by St. Basil of Caesarea and St. Gregory of Nazianzus)

There are three levels of interpretation: the physical-material (literal), the psychological (moral) and the spiritual (allegorical). We could name the physical level, *exoteric*, the psychological, *mesoteric* and the spiritual, *esoteric*. With the term *exoteric*, we mean that it refers to things *outside* us. The term *mesoteric* indicates an intermediate level of our being which is not *exoteric* but neither constitutes our innermost depth. The term *esoteric* refers to our very depth, to *our very selves*.

In the physical-literal level correspond the historical facts that might be real or *fabricated*, that is, *adapted* to the needs of the aiming meaning which is initially the purgation of man (and humanity) and thus his betterment (which includes however the possibility of his worsening, cf. Matthew 12:43-45).

> "Scripture interweaves the imaginative with the historical, sometimes introducing what is utterly impossible, sometimes what is possible but never occurred. Sometimes it is only a few words, not literally true, which have been inserted; sometimes the insertions are of greater length. [...] And not only did the Spirit thus deal with the Scriptures before the coming of Christ, but, inasmuch as He is the same Spirit, and proceedeth from the One God, He has done the same with the Gospels and the writings of the Apostles; for not even they are purely historical, incidents which never occurred being interwoven in the "corporeal" sense."

(Origen, Chapter 1.16 from *The Philocalia of Origen*)

In the psychological level correspond all the moral meanings which aim in the illumination of man and thus relate to his *meta-noia*.

In the spiritual level correspond all the deeper internal meanings which aim in his *metamorphosis* and thus in his *Theosis*. The spiritual meaning is mostly what we call allegorical and refers to two realities, one of which is related directly to our inner world and the other indirectly, since it deals with the illustration and the narration of Jesus Christ's drama.

The material level of interpretation, the literal one, is based on the perception of our physical senses and thus in the *mind of the senses* which is the *carnal mind*. In this level we perceive only what is revealed by our (bodily) senses: what we can see, hear, smell, taste and *touch* (cf. John 20:24-29). Whatever is beyond the world of the senses, *we cannot feel it*. We may "believe" in its existence but in essence we ignore it. *It doesn't touch us.* And this is because it hasn't any access to us, since the necessary organs for its perception are either *asleep* or *deadened.*

The psychological level of interpretation is based on the perception of the psychological organs. That is, it is mostly based on our thinking and feeling. It structures our psychological mind. But this level is not, as it were, entirely *self-luminous*, in the sense that it receives influences either from down below or from high above. It constitutes an intermediate level of our whole being and so it's destined to turn either to one or the other direction. That is why it is influenced from below, from our carnal mind, or from above, from our spiritual mind. And according to the influences it receives, it forms its conclusions, its psychological world.

The spiritual level of interpretation is based on the perception of our spiritual organs which function only when they are connected with their Creator, with the Spirit. There are no words that can describe accurately these organs of perception but there are words that attempt to render something of their function, like *in-tuition, in-sight, awareness.* Therefore, since the spiritual level of interpretation is related directly to the Reality of the Spirit, we could say that its conclusions are based essentially on Divine Revelation and so on Divine Inspiration (*Theopneustia*).

The physical-material (exoteric) level of "interpretation" doesn't need any deepening to understand anything. What it reads, that it is. What is been told, so it is. It *doesn't really interpret* anything; it accepts everything as they "are", *unassimilated.*

The psychological (mesoteric) level searches, learns, asks and struggles to *understand* whether its influences come from below (carnal mind) or from above (spiritual mind). It questions and disbelieves, and *thus* interprets, and *thus* is fed. And according to its final nourishment, carnal or spiritual, brings forth its corresponding fruits.

The spiritual (esoteric) level of interpretation is the deepest one. It struggles with all its strength to transcend all limitations in order to deepen its relationship with the Spirit and thus derive from there its nourishment, its *invigoration*. And this struggle of transcendence takes place internally; it is related directly to *us*, to what we *are*.

In this point we should define a little more what do we mean with the term *inner (esoteric) interpretation* which obviously refers to our *inner* world.

Our carnal mind is incapable of perceiving the notion of an inner world and thinks that the reference to our interior concerns only our inner organs and perhaps our thoughts and feelings which are explained however on the basis of the biochemical procedures of our physical organs.

"What does inner world mean? The interior of my body? But this is so limited... what could happen in there?" is wondering the mind of the senses without being able to grasp that the world of our soul and spirit is vast and incredibly rich.

When we lack the inner understanding of the Holy Scriptures, the inner interpretation of the Divine Words, that is, in what way do the Divine Teachings correspond *inside us*; in what do they aim and in what part *within us* do these narrations address; how do the spiritual revelations map our inner world; then we commit the fatal mistake of interpreting the Holy Scriptures in an *external* way. For example, if they describe battle scenes, we perceive them externally as battles that took place in the past or that will take place in the future, instead of seeing them as *inner battles* that we need to conduct *today* with our own "self".

So when our perspective is thus reversed and from internal becomes external, instead of conducting a Holy War against our ego-centric will in order for the Will of God, that is, Love, to prevail inside us, we conduct instead a "holy" war against the other people, in the name of Love!

And here is detected the basic *sin* (*missing of the Mark*) of christianity: It gave the biggest emphasis to the external, literal (carnal) interpretation and so mutated gradually into "christianity". Considering that the inner interpretation is more *indigestible* from the masses of humanity, it preferred to emphasize the external, literal, interpretation which is more digestible; that means, which doesn't need struggle and effort to be assimilated. Yet, in that way it gradually forgot its deeper interpretation—the one which concerns *ourselves*—and shifted unconsciously all the weight outside us. Everything happened and happens outside us—the

Birth of Christ, His Baptism, Teaching, Transfiguration (Metamorphosis), Crucifixion, Resurrection, Ascension, Second Coming—we don't have to do much; we only need to "believe". In what? In what the Word of God *says*, that is, in Its letter. Yet, what matters is the *Spirit of the Word* and not Its letter.

Our carnal mind studies the "words" and thinks that it will understand. It thinks that it needs to hear, to understand. It's enough to learn in order to know. Not that the words are not important, since when they are distorted they lead to dangerous misunderstandings. Yet, the real essence is to be found in the understanding of the *heart*. Words are important but the *essence* is in their *meanings*, which could be rendered with other words as well, of any language and of any era; and the Divine Meanings aim in building a bridge (or restoring the fallen bridge) between the human spirit and the Divine Spirit. If they succeed then the words are abolished (transcended) and Revelation takes their place.

The Divine Truths are springs of Spirit which aim in (re)creating that Source of Life within our inner world, through which our deadened spirit will be revived. They constitute seeds of Spirit which will grow into the Divine Tree of Life—if they fall on good ground (cf. Matthew 13:3-9), that is, on the well-prepared human soul—from which our starving spirit will be fed.

So we begin to realize deeper that the *Incarnation of the Divine Word (Logos)* is directly related to the *depths* of our inner world. We don't really need the Son of God to explain us the laws of the basic human morality. This is before our sight (theoretically at least...) and is connected mainly with the Old Testament of humanity:

> "Whoever accepts, according to Christ, the Holy Scripture as soul, should also be exercised diligently to the interpretation of the names, so he can decipher all the meaning of what is written in the Scripture; if of course he is interested in the exact understanding of what has been written and not according to the Judaic way to lower the height of Spirit to the body and to the earth and to enclose the divine and immortal promises of the *noetic* goods in the

corruption of the temporary, as some of our own, so called Christians, mistakenly think, declaring thus that their title as Christians is pseudonym, since they appear to have negated completely its strength and walk the opposite to Christ path, as the word shall prove in short.

For if along with the other mysteries, which no word could approach, God came, after He became a man, also for this, to fulfill the law spiritually by abrogating the letter and to establish its life-giving element, I mean of the law, and to elevate it by abolishing the deadly—the deadly element of the law, according to the divine apostle is the letter, and again the life-giving element according to him is the spirit; for he says *"the letter killeth, but the spirit giveth life"* (2 Corinthians 3:6) —so they have clearly undertaken the opposite fate of Christ and they ignored the entire mystery of His incarnation, those who buried the strength of their intellect to the letter only, since they didn't want to be in His image, after His likeness (cf. Genesis 1:26) but because of their relation to earth, which is the letter, they rather preferred to be earth, according to the threat, and to return unto the earth (cf. Genesis 3:19), instead of being caught away into heaven, I mean the Spirit, in the air, that is, the *noetic* illumination, "with the clouds", that is, with the higher contemplations, *"to meet the Lord in the air and so ever be with Him"* (1 Thessalonians 4:17)."

(Maximus the Confessor, *To Thalassius on Various Questions of the Divine Scripture*, Question 50, pp. 357-359, Vol. 14B, Philokalia)

The Divine Word is requisite to explain us the Divine Laws of our inner Conscience, of the Voice of God inside us, when we have lost all touch with Her. The Divine Word is necessary to release us from the captivity to our ego-centric "self". We need Him to teach us anew what we know deep inside us, the Law of Love; and to direct us towards what we have been driven away from as prodigal sons, towards the Kingdom of God. This is truly a worthy reason for the Incarnation of the Divine Word and constitutes a really soul-saving intervention.

On the contrary, the external narrations and the external miracles do not profit us much and often they become a subject of dispute and mockery. That doesn't mean of course that we should reject them or that they do not have their right place, but our priority should be to the *inner meanings* of the Divine History of the Son of God which are truly soul-salutary and cannot be disputed or mocked by whomever experiences them, for then they are raised into objective truths and realities.

These are the *holy* things we should not give to the *dogs*, and the *pearls* we should not cast before the *swine*, which might indeed exist externally but in essence are to be found mainly *internally, within ourselves*:

> "*Do not give what is holy to the dogs; nor cast your pearls before swine, lest they trample them under their feet, and turn and tear you in pieces*" (Matthew 7:6)

The aim of symbolism

"For many reasons, then, the Scriptures hide the sense.
First, that we may become inquisitive, and be ever on the
watch for the discovery of the words of salvation. Then it was
not suitable for all to understand, so that they might not
receive harm in consequence of taking in another sense the
things declared for salvation by the Holy Spirit."

(Clement of Alexandria, *The Stromata*, Book 6, Chapter 15,
p. 509)

Holy Scriptures are named essentially those writings which 1)
derive their origin from the Divine Inspiration, 2) refer to the
transcendental Truth, 3) have a multidimensional meaning, that is,
in many levels at the same time since the transcendental Truth
cannot be expressed directly and entirely through human words.
These particular characteristics of the Holy Scriptures bring forth
the need of symbolism which is used mainly for three reasons:

1) For the protection of their meaning.
2) For its better transmission and assimilation.
3) For lending it a diachronic and universal character.

In the first level, the one of protection, symbolism functions as
the hard shell of a seed. With the use of various allegories and
difficult to understand symbols it attempts to keep away from the
untrained eyes and ears those meanings that they could
misinterpret and distort if they received them unprepared. They
could even mock them or even worse turn against them.

"Divine Scripture is to be interpreted spiritually and the
treasures it contains are revealed only through the Holy Spirit
to the spiritual. Hence the unspiritual [*psychic* (psychological),

in the Greek text] man cannot receive the revelation of these treasures (cf. 1 Cor. 2:14). The ceaseless flow of his own thoughts makes it impossible for him to understand or listen to anything said by someone else. For he lacks the Spirit of God, that searches the depths of God (cf. 1 Cor. 2:10) and knows the things of God. He possesses only the material spirit of the world, full of jealousy and envy, of strife and discord; and for this reason he thinks it foolish to enquire into the sense and meaning of the written word. Unable to understand that everything in divine Scripture concerning things divine and human is to be interpreted spiritually, he mocks those who do interpret it in this way."

(Nikitas Stithatos, *On Spiritual Knowledge, Love and the Perfection of Living*, One Hundred Texts, 78, p. 165, Vol. 4, Philokalia)

For example, the Fall of Adam is presented in an extremely brief and simplistic way, whilst it contains a vast depth of meaning. So for those who are unprepared to perceive its meaning, it remains just a trivial fairy-tale. Or they perceive it literally and without understanding it they reproduce it, contributing thus to its spreading. They might not really understand it but at least do not alter it. They transmit it as they received it; unassimilated on the one hand but on the other intact.

But the most important function of this effort of protection is related again to *ourselves*. The deaf and blind who don't understand are *us*; those sides of us that aren't yet ready to perceive the deeper meaning of the Scriptures. And it is precisely from those sides that the Holy Scriptures need to be protected from, until the stony ground of our soul softens and is able to accept the seeds of the Divine Word.

Inside us are, first and foremost, the dogs which must not be given the holy things and the swine before which we must not cast the pearls so they won't turn and tear us in pieces, which means, to reduce the Divine Meanings into the level of human wisdom and claim proudly, "Jesus says some nice things but others before him have said them as well", "What was Jesus? A good man; a rebel; a philosopher. He didn't say anything remarkable". And so we lose once and for all the chance to be fed from the Divine Word; we pass Him by. We pass by the Tree of Life and we are fed by the tree of knowledge of good and evil, by the worldly and human wisdom, condemning thus our spirit to a perpetual starvation.

If we turn inside us we will locate without difficulty the multitude, the Pharisees and the scribes, etc, which are described in the New Testament, that is, all those aspects, from the courser to the subtlest, which are ready to reduce, to stone and to crucify the Divine Meanings; and then we will understand the initial purpose of the parables and the cryptic symbols which clothe the Holy Scriptures.

In the second level, the symbolisms aim in the deeper assimilation of the Holy Meanings. Initially we understand intellectually and usually we stop there. We think we have understood because we've learned. And very soon we discover the great chasm between our theory and our action. And then we might realize that we haven't felt what we have understood, or what we *think* we have understood, because the next and deeper level of understanding is the one which is related to the heart.

> "The authority of Holy Scripture says on those points on which it would inform us some things so plainly and clearly even to those who are utterly void of understanding, that not only are they not veiled in the obscurity of any hidden meaning, but do not even require the help of any explanation, but carry their meaning and sense on the surface of the words and letters: but some things are so concealed and involved in mysteries as to offer us an immense field for skill and care in the discussion and explanation of them."

(John Cassian, *Conferences*, 8, Chapter 3, p. 376)

Intellect understands through words.

Yet, the heart understands through images and symbols. It is necessary for the intellect to understand so it can participate in the life of the spirit but the real life of the spirit begins when the heart understands the truth. And the understanding of the heart takes place in a deeper than the verbal level. It takes place in the symbolic level which even though it can be expressed again in words, in reality it describes a living image which can enter into the heart and there bring forth its fruits thus creating understanding.

For example, we have the image (which is conveyed of course verbally) of the prodigal son who returns to his Father who accepts him joyfully, forgiving him for everything. The meaning of this narration could be described simplistically with the following words:

Man is alienating from God and spends meaninglessly his God-given potential until he reaches to wretchedness and then decides to return to God, who accepts him back without a second thought and with absolute joy.

The meaning of these words is clear for the intellect but for the heart all this doesn't really mean anything. It doesn't touch her because it doesn't consist of *her language*; so she cannot *see* its meaning for the heart understands through images and not through words. The heart *sees*, she feels; she doesn't *listen*, she doesn't think.

So when she *sees* the image of the prodigal son, which contains a *thousand words*, then and only then she can understand. And the heart feels only what she lives. That is, when we reach to the point of *feeling* as prodigal sons, only then we will truly understand. So the image of the parable of the prodigal son remains stored and protected inside us, and waits for the time that it will find a fertile ground to grow its roots, and then it *is revealed* to us. Then we *see* it, because we feel it. And that's how is explained the paradox of using often images from the Holy Scriptures to describe our experiences whilst we claim that we are non-religious or atheists. We might feel *prodigal sons* (and *daughters*); we might refer to the *cross* we bear; we might talk about the *heaven* or *hell* we experience; without realizing that in this way we testify to the objective value of the Scriptures' symbolism.

We should note here that the images of the Scriptures are offered to the heart through a verbal description and not visually, so the intellect can participate in the work of understanding. The intellect presents the images to the heart and so it understands as well (by rationalizing the meaning of the verbal image). Otherwise, if we were given just a visual image, the intellect would be in danger of being excluded from understanding and sooner or later it would raise its objections. So the verbal images of the Scriptures are one of the most effective ways of teaching.

Of a Teaching that is destined to be diachronic and universal and in this point we come to the third aim of symbolism. The Holy Scriptures are related both to man as a person and to humanity as a whole, so they are obliged to seek a way of expression that transcends the limitations of time and space, of era and place. They address to all men, of all seasons, irrespectively of their manners and customs, their culture and perceptions. They have an objective character because they are related to the expression of the Truth, so they must find a way to transcend the subjective meanings of the human language of every era.

For example, we can easily ascertain the confusion that prevails about the meanings of terms like, spirit, soul, mind (nous). Yet, symbols like, bread, water, wine, vineyard, mountain, valley, night, serpent, fish, remain diachronic and universal, despite their interpretations. When they are placed in the context of a specific Teaching, of a specific expression of the Truth, they can come to life and gradually be experienced by the heart who seeks honestly their correct interpretation. Let us offer a clearer example: The word "soul" which can be found in many passages in the Gospels (cf. Matthew 6:25, 10:39, 16:25-26) is rendered as "life"; but these are two very different words, with very different meanings. Accordingly, there is a very important passage in the Gospel of John which contains a very deep dialogue between Jesus and Peter and uses the words "love" and "philo" ("kissing") altering them very purposefully, but they are both rendered with the word "love" because the word "philo" ("kissing") has a very different meaning in our days. Words like, *philosophy* (love of wisdom), *philology* (love of words), *philokalia* (love of beauty), are examples where the word "philo" is used as a prefix and denotes also *love* but of another kind (or level). We could say perhaps that it has more the sense of affection or caring. In Greek the word for "friend" is "philos" and the word for "kissing" is "philo".

But if we render both words ("love" and "philo") with one and the same word, then a very significant part, if not all, of this dialogue's meaning is lost. Here we use the rendering of the English Majority Text Version of the Bible which attempts to retain something of the original meaning:

> *"So when they had eaten breakfast, Jesus said to Simon Peter, "Simon, son of Jonah, do you love Me more than these?" He said to Him, "Yes, Lord; You know that I care for You" ["philo"—"I have affection for You" in the World English Bible]. He said to him, "Feed My lambs." He said to him again a second time, "Simon, son of Jonah, do you love Me?" He said to Him, "Yes, Lord; You know that I care for You." He said to him, "Shepherd My sheep." He said to him the third time, "Simon, son of Jonah, do you care for Me?" Peter was grieved because He said to him the third time, "Do you care for Me?" And he said to Him, "Lord, You know all things; You know that I care for You." Jesus said to him, "Feed My sheep"* (John 21:15-17).

On the contrary, words like bread, fish, son, Father, mount, etc, cannot be rendered differently and remain intact through the passage of two thousand years both regarding their meaning and their (often manifold) symbolism. Concluding, it becomes obvious when we begin studying the Scriptures with sincerity and as much impartially as we can, that their larger part is not intended to be perceived literally.

> "There are some which, unless they are weakened down by an allegorical interpretation, and softened by the trial of the fire of the spirit cannot become wholesome food for the inner man without injury and loss to him; and damage rather than profit will accrue to him from receiving them: as with this passage: *"But let your loins be girded up and your lights burning;"* (Luke 12:35) and: *"whosoever has no sword, let him*

sell his coat and buy himself a sword;" (Luke 22:36) and: *"whosoever taketh not up his cross and followeth after Me is not worthy of Me"* (Mathew 10:38) a passage which some most earnest monks, having *"indeed a zeal for God, but not according to knowledge"* (Romans 10:2) understood literally, and so made themselves wooden crosses, and carried them about constantly on their shoulders, and so were the cause not of edification but of ridicule on the part of all who saw them."

(John Cassian, *Conferences*, 8, Chapter 3, p. 376)

There are stories which insult not only our reason but often our morality, and are rendered in such a simplistic way as if provoking us to see *behind* or *beyond* their appearance. There are evident exaggerations which reach the limits of naivety for the mind of our senses, which is destined to be offended and abandon his search so that the psychological or spiritual mind will be able to take control. This procedure of course doesn't happen immediately and we might often need even years until our sensual mind abandons the reins and some deeper parts of us take control.

"And who is so silly as to imagine that God, like a husbandman, planted a garden in Eden eastward, and put in it a tree of life, which could be seen and felt, so that whoever tasted of the fruit with his bodily teeth received the gift of life, and further that any one as he masticated the fruit of this tree partook of good and evil? And if God is also said to walk in the garden in the evening, and Adam to hide himself under the tree, I do not suppose that any one will doubt that these passages by means of seeming history, though the incidents never occurred, figuratively reveal certain mysteries."

(Origen, Chapter 1.17 from *The Philocalia of Origen*)

The Scriptures are not meant to make this work easy for us; on the contrary, they are intentionally designed to make our effort as harder as possible in order to awaken our depths. They want to engage our whole being in the effort of their interpretation. They are uncompromised and willing to remain hermetically sealed for us, until we are ready for them; instead of giving in to our downgrading and degeneration. That is why they provoke us on purpose, mainly with their simplicity, but also with their immorality; they confuse us and appear themselves contradictory; until we either abandon or surrender to them with all our soul, and with all our intellect, and with all our heart.

The Image of the New Testament

The external, literal perspective is incapable of making the necessary inner connections. When it sees two externally unlike evidences referring to the same thing, it cannot connect them despite how obvious and simple their inner connection might be; that is, their deeper and essential connection.

For example, some biblical scholars claim that the four Evangelists should be examined separately for only in that way are distinguished their really different points of view and that it is wrong to connect them for in that way we do them an injustice. Many scholars stress the dissimilarity of the Gospels and spot what they perceive as incompatible differences and often as contradictions. But this approach is a characteristic of our physical mind which cannot proceed in non-obvious connections as clear as they might be psychologically and spiritually.

A relative example is the cause of Judas' betrayal. In one Gospel Judas seems to betray Jesus due to his greediness. In another he seems to be carried away by the devil. For the materialistic mind this is an irreconcilable difference (since it can see *only one thing at a time*) and any attempt of synthesis is for it an arbitrary innovation.

The idea that the devil might carried Judas away through his greediness, seems to it an imaginative invention and rejects it, claiming that these kinds of interpretation is like writing our own new gospel which has nothing to do with the intentions of its writers. If next it hears that the material greediness of Judas which is illustrated with the insignificant, for its time, amount of 30 pieces of silver, could consist of a symbol of a psychological greediness, for the physical mind this idea is absolutely *ir-rational* and therefore *sense-less*.

But this is reasonable because anything that doesn't belong in the borders of the "rational" mind is obviously for it *ir-rational*; whatever is beyond the mind of the material senses is *sense-less*. And the borders of the materialistic mind are specific and limited;

they are related only to what can be touched and seen, and this is what the physical mind perceives as "rational".

So it will pose "rational" questions, such as, "And why didn't the writer say clearly that the devil carried Judas away through his greediness? Why shouldn't exist just one Gospel starting its narration in a correct order up to the end, including all the events, instead of having four Gospels, all with different omissions and clear differences? Why didn't they name things for what they are? Why should they write one thing and mean another? One writer says one thing and the other says another." There are "rational" questions of the materialistic mind which can be answered only *psychologically*.

There are three possibilities for man:

One is to *accept* the perspective of the materialistic mind with its clear, tangible limits and reject as non-sense the evangelic narrations.

The other is to *deny* the materialistic perspective based on some undefined notion of "faith"—which in reality will consist of a disguised fear—and answer with the clinching argument, "This is God's will" to all the aforementioned difficult questions. And this will have the unpleasant result of mangling our finite but useful sensual mind.

And our third possibility is to *transcend* (accept *and* deny) the perspective of the materialistic mind by realizing that it might has its uses but at the same time it's very limited, and thus we will penetrate to the deeper layers of our mind.

For it is true that the reason of the materialistic mind is absolutely useful and serves exactly in this, in showing us the obvious: that the narrations of the evangelic stories are indeed "ir-rational" (or rather *super-rational*) and that something is very wrong with their form, structure and content.

This is its work and there it should stop; but if it rules us, it doesn't stop there and continues entering in areas which don't concern it. Seeing all this irrationality of the Gospels' morphology, the materialistic mind decides that they are fairy-tales for children and naïve adults.

"Sometimes the things selected taken literally are not true, but are even unreasonable and impossible [...] but that no one may suppose us to make a sweeping statement and maintain that no history is real, because some is unreal [...] or that what is recorded of the Saviour is true only in a spiritual sense [...] we must add that we are quite convinced of the historical truth of certain passages."

"Still, there are places where the careful reader will be distracted because he cannot without much labour decide whether he is dealing with history in the ordinary sense, or not, and whether a given commandment is to be literally observed, or not. The reader must therefore, following the Saviour's injunction to search the Scriptures, carefully examine where the literal meaning is true, and where it cannot possibly be so."

(Origen, Chapters 1.20, 1.21 from *The Philocalia of Origen*)

But we didn't answer to the question: Why shouldn't there be one Gospel correctly structured from beginning to end, and we have instead four different ones with so many contradictory data? Because what is being given us is in reality an *image* (a puzzle) broken in thousands of pieces which we must reconstruct *inside us*.

And this is the function of our materialistic mind: to let us know that we are faced with a mixed image. Yet, its reconstruction constitutes a function and work of our psychological and spiritual mind. "And if that is so, why are we being given a mixed image? What's the *reason*?" the materialistic mind will hasten to ask.

For *its reconstruction inside us, equals to the (re)structure of our soul*; equals to our cultivation and growth, to our evolution; equals to our metamorphosis or our second birth.

Yet, this answer won't mean anything to the materialistic mind. At first it will startle it and so it will stand in awe for a minute before the unknown, the invisible, the incomprehensible, but soon it will come to it "self" and it will reject this answer as a fanciful non-sense since it will be outside of his sense's range.

That is why the materialistic mind considers itself very intelligent, whilst in reality is itself *sense-less* as *far* as the psychological mind is concerned, in the same way that the psychological mind is *sense-less* as *far* as the spiritual mind is concerned, since each level cannot enter into the range of perception of the mind-level above it.

Still, we should remember the use of the reason of the materialistic mind. When the materialistic mind is healthy and in our service, it informs us that something goes wrong, that things are in disorder; it presents us the obvious unreasonableness of the Gospels and calls us to take a stand.

But if our materialistic mind rules us, it will reject what it doesn't understand; whilst if it is mangled by fear and weakness, it will accept as reasonable something which is clearly unreasonable. In that case, it will still not perform correctly his function because it will perceive the mixed image as a perfect and in order image and it won't get into the trouble of reconstructing it properly.

The materialistic-external mind is called to perceive the obvious external irrationality and then the psychological-internal mind is called to perceive its hidden, internal meaning. For the Gospels do not address to the external man but to the internal (psychological and spiritual) and they are written in a language and in a way that the inner man can grasp. But since the inner man needs the outer one so he can interact with the stimulation and the influences of the outer world, the Gospels are written initially in the form of external language which can be perceived by our external man but in an "irrational" way so they can awaken and attract the internal man which will seek internally now their meaning.

But is this meaning specific and clear? Or each man can derive and perceive his own meaning? The answer is simple and unequivocal. This Meaning is absolutely defined and specific, in other words, *Objective* and in no occasion subjective.

That means that the image which must be recreated internally is predefined. Its tinge or touch, or something similar, might be different but we are always faced with an objective tone of Love. The image which emerges is always an *Image of Love*.

So the criterion in whether the interpretations and the meanings we attribute to these difficult to understand, "irrational", evangelic stories are correct, is in what degree do they make all the more clear the Image of Love inside us or whether they blur and entangle it.

And in this point there cannot also exist any confusion: The more clear and strong is becoming the Image of Love inside us, the more unequivocal and practical are Her results—that is, Her fruits. And the fruits of Love must be clear to all of us:

> *"The Love is long-suffering, it is kind, the Love doth not envy, the Love doth not vaunt itself, is not puffed up, doth not act unseemly, doth not seek its own things, is not provoked, doth not impute evil, rejoiceth not over the unrighteousness, and rejoiceth with the truth; all things it beareth, all it believeth, all it hopeth, all it endureth. The Love doth never fail"* (1 Corinthians 13:4-8, YLT).

As we have already mentioned, the Holy Scriptures of every real spiritual tradition are maps which lead to their treasures. In this work we are dealing of course with the maps of Christianity, the Old and the New Testament. So next we will examine some of the symbols of these Holy Scriptures in order to understand them deeper and be led with greater safety to the treasure of Love.

The Symbols of the Scriptures

There is an extensive bibliography which refers to the symbolism of the Scriptures and which is related to both the more traditional christian sources and the "non-traditional" ones. In this work we will derive our knowledge mostly through the traditional sources but that doesn't mean that the latter don't contain their own wealth or that they contradict the former ones. Now, some of the symbols which are used in the Scriptures can be roughly divided to the following categories:

Human being: woman (female), man (male), mother, father, infant, children, offspring, forefathers
Human body: head, skull, forehead, face, tongue, ears, eyes, heart, hands, right and left hand, feet, heel, bones

Animals: clean and unclean ones, beasts, crow, serpent, dove, donkey (colt), ox, lamb, sheep, lion, bull, eagle
Plants: tree, seed, mustard seed, vineyard, fig-tree, bush
Natural elements: fire, water, earth, air (heaven)
Natural phenomena and relative events: flood, storm, thunder, lighting, cloud, rainbow, shipwreck, fire
Natural sceneries: hill, mount, cliff, valley, plain, wilderness, rivers, lake, sea, spring, cave

Countries and places: Egypt, Babylon, Jericho, (tower of) Babel, Jerusalem, (mount of) Zion, Bethlehem, Nazareth, Golgotha
Peoples: gentiles (heathens), Egyptians, Babylonians, Israelites, Amalekites, Canaanite, Hittite, Girgashites, Amorite, Perizzite, Hivite, Jebusite
Persons and names: Eve, Adam, Cain, Abel, Abraham, Pharaoh, Isaac, Jacob, Noah, Moses, Aaron, Joshua the son of Nun, David, Solomon, Nebuchadnezzar, John the Baptist, Virgin Mary, Jesus Christ, Mary, Martha, Lazarus, John, Peter, James, Judas, Pilate, Paul

Occupations and properties: farmer (husbandman, tiller), vine-dresser, gardener, steward (house-keeper), builder, fisherman, soldier, herdsman, shepherd, swineherd, sadducee, pharisee, scribe, publican, centurion, saint, prophet, apostle, disciple, multitude (crowds)

Acts and relative states: idolatry, adultery, fornication, virginity, marriage, widowhood, circumcision, baptism, alms, fasting, miracles (signs)

Diseases: lame, deaf, blind, possessed, lepers

Foods: bread, manna, quails, meat, honey, milk, wine, water

Clothes: linen, made of hair, girdle (belt), ring, shoes, garment, crown

Objects: ark, sword, purse, staff

Materials and precious stones: myrrh, oil, stone (rock), plinth, gold, sapphire, diamond, jewel, emerald, pearl

Constructions: highway, path, door, gate, bedchamber, closet, city, house, stable, temple, well

Colours

Numbers: 3, 7, 12, 40

Hours and days: darkness, night, day, sunrise, midday, Friday, Saturday

Heavenly bodies: Sun, Moon, stars

Incorporeal beings: angels, archangels, demons, devil

Specific terms: Kingdom of Heaven, Church, Son of God, son of man, son of perdition, Hades, hell, Gehenna, outer darkness, chosen ones, enemies, dead, justice, letter of the law, testament, Passover

The Life of Jesus: Annunciation (Evangelism), Birth, Baptism, Temptations, Teaching, Transfiguration (Metamorphosis), Passion, Crucifixion, Death, Resurrection, Ascension, Second Coming

"None of the persons, places, times, or other things recorded in Scripture—animate and inanimate, sensible and intelligible—has its concurrent literal or spiritual meanings rendered always according to the same interpretive mode.

Whoever, therefore, is infallibly trained in the divine knowledge of the Holy Scripture must, for the diversity of what appears and is communicated therein, interpret each recorded thing in a different way and assign it, according to its place or time, the fitting spiritual meaning."

(Maximus the Confessor, *Ad Thalassium 64, On the Cosmic Mystery of Jesus Christ*)

The magic of the symbols is to be found precisely to the fact that they never symbolize *just one thing* but many objects at the same time. That means that they belong *to many levels simultaneously* and that is what makes them so valuable. If we could substitute each symbol with only one word, then we should really question their essential use and contribution to the rendering of the Divine Meanings. Yet, the truth is that each symbol contains many meanings and often depends on its context. That means that the combination of certain symbols illustrates specific meanings.

At this point we will examine only indicatively some of the aforementioned symbols deriving our knowledge from the traditional christian sources, bearing in mind that the symbolism of the Scriptures is inexhaustible and its essential value is eventually to be found in constituting an internal *experience*, an inner revelation, and not only an intellectual information.

"For this reason the fathers say that we ought to search the Scriptures assiduously, in humility and with the counsel of experienced men, learning not merely theoretically but by putting into practice what we read [...] lest we search the Scriptures simply with our minds and then out of pride think that we have grasped something. For the Lord commands that we should search the Scriptures above all by means of bodily and moral actions, and in this way find eternal life (cf. John 5:39-40)."

(St Peter of Damaskos, *Book I – Spurious Knowledge*,

p. 191, Vol. 3, Philokalia)

Human being

Woman

Let us begin our search with the symbol of woman, giving her thus the honor she deserves and which has essentially been deprived of in so many centuries, often because of the misinterpretation of her symbol. The symbol of woman, to which we will refer more extensively later, was being perceived literally and so it was considered as a reference to the *woman herself* as a being and not (as it should) to the principle that can be expressed through her. The result was her belittlement, or the *justification* of her belittlement, which through its "spiritual" consolation became (and becomes) even more cruel and relentless.

The woman often symbolizes, as the female principle, that is, as the principle of receptivity, the *soul*, in contrast to man, who symbolizes, as the male principle, that is, as the energetic principle, the *spirit*. And so this symbolism indicates the necessary *relationship* between these two parts of our being.

> "And the woman from Samaria and the one who took the seven brothers as her husbands, according to the Sadducees (cf. Matt. 22:25-28), and the one who was diseased with an issue of blood (cf. Matt. 9:20), and the one who was bent over to the earth (cf. Luke 13:11), and the daughter of Jairus (cf. Mk 5:22), and the Syrophenician woman (cf. Mk 7:25), they signify both the whole human nature and the soul of every man."
>
> (Maximus the Confessor, *To Thalassius on Various Questions of the Divine Scripture*, Question 41, p. 263, Vol. 14B, Philokalia)

Infants (little children)

The infants signify the beginning of an inner state; of a thought; of a feeling; which might be good or bad and according which we should have the corresponding attitude.

"Who are the children which the law says "that they should not fall down from the roof?" (Deut. 22:8). The children are the thoughts which come to the soul and which we must keep in humility so that they do not fall down from the roof, which as we have said, is the fulfillment of every virtue."

(Abba Dorotheos, *Practical Teaching on the Christian Life*, Lesson 14, Pgh 151, p. 216)

"Blessed is he that holds little ones and dashes them against the stone" (Psalm 137:9). This means you are happy when your offspring, that is, evil thoughts, are not given the chance to increase even when they are small, before they are fed and multiply against him, but they are held and thrown at the stone, which is Christ. Thus, he destroys them by fleeing to Christ. See how both the elders and Holy Scripture agree in calling "happy" and "blessed", those who struggle to cut out their passions, while they are young, and before they experience the pain and bitterness they cause."

(Abba Dorotheos, *Practical Teaching on the Christian Life*, Lesson 11, Pghs 116-117, p. 181)

Human body

Hands

The hands, as we can easily make out, symbolize our actions and works. The clean hands indicate the clean (good) works whilst the dirty hands signify the unclean (evil) words, hence the expression which is referred to wicked actions, "I don't want to get my hands dirty".

"The hand is the symbol of action."

(Maximus the Confessor, *To Thalassius on Various Questions of the Divine Scripture*, Question 54, p. 31, Vol. 14C, Philokalia)

"Ask, and it will be given to you; seek and you will find; knock, and it will be opened unto you" (Matt. 7:7). It says "ask" so that we will beg through prayer, "seek" so that we shall search for how virtue comes, what brings it about and what we must do to obtain it. The searching in this way each day is the "seek and you shall find". It says, "knock" because this is the practicing of the virtues, since all men knock with their hands and the hands are considered as the means of action."

(Abba Dorotheos, *Practical Teaching on the Christian Life*, Lesson 14, Pgh 154, pp. 218-219)

And accordingly, the folk wisdom has retained the symbolisms of the right and left hand, so it wishes, "Hope everything goes right" meaning, everything goes well.

"His right hands—that is, his holy deeds—are

constantly protected by Him."

(John Cassian, *On Chastity, Twelfth Conference*, from *The Conferences*, p. 440)

"The arm is a symbol of strength; the hands, as we have said in diffirent ways, are considered as symbols of the practical life. The arm is the power of the hand. Thus, they offered the strength of their right hand, that is to say, the action of the good works because they considered the right hand as symbol of good."

(Abba Dorotheos, *Practical Teaching on the Christian Life*, Lesson 17, Pgh 176, pp. 244-245)

"Those are they then who are figuratively spoken of in holy Scripture as ἀμφοτεροδέξιον , i.e., ambidextrous, as Ehud is described in the book of Judges *"who used either hand as the right hand"* (Judges 3:15). And this power we also can spiritually acquire, if by making a right and proper use of those things which are fortunate, and which seem to be "on the right hand," as well as of those which are unfortunate and as we call it "on the left hand," we make them both belong to the right side, so that whatever turns up proves in our case, to use the words of the Apostle, *"the armour of righteousness"* (2 Corinthians 6:7). For we see that the inner man consists of two parts, and if I may be allowed the expression, two hands, nor can any of the saints do without that which we call the left hand: but by means of it the perfection of virtue is shown, where a man by skilful use can turn both hands into right hands."

(John Cassian, *Conferences*, 6, Chapter 10, p. 356)

Tongue, Larynx, Palate

"The tongue is a symbol of the soul's spiritual energy and the larynx a symbol of natural self-love for the body. Thus he who ignobly welds the one to the other (cf. Ps 137:6) cannot give his attention to the tranquil state of virtue and spiritual knowledge, for he sedulously indulges in the confusion of bodily passions."

(St Maximos the Confessor, *Various Texts on Theology, the Divine Economy, and Virtue and Vice*, Second Century, 89, p. 206, Vol. 2, Philokalia)

"As the palate discriminates between different kinds of food (cf. Eccles. 36:18,19), so the spiritual sense of taste clearly and unerringly reveals everything as it truly is."

(St Gregory of Sinai, *On Stillness*, Fifteen Texts, Text 10, p. 270, Vol. 4, Philokalia)

Face, Head

"What does the Gospel indicate, saying, "wash your face and anoint your head"? (cf. Matthew 6:17)

Our "face" is our life, which, just like a face, characterizes who we are "according to the inner self." (cf. Romans 7:22) And so, the passage advises [us] to "wash" it, that is, to purify our life from every stain of sin. And "head" is our *nous*, which the passage urges us to "anoint", that is, to make bright by divine knowledge."

(Maximus the Confessor's, *Questions and Doubts*, Qu. 70, p. 80)

Animals

Animals share with man a common nature but in part since they are deprived of the reason (logic) with which man is endowed, despite of whether he uses or abuses it. So as an esoteric symbol, animals refer in general to the *il-logical* forces or contents of the soul. More specifically, according to their particular characteristics they refer to particular properties of our psychological and spiritual world.

"That none of the irrational animals was allowed to appear on the mountain (cf. Exodus 19:13) signifies, in my opinion, that in the contemplation of the intelligibles we surpass the knowledge which originates with the senses. For it is characteristic of the nature of irrational animals that they are governed by the senses alone divorced from understanding."

(Gregory of Nyssa, *The Life of Moses*, Book II, p. 78)

Beasts

"And once we are filled with darkness all the beasts in the wild places of our heart and our whelp-like passion-imbued thoughts rove raucously through it, seeking to feed on our impassioned proclivities and to despoil the treasure garnered in us by the Spirit (cf. Ps. 104 : 20-21)."

(Nikitas Stithatos, *On the Inner Nature of Things and on the Purification of the Intellect*, One Hundred Texts, 47, pp. 120-121, Vol. 4, Philokalia)

"The 'young of the lion' is the impassible person,

who rules over the beasts that are begotten within him."

(Evagrius of Pontus, *Thirty-three Chapters*, p. 226)

"God said to Job, '*behold the beasts by your side eat*

grass as the oxen' (cf. Job 40:15), which means that the passions have turned from the savage cruelty to a submissive state and in the end they are tamed, even if they still seem to breathe."

(Nilus of Sinai, *Peristeria – To Monk Agathios*, P.G. 79:820)

Sheep, Dog, Wolf, Cock, Leach, Donkey, Herd

"Like a good shepherd it folds the sheep—the divine thoughts—and through refraining from what is harmful it slays licentiousness as if it were a mad dog. It expels stupidity as though it were a fierce wolf, and prevents it from devouring the sheep one by one; but it constantly keeps an eye on such stupidity and reveals it to the intelligence, so that it cannot lie hidden in the moonless dark and infiltrate among our thoughts."

(St Peter of Damaskos, *Book II – Twenty-Four Discourses*, 18,

p. 257, Vol. 3, Philokalia)

"The 'cock' is the spiritual person filled with knowledge and announcing to other souls the good news of the day that has come from the intelligible sun."

(Evagrius of Pontus, *Thirty-three Chapters*, p. 226)

"The 'leech' is the impure nature

that sucks the just blood of rational souls."

(Evagrius of Pontus, *Thirty-three Chapters*, p. 227)

"What is the significance of sitting on a donkey? He sat on a donkey so that the Word of God should bring back the irrational soul (which is like the senseless beasts) and submit it to his deity."

(Abba Dorotheos, *Practical Teaching on the Christian Life*, Lesson 15, Pgh 165, p. 231)

"When the hand of God fell heavy on Pharaoh and his servants and he sought to free the sons of Israel, he said to Moses, *"Go, serve your Lord; only let your flocks and your herds be kept back"* (Ex. 10:24). These denote the thoughts in your understanding that Pharaoh wanted to capture hoping that, through them he could draw back the sons of Israel to himself."

(Abba Dorotheos, *Practical Teaching on the Christian Life*, Lesson 13, Pgh 147, p. 209)

Plants

The vegetable kingdom is used extensively in the Scriptures as a wealthy treasury of symbols concerning our inner world. There are a lot of plants which illustrate states and aspects of our soul but also the more general symbols—as the seed—which run through the Scriptures from beginning to end and refer to specific inner procedures.

Seed, Tree, Fruit

The *seed* (or root) usually symbolizes the beginning of a state. The *tree* symbolizes a state which has grown in us and may have its results, that is, bring its *fruits*.

"Our actions disclose what goes on within us,

just as its fruit makes known a tree otherwise unknown to us."

(St. Thalassios the Libyan, *On Love, Self-Control and Life in Accordance with the Intellect,* Third Century, Text 65, p. 322, Vol. 2, Philokalia)

"Once you have realized that the Amorite within you is '*as strong as an oak*', you should pray fervently to the Lord to dry up 'his fruit from above'— that is, your sinful actions, and '*his roots from beneath*'—that is, your impure thoughts. Ask the Lord in this way to '*destroy the Amorite from before your face*' (Amos 2:9. LXX)."

(St. John of Karpathos, *For the Encouragement of the Monks in India who had Written to Him,* Text 93, p. 320, Vol. 1, Philokalia)

The seed, the tree and the fruit denote the beginning, development and result of a psychological situation. An inner state can begin as a minute thought, emotion, feeling (seed) and if it develops it grows to a way or attitude of life (tree) which brings naturally its results (fruits).

A relative example might be an idea such, "Life has meaning after all" which if develops will lead us in finding the meaning of our life. Or a feeling, "Deep inside everyone is good" which if develops will make us better in our relationships and thus happier. But there could also be a bad seed (weed), a negative feeling, such, "You cannot trust anyone" which if develops inside us will make us in the end suspicious, bad-tempered, isolated and thus miserable.

In the allegory of the Fall, Adam is being given the command, *"And the Lord God commanded the man, saying, "Of every tree of the garden thou mayest freely eat: But of the tree of the knowledge of good and evil, thou shalt not eat of it: for in the day that thou eatest thereof thou shalt surely die"* (Genesis 2:16-17).

With good and evil symbolizing the *duality*, or more generally, the *multiplicity*, the command not to eat from the fruit of the tree of knowledge of good and evil, means not to let grow inside us (tree), the state of duality (which is born—seed—by the perception of the bodily senses), because in that way we will live (eat, taste) its consequences (fruits), that is, division and hostility.

> "By "paradise" I think is indicated the human heart, which is planted in the East, i.e., in the dawning (*anatole*) of the knowledge of God. In the absolute center of it, God planted "the tree of life and the tree of the knowledge of good and evil" (cf. Genesis 2:9). And "the tree of life" is understood as the *logos* of intelligible things, while "[the tree of] the knowledge of good and evil" is understood as the *logos* of perceptible things."

> (Maximus the Confessor's, *Questions and Doubts*, Qu. 44, p. 68)

And of course it is known, that the Kingdom of Heaven is likened to a seed which grows and becomes a tree, *"The kingdom of heaven is like to a grain of mustard seed, which a man took, and sowed in his field: Which indeed is the least of all seeds: but when it is grown, it is the greatest among herbs, and becometh a tree, so that the birds of the air come and lodge in the branches thereof"* (Matthew 13:31-32). And at the same time is being said that, *"The kingdom of God is within you"* (Luke 17:21). So it becomes clear that the Kingdom of Heaven refers to the growth (or recovery) of an inner state of being and perception of things.

Palms, Olive branches

"What is the significance of going to meet Him with palms and olive branches? [...] The palm is the symbol of victory. [...] The olive branches are the symbol of mercy."

(Abba Dorotheos, *Practical Teaching on the Christian Life*, Lesson 15, Pgh 165, p. 231)

Natural elements

Earth

Earth usually symbolizes our body or carnal mind.

"We shall not possess our own earth—that is, the earth of this rebellious body will not be placed under our sway—unless our mind has first been fixed in patient mildness."

(John Cassian, *On Chastity, Twelfth Conference*, from *The Conferences*, p. 440)

'*Put to death therefore whatever is earthly in you: unchastity, uncleanliness, passion, evil desire and greed*' (Col. 3:5). Earth is the name St Paul gives to the will of the flesh. Unchastity is his word for the actual committing of sin. Uncleanness is how he designates assent to sin. Passion is his term for impassioned thoughts. By evil desire he means the simple act of accepting the thought and the desire. And greed is his name for what generates and promotes passion. All these St Paul ordered us to mortify as 'aspects' expressing the will of the flesh."

(St Maximos the Confessor, *Four Hundred Texts on Love*, First Century, Text 83, p. 62, Vol. 2, Philokalia)

Yet, since the earth is also the definition of receptivity and fertility, it often consists of a symbol of our heart, which can also be receptive and fertile.

"If we do not bar our bodily senses, the fountain of that water which the Lord promised to the woman of Samaria will not gush forth in us (cf. John 4:14). This woman, seeking physical water, found the water of life flowing within her. For, as the earth by nature contains water which it pours forth as soon as an outlet is opened, so the earth of the heart by nature contains this spiritual water which gushes forth as soon as this becomes possible, like the light which our forefather Adam lost through transgression."

(Callistus Patriach, *Texts on Prayer*, Chapter 4, p. 271)

"The excellent paradise that was planted wisely by God to Eden in east (cf. Genesis 2:8); is the image of the inner man who has the heart as earth, and as plants [...] he has the various contemplations of God and the divine meanings and the divine revelations [...] For that is what the phrase "to Eden" reveals, which is the heart that is fed according to her nature and has the divine things as evident delight and pleasure."

(Callistus Angelikoudis, *Chapters on Prayer*, Chapter 15, p. 133, Vol. 5, Philokalia)

Heaven (Air)

When the mind of the senses hears heaven being mentioned, he understands the atmosphere which surrounds earth or the ultimate space (!), but for the spiritual mind this kind of interpretation is clearly sense-less. So when it's being said that there was a voice from heaven (cf. Matthew 3:17), the carnal mind interprets this image literally whatever might entail this, whilst the spiritual mind obviously perceives it as a reference to a higher spiritual level.

"God Himself is many times called Heaven, according to the Holy Scripture, as when the great messenger of truth, the forerunner John, says, "*a man can receive nothing, except it be given him from heaven*" (John 3:27), instead of saying "from God", for "*every good gift and every perfect gift is from above, and cometh down from the Father of lights*" (James 1:17). In this chapter we should take the passage of the Scripture according to this meaning.

And again the Scripture is used also in calling heaven the divine powers according to the passage "*the heaven is my throne*" (Isaiah 66:1), for God is resting on the holy and incorporeal natures. And if someone said that heaven is also the human *nous* when it is purged by every material fantasy and adorned with the divine principles (words) of the *noetic* realities, he wouldn't be, on my opinion, outside of the truth. And again if someone names heaven the heights of *noetic* knowledge where people reach to, he won't miss the proper meaning."

(Maximus the Confessor, *To Thalassius on Various Questions of the Divine Scripture*, Question 50, p. 363, Vol. 14B, Philokalia)

Water

Water consists of a multidimensional in its interpretation symbol, with positive and negative tones, according to its form and context. We meet it in the form of sea, lake, flood, cataclysm, storm, river, spring, well, etc. And its contexts are also various. Sometimes it denotes a *food* for man and other times something which he must overcome or transcend.

In the form of sea, it usually signifies something we must transcend. It might refer to temptations, to sin (missing of the mark), to the difficulties of life, to the contents of our soul or to anything we have to face; anything we have to *walk upon it* in order not to *sink* in it.

According to the narration of the Gospels, it wasn't only Jesus that walked on water but Peter as well, even if it only lasted for a little while. We do not give much emphasis in this miracle because in the end he doubted and begun to sink. Yet, even if we took literally this incident, it ought to shock us: how would it be if could walk on water even for a few seconds! But we don't pay so much attention to it, because eventually Peter failed… Nevertheless, the value of this incident and the meaning of its symbolism are to be found precisely to this failure. If this narration is perceived only according to its materialistic interpretation, then it's reasonable to leave us eventually indifferent, simply because it doesn't concern us in the least. In the best case, it might lead us in fabricating ("instructive") stories for other people who walk or even run upon water, and so admire their faith, trying thus to give flesh and bone to an essentially symbolic narration. Yet, inwardly we probably know that we ourselves are never going to walk on water, so this "pious" literal interpretation of this *miracle* (sign), instead of benefiting us, *on the contrary* deprives us of all its worth and use.

For if we perceive it internally and realize that the waters upon which Peter tried to walk are our familiar life's storms or our even more familiar spoons of water in which we are drowning, then we will discover a far more direct connection with this story and its very practical consequences in our lives.

Whatever historic truth these miraculous narrations might contain, their prime value can be traced in their inner symbolism, for only thus they can acquire flesh and bone for us, *right here and right now*. Otherwise they remain external, past (dead) events, something which results in being cut off from the *living* Word of Christ.

So in the cases where the symbol of water refers in efforts of transcendence, these can be either external or internal. That means that we might be called to transcend inner difficulties in order to become masters of our soul or we might have to transcend outer difficulties in order to become masters of our life. In both cases of course (which are closely interrelated) the desired mastership is eventually a fruit of the *synergy* between God and man, as we are taught very eloquently by Peter's effort, "*Lord, if it be thou, bid me come unto thee on the water". And he said, "Come". And when Peter was come down out of the ship, he walked on the water, to go to Jesus. But when he saw the wind boisterous, he was afraid; and beginning to sink, he cried, saying, "Lord, save me". And immediately Jesus stretched forth his hand, and caught him, and said unto him, "O thou of little faith, wherefore didst thou doubt?"* (Matthew 14:28-31).

When water, as a symbol, is connected with something that nourishes us, then it refers essentially to the Spiritual Knowledge, "*Whosoever drinketh of the water that I shall give him shall never thirst; but the water that I shall give him shall be in him a well of water springing up into everlasting life*" (John 4:14), which might be *One* but the levels of Her perceptions are many. So water, when it symbolizes the Spiritual Truth, according to its context, might refer to various levels of understand the *One Truth*.

> "Jacob's well (cf. John 4:5-15) is Scripture. The water is the spiritual knowledge found in Scripture. The depth of the well is the meaning, only to be attained with great difficulty, of the obscure sayings in Scripture."
>
> (St Maximos the Confessor, *Various Texts on Theology, the Divine Economy, and Virtue and Vice*, Second Century, 29, p. 193, Vol. 2, Philokalia)

> "The Lord Himself describes it [the Holy Spirit] as '*a spring of water welling up for eternal life*' (John 4:14)—He refers to the Spirit as water—a source that leaps up in the heart and erupts through the ebullience of its power."

(St Gregory of Sinai, *On the Signs of Grace and Delusion, Written for the Confessor Longinos*, Ten Texts, Text 4, p. 260, Vol. 4, Philokalia)

Fire

Fire has also two internal meanings at least, one good and one "bad", which reflect two of its real functions. Fire can warm us and burn us. So in its positive sense, it symbolizes the inner warmth we experience after we are purged from our uncleanness, and in its "negative" sense, it refers precisely to this procedure of cleansing, which we experience as a "*consuming fire*" (Hebrews 12:29).

"*I have come to cast fire on the earth and how I desire but that it be already enkindled*" (Lk 12:49). For there is a burning of the Spirit which puts hearts on fire. For that reason the immaterial and divine fire enlightens souls and tests them as pure gold is tested in the furnace. But it burns out any evil, as if it were thorns and stubble. For "*our God is a consuming fire*" (Heb 12:29).

(Macarius the Great, *The Fifty Spiritual Homilies*, Homily 25.9, p. 163)

Natural phenomena and relative events

Here we don't really need to say much, it's clear through our everyday talk but mostly through our experience, that the shipwrecks, floods, cataclysms and storms can indicate very accurately our internal or external experiences.

"As I take it, the dark storm which befell St Paul (cf. Acts 28:1-4) is the weight of involuntary trials and temptations. The island is the firm unshakeable state of divine hope. The fire is the state of spiritual knowledge."

(St Maximos the Confessor, *Various Texts on Theology, the Divine Economy, and Virtue and Vice*, Second Century, 23, p. 192, Vol. 2, Philokalia)

"The spirit of scorching heat (cf. Jonah 4:8) signifies not only trials and temptations but also that abandonment by God which deprived the Jews of the gifts of grace. Affinity with the Spirit dissolves the soul's proclivity for the flesh, concentrates our longing on God and binds our will to Him."

(St Maximos the Confessor, *Various Texts on Theology, the Divine Economy, and Virtue and Vice*, Fifth Century, 8, p. 262, Vol. 2, Philokalia)

"Just as no house ever falls to the ground by a sudden collapse, but only when there is some flaw of long standing in the foundation, or when by long continued neglect of its inmates, what was at first only a little drip finds its way through, and so the protecting walls are by degrees ruined, and in consequence of long standing neglect the gap becomes larger, and break away, and in time the drenching storm and rain pours in like a river: for *"by slothfulness a building is cast down, and through the weakness of hands the house shall drop through"* (Eccl. 10:18). And that the same thing happens spiritually to the soul the same Solomon thus tells us in other words, when he says: *"water dripping drives a man out of the house on a stormy day"* (Proverbs 27:15). Elegantly then does he compare carelessness of mind to a roof, and to tiles that have not been looked after, through which in the first instance only very slight drippings (so to speak) of the passions make their way to the soul: but if these are not heeded, as being but small and trifling, then the beams of virtues will decay and be carried away by a great tempest of sins, through which "on a stormy day," i.e., in the time of temptation, the devil's attack will assail us, and the soul will be driven forth from the abode of virtue, in which, as long as it preserved all watchful diligence, it had remained as in a house that belonged to it."

(John Cassian, *Conferences*, 6, Chapter 17, p. 361)

Natural sceneries

Mount

The mountains usually symbolize the higher states of consciousness, "*And having dismissed the crowds, He went up on the mountain privately to pray*" (Matthew 14:23); with the most relevant example being the Sermon on the Mount, "*And seeing the crowds, He went up into the mountain, and after He had sat down, His disciples approached Him*" (Matthew 5:1), which is essentially given from a higher level of consciousness and not necessarily upon a physical mountain!

And again, when Jesus leads His triad of disciples up to a *high* mountain, in order to reveal them His real face, that doesn't necessarily mean that they truly ascended to a mountain, without of course this being excluded, "*After six days Jesus took Peter, James, and John, and led them up into a high mountain alone by themselves. And He was transfigured before them*" (Mark 9:2).

"Interpretation of the outward form of Scripture according to the norms of sense-perception must be superseded, for it clearly promotes the passions as well as proclivity towards what is temporal and transient. That is to say, we must destroy the impassioned activity of the senses with regard to sensible objects, as if destroying the children and grandchildren of Saul (cf. 2 Sam. 21:1-9); and we must do this by ascending to the heights of natural contemplation through a mystical interpretation of divine utterances, if in any way we desire to be filled with divine grace."

(St Maximos the Confessor, *Various Texts on Theology, the Divine Economy, and Virtue and Vice*, Fifth Century, 36, p. 269, Vol. 2, Philokalia)

"Mountains (cf. 2 Chronicles 26:10), says in general the high spiritual contemplation of nature which is cultivated by those who are released from the imaginations of the sensible things and have ascended through the virtues to the *noetic* principles (words) themselves."

(Maximus the Confessor, *To Thalassius on Various Questions of the Divine Scripture*, Question 48, Comment 11, p. 325, Vol. 14B, Philokalia)

"The peace of God dawns in the soul and the ineffable joy and inexpressible rejoicing of the Holy Spirit flows in her as she chants silently being seized by the unknowable surprise that, not in the future but from now the God of gods appears in Zion (cf. Psalm 84:7-8), that is, in the *nous* that reaches heaven and oversees the higher things."

(Callistus Katafygiotis, *On Union with God, and Life of Theoria*, Chapter 51, p. 250, Vol. 5, Philokalia)

"The knowledge of God is a mountain steep indeed and

difficult to climb—the majority of people scarcely reach its base."

(Gregory of Nyssa, *The Life of Moses*, Book II, p. 78)

Yet, at the same time, according to its context, the mountain can signify the mountain of our egoism, or a mountain of difficulties, *"If you have faith like a mustard seed, you shall say to this mountain, "Be moved from here to there," and it shall move; and nothing shall be impossible for you"* (Matthew 17:20).

"The grain of mustard seed is the Lord, who by faith is sown spiritually in the hearts of those who accept Him. He who diligently cultivates the seed by practicing the virtues moves the mountain of earth-bound pride and, through the power he has gained, he expels from himself the obdurate habit of sin. In this way he revives in himself the activity of the principles and qualities or divine powers present in the commandments, as though they were birds."

(St Maximos the Confessor, *On Theology and the Incarnate Dispensation of the Son of God*, Second Century, Text 11, p. 140, Vol. 2, Philokalia)

Valley

Having in mind the aforementioned symbolism of the mountain, we can easily perceive that the symbol of the valley refers to a lower state of consciousness.

"The 'valleys' are the rational souls that have been

hollowed out by vice and ignorance."

(Evagrius of Pontus, *Thirty-three Chapters*, p. 227)

Wilderness

It's true that we all have needs which must be fulfilled: physical, psychological and spiritual ones. But there are three ways of fulfilling them: the ego-centric, the human-centric and the God-centric. The first one leaves us eventually empty. The second one is fickle and transient. The third one completes us.

Every real need creates a *constant* void inside us. For the void creates the possibility of motion (action) and of the subsequent fulfillment. If something was filled forever, that would be mean the end of all its activity, since it would not need anything else. Yet, it is known that "everything changes, and no thing abides" if they want to remain alive. So what is filled is emptied again, to be refilled, and thus to grow.

Our body wearies; rests; wearies; and thus it strengthens. Our stomach fills; empties; fills; and thus lives. Our soul searches; finds; loses; and all over again; and thus matures. Our spirit prays; becomes heavy; prays; and thus is Deified.

So the creation of this constant void is what motivates us and keeps us alive. This emptiness, this kenosis, is necessary for the birth or the retaining of anything new, and is expressed as an inviolate law, "*No man puts a bit of new cloth on an old coat, for by pulling away from the old, it makes a worse hole. And men do not put new wine into old wine-skins; or the skins will be burst and the wine will come out, and the skins are of no more use: but they put new wine into new wine-skins, and so the two will be safe*" (Matthew 9:14-17). In life we need deprivations otherwise nothing can exist; nothing new can be born.

A life without deprivations is a poor life.

That is why *fasting* (deprivation) is defined as a necessary condition for our physical, psychological and spiritual health and is related directly to the experience of this *void*, of this *wilderness*, "*Then was Jesus led up of the Spirit into the wilderness to be tempted of the devil. And when he had fasted forty days and forty nights, he was afterward an hungred*" (Matthew 4:1).

The wilderness symbolizes internally this void that we need to *endure* in order to *transcend* it and thus *go deeper*; so we can enter into our Promise Land.

When we have patience in the wilderness, what we gain is subtle and imperceptible, it's like... nothing! Yet, in reality we gain space, purification, strength, we are "*as having nothing, and yet possessing all things"* (2 Corinthians 6:10). On the contrary, when we give in to the passions of Egypt, what we gain is coarse and visible, whilst it's nothing, it seems like everything!

"Hast thou taken us away to die in the wilderness? Wherefore hast thou dealt thus with us, to carry us forth out of Egypt? [...] For it had been better for us to serve the Egyptians, than that we should die in the wilderness [...] And the whole congregation of the children of Israel murmured against Moses and Aaron in the wilderness. And the children of Israel said unto them, "Would to God we had died by the hand of the Lord in the land of Egypt, when we sat by the flesh pots, and when we did eat bread to the full; for ye have brought us forth into this wilderness, to kill this whole assembly with hunger" (Exodus 14:11-12, 16:2-3).

On the former occasion we are led, through the seeming "nothing", to the freedom from everything; we are elevated to the Promised Land. On the latter occasion we are led, through the seeming "everything" into the captivity of anything; we are lowered to the slough of weakness.

The *wilderness* symbolizes a very specific inner stage which all of us have experienced more or less, whenever we have tried to *turn inside* us, to enter inside us, or just to be *alone* with ourselves. And precisely because it seems like absolute nothing, it ends up being an impenetrable impediment to our deepening. The wilderness (the void) is full of *temptations*. Due to the needs that it creates, it makes our attention to be turned outwards more than ever. So it provides a valuable *experience* regarding our strongest weaknesses, that is, our *ego-centric needs*.

"Every affliction tests our will, showing whether it is inclined to good or evil. This is why an unforeseen affliction is called a test [temptation (*peirasmos*) in the Greek text which means *"to acquire experience (peira)"* of something] because it enables a man to test [*experience-peira*] his hidden desires."

(St. Mark the Ascetic, *226 Texts*, 204, p. 143, Vol. 1, Philokalia)

When we attempt to return to our inner abode, after we have been tired from our enslavement to the external passions, we are necessarily faced with the wilderness. And that is why we have difficulty in entering to our internal because the experience of the wilderness, of nothing, frightens us and makes us hasten even more to our old "self" which we feel as incredibly familiar, "*And a man's foes shall be they of his own household*" (Matthew 10:36).

But if we remain in the void, we will begin transcending it as we will experience its necessary procedure of purification with the result of getting to our Promised Land which entails our completion.

If we *try* to fill it (succumbing to the temptations), that means essentially that we will *avoid* it, and thus we will return automatically to the surface of our "self", that is, to non-existence, and eventually we will be left really *empty* and *shallow*.

Jesus stayed in the wilderness for 40 days and nights and Israel spend 40 years of wondering in the wilderness. Jesus is baptized in Jordan before being led into the wilderness and Israel crosses the Red Sea before traveling through the wilderness, and later on crosses Jordan in order to enter into the Promised Land. So it becomes obvious that both narrations are describing this requisite stage in our inner evolution (return) and provide us with the necessary instructions in order to be able to *not avoid it* but instead transcend it in order to be led to our Fulfillment.

Countries and places

Cities, countries and other places symbolize again our soul's states, positive and negative, and often contain more meanings than one which are interconnected.

"He who still satisfies the impassioned appetites of the flesh dwells in the land of the Chaldeans as a maker and worshipper of idols. But when he has begun to discern what the situation is and has gained some insight into the mode of life which nature demands, he leaves the land of the Chaldeans and comes to Haran in Mesopotamia (cf. Gen. 11:31). By Haran I mean that intermediate state between virtue and vice—a state not yet purified from the delusion of the senses. But if he goes beyond that moderate understanding of goodness which he has attained through the senses, he will hasten towards the blessed land, that is, to the state free from all sin and ignorance which God, who does not lie, manifests to those who love Him, promising to give it to them as a reward for their virtue."

(St Maximos the Confessor, *On Theology and the Incarnate Dispensation of the Son of God*, Second Century, Text 26, p. 143, Vol. 2, Philokalia)

Jerusalem

"Jerusalem means "place of peace" and is a type of the place of God, that is, of the soul who possesses the peace in Christ. But not all souls can possess the peace in Christ and bear the name of peace, only the soul that is built as a city on the precious corner-stone that God laid in Zion, as He promised (cf. Isaiah 28:16). Zion is the highest hill, the watch tower of Jerusalem, which is a type of the contemplative *nous* of the peaceful soul."

(Callistus Angelikoudis, *Chapters on Prayer*, Chapter 53, p. 175, Vol. 5, Philokalia)

"Jerusalem is the celestial knowledge of immaterial beings;

within it the vision of peace can be contemplated."

(St. Thalassios the Libyan, *On Love, Self-Control and Life in Accordance with the Intellect,* Second Century, Text 31, p. 314,

Vol. 2, Philokalia)

"The intellect [*nous*] of every true philosopher and gnostic possesses both Judah and Jerusalem; Judah is practical philosophy and Jerusalem is contemplative intuition."

(St Maximos the Confessor, *Various Texts on Theology, the Divine Economy, and Virtue and Vice*, Third Century, 11, p. 211, Vol. 2, Philokalia)

Egypt

Egypt consists of a symbol which is mentioned very often in the patristic texts and symbolizes overall the *enslavement*: to the carnal mind, to the passions, to the world. Besides, we all know that from Egypt begins the great adventure of the chosen people who seeks the Promised Land; a story filled with allegories and symbols which illustrates the inner journey of return which all of us experience from the moment we decide to be freed from the state of captivity to our lower sides.

"The Egypt of the spirit is the darkness of the passions."

(St. Thalassios the Libyan, *On Love, Self-Control and Life in Accordance with the Intellect,* Second Century, Text 35, p. 315, Vol. 2, Philokalia)

"What the Fathers call "Egypt" is the bodily desire which inclines us towards bodily comfort and trains our *nous* to love pleasure."

(Abba Dorotheos, *Practical Teaching on the Christian Life*, Lesson 13, Pgh 142, p. 206)

"Egypt has also many meanings, sometimes is interpreted as the present world, sometimes as flesh, sometimes as sin, sometimes as ignorance, sometimes as hardship."

(Maximus the Confessor, *On Various Questions of St. Denys and St. Gregory*, Question 100, p. 415, Vol. 14D, Philokalia)

"From the moment that harmful fantasies appear we should deny them entry into our mind. We should not allow it to 'go down into Egypt', for from there it is led away into captivity by the Assyrians (cf. Jer. 42:19; 43:2-3). For when the mind descends into the darkness of impure thoughts—and that is what Egypt means—then the passions drag it forcibly and against its will into their service."

(St. Neilos the Ascetic, *Ascetic Discourse*, p. 226, Vol. 1, Philokalia)

Babylon

"*And he cried mightily with a strong voice, saying, "Babylon the great is fallen, is fallen, and is become the habitation of devils, and the hold of every foul spirit, and a cage of every unclean and hateful bird. For all nations have drunk of the wine of the wrath of her fornication, and the kings of the earth have committed fornication with her, and the merchants of the earth are waxed rich through the abundance of her delicacies". And I heard another voice from heaven, saying, "Come out of her, my people, that ye be not partakers of her sins, and that ye receive not of her plagues. For her sins have reached unto heaven, and God hath remembered her iniquities*" (Apocalypse 18:2-5).

We could attempt an *inner* interpretation of this passage by saying that the *earth* symbolizes our lower, physical self; *heaven* our higher, spiritual self; and *Babylon* our false self.

The sides of our physical self—the kings and the merchants of the earth—become greedy and fornicate with Babylon and so they are waxed "rich" by tasting the delicacies of our egoistic, false self.

> "The prophet commanded the Israelites to 'destroy the seed from Babylon' (Jer. 50:16 [27:16. LXX]), meaning that we should erase sense-impressions before they penetrate into the mind."
>
> (St. Neilos the Ascetic, *Ascetic Discourse*, p. 233, Vol. 1, Philokalia)

But when the sins of Babylon, of our false self, reach unto our spiritual self, our heaven, then he cries to our lower (physical) self, *"be not partaker of her sins"* and calls all the healthy and true parts that belong to him, that is, his *people*, to come out of Babylon (egoism). And of course we can attribute this heavenly call both to the spirit inside us and to the Spirit outside us which again calls us *internally* and names us *His people*.

> "When a sinful soul does not accept the afflictions that come to it, the angels say: 'We would have healed Babylon, but she was not healed' (Jer. 51:9)."
>
> (St. Mark the Ascetic, *226 Texts*, 82, p. 132, Vol. 1, Philokalia)

Peoples

The various peoples symbolize also internal states of the soul, with the most familiar symbol being the one of the *chosen people*, of Israel, which are the chosen people of God precisely because this people (this side of ours) is the one which *chooses* the One Real God.

'His majesty is upon Israel' (Ps. 68:34. LXX)—that is, upon the intellect that beholds, so far as this is possible, the beauty of the glory of God Himself."

(St. Hesychios the Priest, *On Watchfulness and Holiness*, Section 35, p. 168, Vol. 1, Philokalia)

'God is known in Judah' (Ps 76:1a.) —that is, in the soul that is still held under the confession of sin, since Judah means confession. But 'in Israel'—that is, in the one who sees God or, as some people interpret it, God's most righteous one—he is not only known but also 'his name is great' (Ps 76:1b.).

(John Cassian, *On Chastity, Twelfth Conference*, from *The Conferences*, p. 448)

'He is not a real Jew who is one outwardly,' says St Paul, 'nor is true circumcision something external and physical; he is a Jew who is one inwardly, and real circumcision is a matter of the heart, spiritual and not literal' (Rom. 2:28-29)."

(Nikitas Stithatos, *On Spiritual Knowledge, Love and the Perfection of Living*, One Hundred Texts, 69, p. 161, Vol. 4, Philokalia)

"There are eight principal faults which attack mankind; viz., first gastrimargia, which means gluttony, secondly fornication, thirdly philargyria, i.e., avarice or the love of money, fourthly anger, fifthly dejection, sixthly acedia, i.e., listlessness or low spirits, seventhly cenodoxia, i.e., boasting or vain glory; and eighthly pride."

(John Cassian, *Conferences*, 5, Chapter 2, p. 339)

"And in reference to these eight faults we also have the following in the gospel: *"But when the unclean spirit is gone out from a man, he walketh through dry places seeking rest and findeth none. Then he saith, I will return to my house from whence I came out: and coming he findeth it empty, swept, and garnished: then he goeth and taketh seven other spirits worse than himself, and they enter in and dwell there: and the last state of that man is made worse than the first"* (Mathew 7:43-45). Lo, just as in the former passages [Deuteronomy] we read of seven nations besides that of the Egyptians from which the children of Israel had gone forth, so here too seven unclean spirits are said to return beside that one which we first hear of as going forth from the man. And of this sevenfold incentive of sins Solomon gives the following account in Proverbs: *"If thine enemy speak loud to thee, do not agree to him because there are seven mischiefs in his heart"* (Proverbs 26:25)

(John Cassian, *Conferences*, 5, Chapter 25, p. 350)

"These [faults] are the seven nations whose lands the Lord promised to give to the children of Israel when they came out of Egypt. And everything which, as the Apostle says, happened to them "in a figure" (Cf. 1 Corinthians 10:6) we ought to take as written for our correction. For so we read: *"When the Lord thy God shall have brought thee into the land, which thou art going in to possess, and shall have destroyed many nations before thee, the Hittite, and the Girgashites, and the Amorite, the Canaanite, and the Perizzite, and the Hivite, and the*

Jebusite, seven nations much more numerous than thou art and much stronger than thou: and the Lord thy God shall have delivered them to thee, thou shalt utterly destroy them" (Deut. 7:1-2)

(John Cassian, *Conferences*, 5, Chapter 16, p. 347)

Persons and names

"When the Lord says to Nathanael, 'Behold, a true Israelite, in whom there is no guile' (John 1: 47), he thereby proclaims the virtue of the man; for Nathanael means 'zeal for God'. The name given him by his family was 'Simon'; he was called 'the Canaanite' because he came from Cana of Galilee, and 'Nathanael' because of his virtue. Thus the Israelite—that is to say, the intellect [*nous*] that sees God—is without guile. For, according to St Basil the Great, it is usual in the divine Scripture to call a man by a name expressing his particular virtue, rather than by the name given him at birth."

(St Peter of Damaskos, *Book I – How It Is Impossible To Be Saved Without Humility*, pp. 180-181, Vol. 3, Philokalia)

Moses

"The Fathers regard Moses the Lawgiver as an icon of the intellect [*nous*]. He saw God in the burning bush (cf. Exod. 3:2-4:17); his face shone with glory (cf. Exod. 34:30); he was made a god to Pharaoh by the God of gods (cf. Exod. 7:1); he flayed Egypt with a scourge; he led Israel out of bondage and gave laws. These happenings, when seen metaphorically and spiritually, are activities and privileges of the intellect [*nous*]."

(St. Hesychios the Priest, *On Watchfulness and Holiness*,

Section 164, p. 186, Vol. 1, Philokalia)

Pilate

Whilst Pilate was historically a very cruel governor; traditionally, due to his inner symbolism, he has been considered partially innocent regarding the responsibility of Jesus' death. He constitutes an aspect of ours which isn't directly hostile to the Divine Meanings but it certainly doesn't understand them because of the lower level to which it belongs; therefore it leads them to crucifixion.

"Pilate is a type of the natural law; the Jewish crowd is a type of the written law. He who has not risen through faith above the two laws cannot therefore receive the truth which is beyond nature and expression. On the contrary, he invariably crucifies the Logos, for he sees the Gospel either, like a Jew, as a stumbling-block or, like a Greek, as foolishness (cf. 1 Cor. 1:23)."

(St Maximos the Confessor, *On Theology and the Incarnate Dispensation*

of the Son of God, First Century, Text 71, p. 128, Vol. 2, Philokalia)

"Herod exemplifies the will of the flesh; Pilate, the senses; Caesar, sensible things; and the Jews, the soul's thoughts. When the soul through ignorance associates with sensible things, it betrays the Logos into the hands of the senses to be put to death and proclaims within itself the kingship of perishable things. For the Jews say, 'We have no king but Caesar' (John 19:15)."

(St Maximos the Confessor, *On Theology and the Incarnate*

Dispensation of the Son of God, First Century, Text 75, p. 129, Vol. 2, Philokalia)

Cain and Abel

"Cain is the law of flesh which was born first from Adam when he transgressed the divine commandment. Abel is the mind of spirit which was born from Adam after he repented."

(Maximus the Confessor, *To Thalassius on Various Questions of the Divine Scripture*, Question 49, Comment 20, p. 355, Vol. 14B, Philokalia)

Noah, Job, Daniel

"It is written, "There were these three men: Noah, Job and Daniel" (Ezek. 14:14). Noah represents indifference to material goods, Job toil, and Daniel discretion. If there are these three activities in a person, God is dwelling in him."

(Abba Poemen, *The Book of the Elders*, p. 12)

Melchisedec

"Each one who has deadened his members which are upon the earth (cf. Colossians 3:5) and has extinguished his entire carnal mind and has shaken off completely his relationship to the flesh—for the sake of which the love we owe only to God is divided—and has repudiated all the traits of the flesh and of the world for the Divine Grace, so he can say along with the blessed apostle Paul, "*Who shall separate us from the love of Christ?*" (Romans 8:35); he has become without father and without mother and without generation as the great Melchisedec, because flesh and nature cannot hinder him due to his union with the Spirit."

(Maximus the Confessor, *On Various Questions of St. Denys and St. Gregory*, Question 26, pp. 175-177, Vol. 14D, Philokalia)

Occupations and properties

The various activities or properties which are mentioned in the Scriptures, usually illustrate activities or properties of our soul.

"Outwardly men follow different occupations: there are money-changers, weavers, fowlers, soldiers, builders. Similarly, we have within us different types of thoughts: there are gamblers, poisoners, pirates, hunters, defilers, murderers, and so on. Rebutting such thoughts in prayer, the man of God should immediately shut the door against them—arid most of all against the defilers, lest they defile his inward sanctuary and so pollute him."

(St. John of Karpathos, *For the Encouragement of the Monks in India who had Written to Him*, Text 55, p. 311, Vol. 1, Philokalia)

Fisherman

There is a generalized tendency, which is due to the literal interpretation of the New Testament, to present the twelve disciples of Jesus as some simplistic men without much knowledge and often without acute perception who accepted the Divine Call and became as if by magic the known to all Twelve Apostles. Yet, it is very probable that the truth is far from this simplistic interpretation. Still, the fact is that in the Gospels there are not enough details regarding the special characteristics of the twelve disciples. There are mostly incidents in which the closest disciples of Christ are involved which are intended to carry us beyond any superficial perception of them to a deeper inner correlation with them.

A special mention which is being made for some disciples is that they were fishermen before the call of Jesus. One esoteric meaning of their property is mentioned by Jesus Himself, when He says that he will make them *fishers of men*, *"Follow me, and I will make you fishers of men"* (Matthew 4:19).

The characteristic of a fisherman is that he seeks his capture in the *depths* (of the *water*). The results of his search are uncertain, but if he shows perseverance (faith) and patience (hope) then it's almost certain that he will be rewarded.

> "For myself, I cannot deny that although I have worked hard all night I have caught nothing. Yet at your suggestion I have again let down the nets, and I have made a large catch. They are not big fish, but there are a hundred and fifty-three of them (cf. John 21:11). These, as you requested, I am sending you in a creel of love, in the form of a hundred and fifty-three texts."
>
> (Evagrios the Solitary, *On Prayer*, *153 Texts*, p. 55, Vol. 1, Philokalia)

There is an excellent narration in the end of John's Gospel which is usually appreciated only in relation to the appearance of Christ to his disciples, after His resurrection. So the rest of its elements are ignored as decorative which simply frame the miraculous event of His resurrection. But this profound narrative is full of symbols (sea, boat, night, morning, nets, right side of the boat, fishes (153), nakedness, garment, little boat, land, bread, fire, food) and if they are been given their proper value, they can revive inside us this brief incident and its deep meaning.

> "*After these things Jesus showed Himself again to the disciples at the Sea of Tiberias, and in this manner He showed Himself: Simon Peter, Thomas called the Twin, Nathanael of Cana in Galilee, the sons of Zebedee, and*

two others of His disciples were together. Simon Peter said to them, "I am going fishing." They said to him, "We are coming with you also." They went out and immediately got into the boat, and that night they caught nothing. But as daybreak had already come, Jesus stood upon the shore; however the disciples did not know that it was Jesus. Then Jesus said to them, "Children, have you any food?" They answered Him, "No." And He said to them, "Cast the net on the right side of the boat, and you will find some." Therefore they cast, and they were not able to haul it in because of the multitude of fish. Therefore that disciple whom Jesus loved said to Peter, "It is the Lord!" Now when Simon Peter heard that it was the Lord, he put on his outer garment (for he had removed it), and he threw himself into the sea. But the other disciples came in the little boat (for they were not far from the land, but about two hundred cubits), dragging the net with fish. Then as they got off onto the land, they saw a charcoal fire laid there, and fish placed on it, and bread. Jesus said to them, "Bring some of the fish which you have just caught." Simon Peter went up and hauled the net onto the land, full of large fish, one hundred and fifty-three; and although there were so many, the net was not torn. Jesus said to them, "Come, eat breakfast." Yet none of the disciples dared to question Him, "Who are You?" knowing that it was the Lord. Jesus then came and took the bread and gave it to them, and likewise the fish. This was now the third time Jesus was manifested to His disciples, having been raised from the dead" (John 21:1-14, EMTV).

One interpretation for the net is given by Jesus Himself, *"Again, the kingdom of heaven is like unto a net, that was cast into the sea, and gathered of every kind: Which, when it was full, they drew to shore, and sat down, and gathered the good into vessels, but cast the bad away"* (Matthew 13:47-48).

"If any of the inspired words are required to aid our pleading, the Truth (John 14:6) Itself will be sufficient to corroborate the truth when It inculcates this very kind of teaching in the veiled meaning of a Gospel Parable: the good and eatable fish are separated by the fishers' skill from the bad and poisonous fish, so that the enjoyment of the good should not be spoilt by any of the bad getting into the "vessels" with them. The work of true sobriety is the same; from all pursuits and habits to choose that which is pure and improving, rejecting in every case that which does not seem likely to be useful, and letting it go back into the universal and secular life, called "the sea" (Matt. 13:47-48), in the imagery of the Parable."

(St. Gregory of Nyssa, *On Virginity*, Chapter 18, p. 364)

So gradually we perceive that the various symbols of the Scriptures compose an inner picture which contains much more than a thousand words.

"A heart that has been completely emptied of mental images gives birth to divine, mysterious intellections that sport within it like fish and dolphins in a calm sea."

(St. Hesychios the Priest, *On Watchfulness and Holiness*, Section 156, p. 190, Vol. 1, Philokalia)

Farmer (Husbandman, Tiller)

"Elsewhere St Paul, calling the teachers tillers and their pupils the fields they till (cf. 2 Tim. 2:6), wisely presents the former as plowers and sowers of the divine Logos and the latter as the fertile soil, yielding a rich crop of virtues. True ministry is not simply a celebration of sacred rites; it also involves participation in divine blessings and the communication of these blessings to others."

(St Gregory of Sinai, *One Hundred and Thirty-Seven Texts,* Text 93, p. 231, Vol. 4, Philokalia)

"Uzziah, it says, is a husbandman (cf. 2 Chronicles 26:10) because each *nous* that is contemplative by God's strength and is a real husbandman, guards with attention and care the divine seeds of the goods so they can be kept clean from weeds, until he obtains the remembrance of God to preserve him."

(Maximus the Confessor, *To Thalassius on Various Questions of the Divine Scripture*, Question 48, p. 321, Vol. 14B, Philokalia)

Vine-dresser

"Vine-dressers in the mountains (cf. 2 Chronicles 26:10) are those godly thoughts that insist in the heights of contemplation and love the beauty of the ecstatic and secret knowledge."

(Maximus the Confessor, *To Thalassius on Various Questions of the Divine Scripture*, Question 48, p. 321, Vol. 14B, Philokalia)

Herdsman, Shepherd

"The herdsman signifies the man practicing the virtues, for moral achievements may be represented by cattle. That is why Jacob said, *'Your servants are herdsmen'* (Gen. 46:34). The shepherd signifies the gnostic, for sheep represent thoughts pastured by the intellect on the mountains of contemplation."

(St Maximos the Confessor, *Four Hundred Texts on Love,* Second Century, Text 55, pp. 74-75, Vol. 2, Philokalia)

Deacon, Priest, Bishop

"He who anoints his intellect for spiritual contest and drives all impassioned thoughts out of it has the quality of a deacon. He who illuminates his intellect with the knowledge of created beings and utterly destroys false knowledge has the quality of a priest. And he who perfects his intellect with the holy myrrh of the knowledge and worship of the Holy Trinity has the quality of a bishop."

(St Maximos the Confessor, *Four Hundred Texts on Love*, Second Century, Text 21, p. 68, Vol. 2, Philokalia)

"We give the name of Levites and priests to those who dedicate themselves totally to God, alike through the practice of the virtues and through contemplation."

(St. John of Karpathos, *For the Encouragement of the Monks in India who had Written to Him*, Text 78, p. 316, Vol. 1, Philokalia)

Pharisees

Pharisees weren't all bad. Historically they constituted a religious group who tried through its own perception to be pleasing to God. An example of a good Pharisee is Nicodemus (who came to Jesus by *night*) who consists one of the most known *hidden* disciples of Jesus. Yet, other than that, Pharisees were also one established religious authority who had gradually distorted the Divine Word, mostly through their *actions* and these are attacked "relentlessly" by Christ.

"At first sight it seems that the only teachers our Lord had in mind were the Pharisees when He said: '*Woe to you, scribes* and Pharisees, hypocrites! For you scour sea and land to gain one proselyte, and when he is gained, you make him twice as much the child of hell as yourselves' (Matt. 23:15) But in reality, by rebuking the Pharisees in this way, He was warning those who in the future would fall into the same mistake."

(St. Neilos the Ascetic, *Ascetic Discourse*, p. 216, Vol. 1, Philokalia)

So the Pharisee is the diachronic symbol of hypocrisy but also of the general inadequacy of man to *put theory into practice*. We usually think that the symbol of Pharisee refers to *intentional* hypocrisy and so we believe that it doesn't concern us directly, since none of us believes for himself that he chooses hypocrisy (and this might be true, though very easily we blame others for deliberate hypocrisy). Yet, the deeper value of this meaning is to be found in the fact that it constitutes a picture of the *unconscious* hypocrisy that possesses us all. The Pharisee exalts himself feeling *righteous* without necessarily seeing any contradiction between his words and actions.

So how many of us do we fall to this sin (missing of the mark)? How many of us do we self-justify *without even* knowing it? And specifically in relation to the things of God; how many of us do we feel *true Christians* and *Orthodox* and guardians of Jesus' tradition? For the same did the Pharisees believe; they considered themselves guardians of their tradition and heard the famous: "*O generation of vipers, who hath warned you to flee from the wrath to come? Bring forth therefore fruits worthy of repentance [metanoia], and begin not to say within yourselves, "We have Abraham to our father": for I say unto you, "That God is able of these stones to raise up children unto Abraham*" (Luke 3:7-8).

As long as our works (fruits) are not according to our faith, we cannot claim the parentage of any Christian (Orthodox) Tradition, for thus we are, *unconsciously*, proved to be hypocrites (Pharisees), "*They answered and said unto him, "Abraham is our father." Jesus saith unto them, "If ye were Abraham's children, ye would do the works of Abraham*" (John 8:39). And the less we feel that the notion of the Pharisee concern us, the more certain can we be that is referring precisely to us!

> "*And he spake this parable unto certain which trusted in themselves that they were righteous, and despised others: Two men went up into the temple to pray; the one a Pharisee, and the other a publican. The Pharisee stood and prayed thus with himself, "God, I thank thee, that I am not as other men are, extortioners, unjust, adulterers, or even as this publican. I fast twice in the week, I give tithes of all that I possess." And the publican, standing afar off, would not lift up so much as his eyes unto heaven, but smote upon his breast, saying, "God be merciful to me a sinner." I tell you, this man went down to his house justified rather than the other: for every one that exalteth himself shall be abased; and he that humbleth himself shall be exalted*" (Luke 18:9-14)

So let us be careful lest we "thank" God for making us "christians", "orthodox", etc, and not as the others, so we won't hear the according harsh words: "O generation of vipers, who hath warned you to flee from the wrath to come? Bring forth therefore fruits worthy of repentance [*metanoia*], and begin not to say within yourselves, "We are Christians": for I say unto you, "That God is able of these stones to raise up Christians".

For with our words we might confess Jesus Christ, saying, "Lord, Lord", but we do not confess Him with our actions, "*And why call ye me, Lord, Lord, and do not the things which I say?*" (Luke 6:46). Our *Being* denies Him before men, so let us not be taken aback if Jesus doesn't confess us before the Father as well, "*Whosoever therefore shall confess me before men, him will I confess also before my Father which is in heaven. But whosoever shall deny me before men, him will I also deny before my Father which is in heaven*" (Matthew 10:32-33).

Despite how *correct* (*orthos*) our *belief* (*doxa*) might be, if our actions are not in the same level of correctness then we shouldn't wonder if we hear that, "*The kingdom of heaven is at hand*" (Matthew 4:17) but in essence is nowhere to be found; not even in our far horizon; for His instructions are pretty distinct, "*Not every* one that saith unto me, *"Lord, Lord"*, *shall enter into the kingdom of heaven; but he that doeth the will of my Father which is in heaven"* (Matthew 7:21).

Multitude (Crowds)

It can be easily grasped that the multitudes (crowds) symbolize internally the lack of understanding of the Truth, which leads in Her superficial embracement or in Her stoning. But at the same time, they symbolize also our inner multiplicity. That is to say, they symbolize our inner fragmentation (disintegration) that results in the existence of a plethora of contradictory "personalities" (false sides) within us, which all claim the primacy, the place of our Real Self.

This inner multiplicity has been termed in the Gospels as *Legion*: *"For he said unto him, "Come out of the man, thou unclean spirit." And he asked him, "What is thy name?" And he answered, saying, "My name is Legion: for we are many"* (Mark 5:8-9).

Centurion

"Of this perfect mind then there is an excellent figure drawn in the case of the centurion in the gospel; whose virtue and consistency, owing to which he was not led away by the rush of thoughts, but in accordance with his own judgment either admitted such as were good, or easily drove away those of the opposite character, are described in this tropical form: *"For I also am a man under authority, having soldiers under me: and I say to this man, Go, and he goeth; and to another, Come, and he cometh; and to my servant, Do this, and he doeth it"* (Mathew 8:9). If then we too strive manfully against disturbances and sins and can bring them under our own control and discretion, and fight and destroy the passions in our flesh, and bring under the sway of reason the swarm of our thoughts, and drive back from our breast the terrible hosts of the powers opposed to us by the life-giving standard of the

Lord's cross, we shall in reward for such triumphs be promoted to the rank of that centurion spiritually understood, who, as we read in Exodus, was mystically pointed to by Moses: "Appoint for thee rulers of thousands, and of hundreds, and of fifties and of tens" (Exodus 18:21).

(John Cassian, *Conferences*, 7, Chapter 5, pp. 363-364)

"And what is the character of the arms of this centurion, and for what use in battle they are, hear the blessed Apostle declaring: *"The arms,"* he says *"of our warfare are not carnal, but mighty to God"* (2 Corinthians 10:4). He tells us their character; viz., that they are not carnal or weak, but spiritual and mighty to God. Then he next suggests in what struggles they are to be used: *"Unto the pulling down of fortifications, purging the thoughts, and every height that exalteth itself against the knowledge of God, and bringing into captivity every understanding unto the obedience of Christ, and having in readiness to avenge all disobedience, when your obedience shall be first fulfilled"* (2 Corinthians 10:4-6).

(John Cassian, *Conferences*, 7, Chapter 5, p. 364)

Acts and relative states

Baptism

Baptism essentially means submersion, plunging; and in its inner dimension refers to an inner pervasion (saturation), to an inner deepening which transforms us, which acts in our *whole* Being.

The external picture of the baptism illustrates precisely this internal *mystery*; that is why man must get *whole* into the water. This is a picture of what is to take place in our internal. Our Being must sink *wholly* into the *water* of Life, into the spiritual Truth; which has many levels that is why there are mentioned at least four different levels of baptism in the Gospels.

> "Some are reborn through water and the spirit (cf. John 3:5); others receive baptism in the Holy Spirit and in fire (cf. Matt. 3:11). I take these four things—water, spirit, fire and Holy Spirit—to mean one and the same Spirit of God. To some the Holy Spirit is water because He cleanses the external stains of their bodies. To others He is simply spirit because He makes them active in the practice of virtue. To others He is fire because He cleanses the interior defilement which lies deep within their souls. To others, according to Daniel, He is Holy Spirit because He bestows on them wisdom and spiritual knowledge (cf. Dan. 1:17; 5:11-12). For the single identical Spirit takes His different names from the different ways in which He acts on each person."

> (St Maximos the Confessor, *On Theology and the Incarnate Dispensation of the Son of God*, Second Century, Text 63, p. 152, Vol. 2, Philokalia)

And there is of course the baptism of the Lord which can also be interpreted variously.

> "The baptism of the Lord (cf. Matt. 20:22) is the utter mortification of our propensity for the sensible world; and the cup is the disavowal of our present mode of life for the sake of truth.

> The baptism of the Lord typifies the sufferings we willingly embrace for the sake of virtue. Through these sufferings we wash off the stains in our conscience and readily accept the death of our propensity for visible things. The cup typifies the involuntary trials which attack us in the form of adverse

circumstances because of our pursuit of the truth. If throughout these trials we value our desire for God more than nature, we willingly submit to the death of nature forced on us by these circumstances.

The baptism and the cup differ in this way: baptism for the sake of virtue mortifies our propensity for the pleasures of this life; the cup makes the devout value truth above even nature itself."

(St Maximos the Confessor, *Various Texts on Theology, the Divine Economy, and Virtue and Vice*, First Century, 98-100, p. 187, Vol. 2, Philokalia)

So baptism, in its inner (spiritual) senses, constitutes a soul-saving experience that we need to experience *constantly* (in different levels) and not just an accomplished past event regarding which we do not retain any conscious memory.

"Baptism doth also now save us, not the putting away of the filth of the flesh, but the answer of a good conscience toward God, by the resurrection of Jesus Christ" (1 Peter 3:21)

Circumcision

"Circumcision signifies the quelling of the soul's

impassioned predilection for things subject to generation."

(St Maximos the Confessor, *On Theology and the Incarnate Dispensation of the Son of God*, First Century, Text 40, p. 122, Vol. 2, Philokalia)

Marriage

Marriage means *union*; and internally symbolizes the union of our soul with our spirit which have been cut off and fragmented, or the union of our spirit with the Spirit.

"The grace of the Holy Spirit is given as a pledge to souls that are betrothed to Christ; and just as without a pledge a woman cannot be sure that her union with her man will take place, so the soul will have no firm assurance that it will be joined for all eternity with its Lord and God, or be united with Him mystically and inexpressibly, or enjoy His unapproachable beauty, unless it receives the pledge of His grace and consciously possesses Him within itself. Just as an engagement is not binding unless the documents of the contract bear the signatures of trustworthy witnesses, so the illumination of grace is dependent upon the practice of the commandments and the actualization of the virtues. What witnesses are to a contract, the virtues and the practice of the commandments are to spiritual betrothal: through them everyone who is going to be saved secures the consummation of the pledge. It is as if the contract were written through the practice of the commandments and then signed and sealed by the virtues. Only then does Christ, the bridegroom, give His ring—the pledge of the Holy Spirit—to the soul that is His bride-to-be."

(St. Symeon the New Theologian, *One Hundred and Fifty-Three Practical and Theological Texts*, 76-78, pp. 40-41, Vol. 4, Philokalia)

Widowhood

So widowhood symbolizes the exactly opposite state.

"St Paul has taught us that the soul endowed with intelligence can be as if dead even though it possesses life as its being; for he writes, '*The self-indulgent widow is dead while still alive*' (1 Tim. 5:6). He could not have said worse than this about the present subject of our discourse, namely, the soul endowed with intelligence. For if the soul deprived of the spiritual Bridegroom does not humble itself and mourn, and does not adopt the strait and grievous life of repentance, but is, on the contrary, profligate, sunk in sensual pleasure and self-indulgence, it is dead even while it lives and even though it is immortal in essence."

(St Gregory Palamas, *Topics of Natural and Theological Science and on the Moral and Ascetic Life*, One Hundred and Fifty Texts, Text 45, pp. 365-367, Vol. 4, Philokalia)

"A passion and sin-loving soul, shorn of grace and

divorced from God, is the haunt of passions"

(St Gregory of Sinai, *One Hundred and Thirty-Seven Texts*, Text 12, p. 214, Vol. 4, Philokalia)

"Since salvation comes to you as a free gift, give thanks to God your savior. If you wish to present Him with gifts, gratefully offer from your widowed soul two tiny coins, humility and love, and God will accept these in the treasury of His salvation more gladly than the host of virtues deposited there by others (cf. Mark 12:41-43)."

(St Theognostos, *On the Practice of the Virtues, Contemplation and the Priesthood*, Chapter 45, p. 369, Vol. 2, Philokalia)

Adultery

"And this care of His and providence with regard to us the Divine word has finely described by the prophet Hosea under the figure of Jerusalem as an harlot, and inclining with disgraceful eagerness to the worship of idols, where when she says: "*I will go after my lovers, who give me my bread, and my water, and my wool, and my flax, and my oil, and my drink*" (Hosea 2:7) the Divine consideration replies having regard to her salvation and not to her wishes: "*Behold I will hedge up thy way with thorns, and I will stop it up with a wall, and she shall not find her paths. And she shall follow after her lovers, and shall not overtake them: and she shall seek them, and shall not find them, and shall say: I will return to my first husband, because it was better with me then than now*" (Hosea 2:8-9). And again our obstinacy, and scorn, with which we in our rebellious spirit disdain Him when He urges us to a salutary return, is described in the following comparison: He says: "*And I said thou shalt call Me Father, and shalt not cease to walk after Me. But as a woman that despiseth her lover, so hath the house of Israel despised Me, saith the Lord*" (Jeremiah 3:19-20). Aptly then, as He has compared Jerusalem to an adulteress forsaking her husband, He compares His own love and persevering goodness to a man who is dying of love for a woman. For the goodness and love of God, which He ever shows to mankind,— since it is overcome by no injuries so as to cease from caring for our salvation, or be driven from His first intention, as if vanquished by our iniquities,—could not be more fitly described by any comparison than the case of a man inflamed with most ardent love for a woman."

(John Cassian, *Conferences*, 13, Chapter 8, p. 426)

"He who secretly mingles his own wishes with spiritual counsel is an adulterer, as the Book of Proverbs indicates (cf. Prov. 6:32-33)."

(St. Mark the Ascetic, *On the Spiritual Law*, Text 124, p. 118, Vol. 1, Philokalia)

Fasting

Fasting is related with the abstinence which contributes to cleansing and revival. There are three levels of fasting: the physical, the psychological (moral) and the spiritual (Divine). There is fasting from material food; fasting from negative thoughts, negative feelings and negative words; and fasting from all the physical and psychological data in order to be made space for the spiritual nourishment.

"As we fast with our stomach, we must fast with our tongue, abandoning slander, lies, idle chatter, reproach, anger and basically any sin that is commited by the tongue. Likewise, we must fast with our eyes so that we do not see idly, nor do we act boldly with the eyes looking impudently. Also, we must prevent our hands and feet from perfoming any evil. This fasting, as St. Basil says, is an acceptable fast, as we abstain from every evil manifested through all the senses."

(Abba Dorotheos, *Practical Teaching on the Christian Life*, Lesson 15, Pgh 164, p. 230)

"The fasting which you think you observe is not a fasting. But I will teach you what is a full and acceptable fasting to the

Lord. Listen," he continued: "God does not desire such an empty fasting. For fasting to God in this way you will do nothing for a righteous life; but offer to God a fasting of the following kind: Do no evil in your life, and serve the Lord with a pure heart: keep His commandments, walking in His precepts, and let no evil desire arise in your heart; and believe in God. [...] Thus, then, shall you observe the fasting which you intend to keep. First of all, be on your guard against every evil word, and every evil desire, and purify your heart from all the vanities of this world."

(The Pastor of Hermas, *Similitude 5th*, Chapters 1 & 3, pp. 33-34)

Mercifulness (Alms)

Mercifulness (alms) constitutes a very big chapter in our spiritual course and that is why it has been considered as decisive for our inner progress, "*Redeem thou thy sins with alms*" (Daniel 4:27, DRC). Usually the emphasis is given to the material alms (mercifulness) but it's self-evident that there is also psychological alms (mercifulness):

"God gave us the power, if we wish to use it, to forgive each other's sins. Not having the power to show mercy to his body, you help his soul and what is greater mercy than that shown to the soul? As the soul is more valuable than the body, it is the same with the mercy shown to the soul, which is greater than that shown to the body. Therfore, nobody can say, "I cannot show mercy". Each person can, according to his ability, but he must try to make sure that he does good consciously."

(Abba Dorotheos, *Practical Teaching on the Christian Life*, Lesson 14, Pgh 158, p. 222)

Now, the material alms (mercifulness) is also a big chapter by itself and it must certainly not be neglected, even if the psychological charity is on a higher level and transcends it in essence and value. Yet, one "impediment" we often face regarding the practice of material alms, is our familiar lack of discernment when we are faced with a fellow-man of ours who is asking help and we are not sure whether he really needs it or whether he deceives us.

In this point we must turn again to the three levels of perception that we have in our disposal. There is the materialistic (physical) perception which cannot feel in essence anyone and anything else beyond itself. Then we have the psychological perception which feels and thinks about the others but still perceives them as different, as *others* than itself. It sympathizes and rejoices with them but it doesn't feel one with them. Finally, we have the spiritual perception which perceives everything and everyone as One.

So if the materialistic perception prevails in us, when we walk by someone who asks for help, we cannot *feel* anything in relation to him. We see him as completely separated from us. So basically we feel that he *bothers* us because he wants something from us. If we give him a minimum part of our material wealth, this will be from guilt, from annoyance, or for the eyes of men. And certainly we are not in any position to understand (to feel) whether he is deceiving us or not, but that doesn't matter after all because even if he is really in need, we cannot feel it with our materialistic organs of perception, so we are just *not moved* by it in the least.

"You see on the ground, in the middle of the market, your fellow-man lying homeless, without permanent residence, hungry, without having below him a rag to intervene between the earth and his melted ribs, nor above him a cover to protect him from the cold or the heat, in the open-air, exposed equally to the snowfall and the sun's rays, defeating naked the nature's mysteries, without being able, due to his hunger, to use even his own voice to beg, making the sign of his begging by gesturing only with his hand and beckoning with his eyes, which are just moving, reaching to his end, dying from poverty, and you pass him by, pressured perhaps by your eating time, and not even your own passion can't make you give in so you can feel sympathy for him, nor hunger makes you understand the one who is hungry."

(Nilus of Sinai, *Peristeria – To Monk Agathios*, P.G. 79:868-869)

If the psychological perception prevails in us, then we can feel more or less his real situation, but the important thing is that we *care* to feel it, simply because… we *feel*. So we will look at him, we will be troubled and we will ponder; and according to the degree that our psychological organs of perception are awakened and alive, we will feel what we think we should do in relation to that *other* man. Because as much sympathy as we might feel for him, we will still feel him as separated from us but very close to us. He is our fellow-man, but not us. He is one human being and we are *another* human being.

If the spiritual perception prevails, then we can feel to the utmost degree the need of our fellow-man, but what is most important is that we do not perceive him as separated from us; we perceive him as One with us. That is why when Jesus says, "*And if a man will contend with thee in judgment, and take away thy coat, let go thy cloak also unto him. And whosoever will force thee one mile, go with him other two, give to him that asketh of thee and from him that would borrow of thee turn not away*" (Matthew 5:40-42), He is referring precisely to this *spiritual* view of things. He tells us in essence that what we do to others, we do it to ourselves. If we give them, we give to ourselves, so what do we expect to get back? The others are us and we are them. And in the case we are faced with someone who is pretending to be in need, if we don't "help" him, it will be for his own good and not to save our minimum material wealth.

> "The compassionate is he, whose spirit does not distinguish,
>
> when practicing compassion, any of the classes of men.
>
> (Isaac of Nineveh, *Mystic Treatises*, VI, p. 57)

> "And what is a merciful heart? He replied: The burning of the heart unto the whole creation, man, fowls and beasts, demons and whatever exists so that by the recollection and the sight of them the eyes shed tears on account of the force of mercy which moves the heart by great compassion.
>
> (Isaac of Nineveh, *Mystic Treatises*, LXXIV, p. 341)

So this *heavenly* perspective which conceives everything as One, "*Love your enemies: do good to them that hate you: and pray for them that persecute and calumniate you: that you may be the children of your Father who is in heaven, who maketh his sun to rise upon the good, and bad, and raineth upon the just and the unjust*" (Matthew 5:44-45), is the most "difficult" one, simply because the corresponding spiritual organs of perception are not awakened. Our materialistic (physical) senses usually occupy the prominent place inside us, whilst our psychological organs of perception are more or less awakened and function more or less normally.

> "But when it is necessary, we will not neglect mercifulness, compelling ourselves perpetually to be inwardly full of mercy toward all kinds of rational beings, at all times."

(Isaac of Nineveh, *Mystic Treatises*, LXXXI, p. 379)

Miracles

As with everything else, miracles (signs) can also take place in three levels: in the physical (material), the psychological and the spiritual one. And as it is with everything else, the psychological and spiritual levels are higher than the physical one. Nevertheless, since our carnal mind (the mind of the senses) rules us, we ought to admit that we are much more incredulous toward the material miracles and those are the ones which impress us more. Yet, Jesus taught again with His attitude that the internal miracles are the essential ones whilst the desire for external miracles (signs) is often harmful and reprehensible.

> *"Then some of the scribes and Pharisees answered him, saying: Master we would see a sign from thee. Who answering said to them: An evil and adulterous generation seeketh a sign: and a sign shall not be given it"* (Matthew 12:38-39).

And since we are dominated by the materialistic perception, which one is the miracle (sign) that impresses us more than anything else? The resurrection of a dead man, of course; the return to life of a dead *body*. Unfortunately though, our obsession with the material dimension of miracles—as much as they impress us and seem to us literally unbelievable—overshadows the benefit of the rest dimensions that are included in the narrative of a miracle. For an external to us miracle, even if it is about the resurrection of a dead (body), objectively it doesn't affect us in essence; it doesn't change us. Whilst the psychological and spiritual dimensions of a miracle concerns us directly.

> "When the Logos of God enters a fallen soul—as He entered the city of Bethany (cf. John 11:17)—in order to resurrect its intellect [*nous*], sin-slain and buried under the corruption of the passions, then sound understanding and

justice, plunged into grief by the intellect's [*nous'*] death, come as mourners to meet Him, and they say, 'Hadst Thou been here with us, guarding and keeping watch, our brother intellect [*nous*] would not have died because of sin' (cf. John 11:32)."

(Nikitas Stithatos, *On the Inner Nature of Things and on the Purification of the Intellect*, One Hundred Texts, 98, pp. 120-121, Vol. 4, Philokalia)

The most noted miracle in the Gospels is the resurrection of Lazarus and this is because it's about, as we already mentioned, the return of a dead *body (flesh)* to life. Yet, we should wonder about the enormous emphasis that is being given to the material dimension of this miracle, when all the Christian Teaching revolves around the priority of the soul and spirit to the body, *"the spirit it is that is giving life; the flesh doth not profit anything"* (John 6:63, EMTV) and the transcendence of every materialistic perception, even of the natural desire (and subsequent fear, cf. Matthew 10:28) for bodily life itself.

In the narration of the Gospels, Jesus is informed about the *sickness* of Lazarus and claims that this sickness is not to death, *"The sisters therefore sent to him, saying, "Lord, behold, he for whom you have great affection [phileis—from philo] is sick." But when Jesus heard it, he said, "This sickness is not to death, but for the glory of God, that God's Son may be glorified by it"* (John 11:3-4, WEB). Nevertheless, he deliberately delays to visit him, *"When therefore he heard that he was sick, he stayed two days in the place where he was"* (John 11:6, WEB); and after he foresees that Lazarus has fallen *asleep*, He decides to visit him, *"Our friend, Lazarus, has fallen asleep, but I am going so that I may awake him out of sleep." The disciples therefore said, "Lord, if he has fallen asleep, he will recover." Now Jesus had spoken of his death, but they thought that he spoke of taking rest in sleep. So Jesus said to them plainly then, "Lazarus is dead"* (John 11:11-14, WEB). And whilst He *knew from the start* the imminent sleep (death) of Lazarus, nevertheless, when He approaches to his tomb He weeps! *"Jesus wept"* (John 11:35).

All this narration of the resurrection of Lazarus is indeed very strange, especially if we bear in mind that before this resurrection, two more resurrections have been preceded: the resurrection of the widow's son (cf. Luke 7:11-17) and the resurrection of Jairus' daughter (cf. Luke 8:41-56). Yet, if we understand the constant peculiarity of the Gospels, it won't be difficult to realize that each one of their narrations is multidimensional and always contains a message that concerns us *directly*.

> "Dead through the passions, pray like Lazarus to be brought to life again, sending to God these two sisters [humility and love] to intercede with Him (cf. John 11:20-44); and you will surely attain your goal."
>
> (St Theognostos, *On the Practice of the Virtues, Contemplation and the Priesthood*, Chapter 45, p. 369, Vol. 2, Philokalia)

And we should have the same multidimensional perception towards all accounts of miracles that are taking place in the Scriptures, in order to be able to draw also their deeper meanings which affect us internally.

> "According to the Gospel, the person who is simply a man of faith can remove the mountain of his sin through the practice of the virtues (cf. Matt. 17:20), thus freeing himself from his former attachment to the restless gyration of sensible things. If he has the capacity to be a disciple he receives fragments of the loaves of spiritual knowledge from the hands of the Logos and feeds thousands of people (cf. Matt. 14:19-20), demonstrating by his action how the power of the Logos is increased and multiplied by the practice of the virtues. If he also has the strength to be an apostle he cures every disease and infirmity: he casts out demons (cf. Matt. 10:8; Luke 10:17), that is, he banishes the activity of the passions; he heals the sick, through hope restoring a state of devotion to those who have lost it,

and through his teaching about judgment stiffening the resolve of those who have been softened by sloth. For, since he has been commanded *'to tread on serpents and scorpions'* (Luke 10:19), he destroys the beginning and end of sin."

(St Maximos the Confessor, *On Theology and the Incarnate Dispensation of the Son of God*, First Century, Text 33, pp. 120-121, Vol. 2, Philokalia)

Otherwise, we are disorientated from our materialistic perception which is impressed by the external dimension of these miraculous phenomena and thus we remain in essence unaffected by their psychological and spiritual benefit.

"How would one not tremble before the power of the Lord when he sees that people who once were harsh and cruel and who used to fall into an ungovernable rage even at the most cringing submission of their inferiors have become so gentle that they are not only unmoved by any insults but even rejoice with the loftiest high-mindedness when they suffer them? Who would not wonder thoroughly at the works of God and cry out with his whole being: *'I know that the Lord is great,'* (Ps 135:5) when he sees that he or someone else has gone from grasping to generous, from wasteful to abstinent, from proud to humble, from delicate and refined to filthy and rough, even gladly enjoying poverty and the scarcity of temporal things?

These are truly the marvelous works of God, which the soul of the prophet and of others like him knows specially by the dumbstruck gaze of a wondering contemplation. These are the prodigies that he has wrought upon the earth, which the same prophet, reflecting upon them, calls all people to admire when he says: *'Come and see the works of God, the prodigies that he has wrought upon the earth, making wars cease to the ends of the earth. He destroys the bow and shatters the weapons and burns the shields with fire.'* (Ps 46:8-9)

What could be a greater prodigy than that in a brief moment grasping tax-collectors would become apostles and harsh persecutors would be turned into the most patient preachers of the Gospel, such that they would spread the faith which they used to persecute even to the shedding of their own blood? These are the works of God which the Son declares that he does every day, together with his Father, when he says: *'My Father is working until today, and I am working.'* (Jn 5:17) The blessed David, singing in spirit, says of these works of God: *'Blessed be the Lord, the God of Israel, who alone does great marvels.'* (Ps 72:18) The prophet Amos says about them: *'He does all things and changes them. He changes the shadow of death into morning.'* (Am 5:8 LXX) This, namely, is the *'changing of the right hand of the Most High.'* (Cf. Ps 77:10). Concerning this saving work of God the prophet prays to the Lord and says: *'Confirm, O God, what you have worked in us'* (Ps 68:28).

Let me pass over those secret and hidden dispensations of God which each holy person's mind sees operative in a special way within itself at given moments; over that heavenly inpouring of spiritual gladness by which the downcast mind is uplifted by an inspired joy; over those fiery ecstasies of heart and the joyful consolations at once unspeakable and unheard of, by which those who occasionally fall into a listless torpor are raised as out of the deepest sleep to the most fervent prayer. This indeed is the joy which, the blessed Apostle says, *'eye has not seen nor ear heard nor has it entered into the heart of man'* (1 Cor 2:9)."

(John Cassian, *On Chastity, Twelfth Conference,* from *The Conferences,* pp. 450-451)

Yet, our carnal mind, as *cunning* as it is, will surely raise its final objection: "Cannot the material miracles also change a man? They cannot make him believe?" The answer is again given through the Gospels' Teachings and is really diachronic: A man who doesn't want to believe, cannot be made to believe by any material miracle.

It is very interesting the fact that every spiritual tradition claims essentially the same signs which testify to its genuineness. In every tradition are mentioned exactly the same miracles: cures of all kinds, resurrections of dead, transcendences of all known physical (material) laws, near-death experiences, visions, prophecies. And these references are usually relevant if not completely similar. Very often though, all the miraculous dimension of some tradition is reduced to demonic by its opponents!

Jesus didn't give to disbelievers or unbelievers the signs they were seeking, "*And the Pharisees came forth, and began to question with him, seeking of him a sign from heaven, tempting him. And he sighed deeply in his spirit, and saith, "Why doth this generation seek after a sign? Verily I say unto you, There shall no sign be given unto this generation." And he left them, and entering into the ship again departed to the other side*" (Mark 8:11-13), for He knew from first hand experience that not only this wouldn't make them believe but it could also become a cause of accusation, "*But some of them said, "He casteth out devils through Beelzebub the chief of the devils*" (Luke 11:15).

So the answer that is being given in the Gospels is clear: the "signs and wonders", when they are perceived only carnally (materialistically) can truly do harm instead of good, whilst when they are conceived internally, they can *metamorphose*.

Diseases

It's obvious that the diseases of the body can easily consist of symbols for the according diseases of the soul.

"Blind is the man crying out and saying: 'Son of David, have mercy on me' (Luke 18:38). He prays with the body alone, and not yet with spiritual knowledge."

(St. Mark the Ascetic, *On the Spiritual Law*, Text 13, p. 111, Vol. 1, Philokalia)

"Blindness is the ignorance of the mind that does not attend to the virtues of the practical life and the contemplation of beings. Paralysis is the immobility of the rational soul with regard to the virtues of the practical life. Gonorrhoea is the laziness of the rational soul in which it has the habit of discarding the words of spiritual teaching. [...] Leprosy is the unbelief of the rational soul in which it finds no assurance even after it has touched the reasons. [...] Mutilation of the ear is the obduracy of the rational soul that resists spiritual teaching. [...] Lameness is the incapacity of the rational nature with respect to the work of virtue."

(Evagrius of Pontus, *Thirty-three Chapters*, p. 225)

"These are the signs which our Lord Jesus performed before ascending the cross, for he says, '*Go and tell John what you have heard and seen. The blind receive their sight, the lame walk, the lepers are cleansed, the dead are raised, the poor have good news brought to them, and blessed is anyone who takes no offense at me*' (Mt 11:4-6; Lk 7:22-23). Since John baptized the Lord Jesus, this word assumes a symbolical meaning, because the one who is baptized must confess the significance of his action. *The signs performed by the Lord Jesus were many* (Jn 20:30). However, the phrase, '*the blind receive their sight*' refers to the blindness of someone who attends to the hope of this world. If this person renounces it and beholds the expected hope <of the future world>, then he receives his sight. Similarly, the phrase, '*the lame walk*' signifies that someone desiring God but loving the fleshly cares of the heart is, in fact, lame. If this person renounces these and loves God with all his heart, he is able to walk. Likewise, the phrase, *'the deaf hear'* refers to the person who is distracted <by worldly cares>, who is deaf on account of captivity <to such thoughts> and forgetfulness. If he acquires stillness in knowledge, he is able to hear. Again, the phrase, *'the lepers are cleansed'* has the following meaning. Since it is written in the law of Moses that 'an unclean person will not enter the house of the Lord' (cf. Lv 15:31; Nm 5:3), this includes whoever holds enmity, or hatred, or envy, or slander against his neighbor, but if this person renounces these, he is cleansed. Therefore, if the blind person sees, the lame walks, <the deaf hears>, and the leper is cleansed, anyone who dies spiritually on account of these, at a time of negligence, may be raised from the dead and renewed, proclaiming the good news to his senses which have been impoverished through a lack of holy virtues, and declaring that this person is now able to see, and walk, and be cleansed. This is the confession that you have offered to the one who baptized you.

By baptism I mean humble endurance of suffering, and silence, for it is written about John that, *'He wore clothing of camel's hair, with a leather belt around his waist'*, and lived in the desert (Mt 3:4, 1). This is the sign of endurance: first it cleanses a person, and, if he labors, then he acquires it. When one acquires it within, he is able to ascend the cross in stillness."

"Abba Isaiah of Scetis, *Ascetic Discourses*, pp. 105-106)

Foods

The foods that are mentioned in the Scriptures, in their inner interpretation, refer to our internal feeding (assimilation); to anything (good or bad) which *feeds* our inner man. Very often they refer specifically to our Divine nourishment, to the Divine Word which revives us.

Bread

Bread is the principal symbol of the inner nourishment. Yet, as clear and obvious as its inner symbolism might be, for our carnal mind it remains equally hard to understand, so it insists perceiving the heavenly (*epiousios*) bread we ask in the Lord's Prayer, as our daily bread!

> "For those still mainly concerned with the bodily forms of virtue, the Logos of God becomes hay and straw, sustaining the passible aspect of their souls and guiding it to the service of the virtues. For those who have advanced to the true contemplation of divine things, the Logos is bread, sustaining the intellective [*noetic*] aspect of their souls and guiding it to a godlike perfection."

> (St Maximos the Confessor, *On Theology and the Incarnate Dispensation of the Son of God*, Second Century, Text 66, p. 153, Vol. 2, Philokalia)

> "You have been sentenced to eat the bread of spiritual knowledge
>
> with toil, struggle and the sweat of your face (cf. Gen. 3:19)."

> (St. Thalassios the Libyan, *On Love, Self-Control and Life in Accordance with the Intellect,* Fourth Century, 22, p. 326, Vol. 2, Philokalia)

Wine

It is known, that wine can *"maketh glad the heart of man"* (Psalms 104:15), so it signifies the same function as an inner symbol. Wine stands for the higher spiritual knowledge which leads to the internal intoxication, to the internal ecstasy that carries man beyond the familiar limits of his ordinary "self".

"When the soul having sensed the truth feels intoxicated by the cup of grace as if by the strongest wine, then it is time for silence."

(Callistus Katafygiotis, *On Union with God, and Life of Theoria*, Chapter 65, p. 254, Vol. 5, Philokalia)

"The vineyard makes wine, wine causes intoxication, and intoxication causes ecstasy. So the active word which is the vineyard, if it is cultivated with the virtues brings forth the knowledge, knowledge brings forth the good ecstasy which carries the *nous* beyond its relationship with the senses."

(Maximus the Confessor, *To Thalassius on Various Questions of the Divine Scripture*, Question 48, Comment 18, p. 327, Vol. 14B, Philokalia)

Yet, since *intoxication* has also a negative side, when it indicates dizziness and lack of self-control, wine can also symbolize internally the man who has lost his real aim in this life and "lives" meaninglessly, bewildered by the impressions of the world and the senses, prey to his passions and weaknesses.

Honey and Milk

"If you want the body of the commandments to nourish, you must zealously desire the pure spiritual milk of maternal grace (cf. 1 Pet. 2:2); for it is on this milk of grace that you must suckle yourself if you wish to increase your stature in Christ. Wisdom yields fervor from her breasts as milk that helps you to grow; but to nourish the perfect she gives them the honey of her purifying joy. *'Honey and milk are under your tongue'* (Song of Songs 4:11): by 'milk' Solomon means the Spirit's nurturing and maturing power, while by 'honey' he means the Spirit's purificatory power. St Paul likewise refers to the differing functions of these powers when he says, *'I have fed you as little children with milk and not with meat'* (cf. 1 Cor. 3:2)."

(St Gregory of Sinai, *One Hundred and Thirty-Seven Texts,* Text 21, p. 216, Vol. 4, Philokalia)

Manna

"The manna which was given to Israel in the desert (cf. Exod. 16:14-35) is the Logos of God. Those who eat it find that it supplies every spiritual delight. It is blended to suit every taste in accordance with the different desires of those who eat it, for it has the quality of every kind of spiritual food. Thus, to those who through the Spirit have been born from above by means of incorruptible seed (cf. John 3:3-5), it comes as pure spiritual milk (cf. 1 Pet. 2:2); to the weak it comes as vegetables (cf. Rom. 14:2) sustaining the soul's passible aspect; to those in whom the soul's organs of perception have been trained by long practice to distinguish between good and evil it serves as solid food (cf. Heb. 5:14)."

(St Maximos the Confessor, *On Theology and the Incarnate Dispensation of the Son of God*, First Century, Text 100, p. 135, Vol. 2, Philokalia)

Husks

"After those husks which the swine ate, satisfaction from which was denied to him, i.e., the disgusting food of sin, as he "came to himself," and was overcome by a salutary fear, he already began to loathe the uncleanness of the swine, and to dread the punishment of gnawing hunger."

(John Cassian, *Conferences*, 11, Chapter 7, p. 417)

Spiritual Nourishment

So the inner interpretation of the foods which are mentioned in the Scriptures, can also lead us to the inner interpretation of some miracles attributed to Jesus, like the miracle of turning water into wine (cf. John 2:1-11) or the miracle of the feeding of the multitude (crowds):

"Jesus went over the Sea of Galilee, that is, of Tiberias. And a large crowd was following Him, because they were seeing His signs which He was doing upon those who were sick. And Jesus went up on the mountain, and there He sat down with His disciples. Now the Passover, the feast of the Jews, was near. Then Jesus lifted up His eyes, and seeing that a large crowd was coming toward Him, He said to Philip, "Where shall we buy bread, that these people may eat?" But this He said to test him, for He Himself knew what He was about to do. Philip answered Him, "Two hundred denarii worth of bread is not enough for them, that each of them might receive a little." One of His disciples, Andrew, Simon Peter's brother, said to Him, "There is a little boy here who has five barley loaves and two small fish, but what are they for so many?" Then Jesus said, "Make the people to recline." Now there was much grass in that place. Therefore the men reclined, in number about five thousand. And Jesus took the loaves, and having given thanks He distributed them to the disciples, and the disciples to those who were reclining;

and likewise of the fish, as much as they wished. But when they were filled, He said to His disciples, "Gather up the leftover fragments, so that nothing may be lost." Therefore they gathered them up, and they filled twelve baskets of fragments from the five barley loaves which were left over by those who had eaten. Then those men, when they had seen the sign that Jesus did, said, "This is truly the Prophet who is to come into the world." Therefore Jesus, knowing that they were about to come and seize Him, that they might make Him king, withdrew to the mountain by Himself. [...] On the next day, when the crowd which had remained on the other side of the sea, having seen that there was no other boat there, except that one in which His disciples had entered, and that Jesus had not entered into the boat with His disciples, but His disciples had gone away alone—however, other boats came from Tiberias, near the place where they ate bread after the Lord had given thanks—when the crowd therefore saw that Jesus was not there, nor His disciples, they got into boats and came to Capernaum, seeking Jesus. And having found Him on the other side of the sea, they said to Him, "Rabbi, when did You come here?" Jesus answered them and said, "Most assuredly I say to you, you seek Me, not because you saw the signs, but because you ate from the loaves and were satisfied. Work not for the food which perishes, but for the food which abides unto everlasting life, which the Son of Man will give to you; for upon Him God the Father has set His seal" (John 6:1-27, EMTV).

In this evangelic narration, Jesus is almost denying the performance of some external miracle (sign), *"not because you saw the signs"* and refers clearly to the inner feeding, *"but because you ate from the loaves and were satisfied"*, since He places evident priority to the *"food which abides unto everlasting life"* which He has been sent to provide to those who will work for it, *"And Jesus said unto them, I am the bread of life: he that cometh to me shall never hunger; and he that believeth on me shall never thirst"* (John 6:35).

"So the five barley loaves stand for the rough words of natural contemplation (theoria). The five thousand men that are filled by them signify the ones who move according to nature but they're not completely purged from the disposition which is related to the passive (passible) and irrational part of the soul (cf. Matthew 14:15-21). [...] The seven loaves of the four thousand men (cf. Matthew 15:32-38), signify, as I think, the mystagogy of the law, that is, the more divine words. The Word provides it mystically to those who wait for three days, which means, who suffer patiently the labor which is caused around the moral and natural and theological philosophy."

(Maximus the Confessor, *On Various Questions of St. Denys and St. Gregory*, Questions 159, 169, pp. 143, 155, Vol. 14E, Philokalia)

Jesus didn't come to feed the hungry and thirsty in the flesh; that is why He refused all earthly offices (cf. John 6:15). He came to feed the hungry and thirsty in the soul and spirit, for that was and is the truly miraculous work of God (cf. John 6:1-59).

"The Christian religion is a food and drink. The more one eats of it, the more strongly his mind is enticed by its sweetness, so much so that he can never be restrained or satisfied, but insatiably asks for more and continually eats more."

(Macarius the Great, *The Fifty Spiritual Homilies*, Homily 17.13, p. 140)

The Flesh and Blood of the Lord

"For My flesh truly is food, and My blood truly is drink" (John 6:55, EMTV).

These two terms (cf. John 6:53-55) have generated endless discussions and arguments, but whatever they might really signify, it is a fact that their multidimensional *inner* interpretation has been completely forgotten:

> "And again; flesh of the Lord is the true virtue, blood is the perfect knowledge. [...] If again someone says that the flesh and blood are the words on judgment and providence, because we will definitely eat them and drink them someday [...] he is not outside, I think, of the correct boundaries. [...] And again the flesh of the Word might be the perfect return and restoration of nature to herself through virtue and knowledge, and blood the future *theosis* which is sustained by Grace for the eternal beatitude. [...] But if someone suggests the easier that the flesh is the voluntary necrosis (mortification) through the virtues, and blood the perfection through death in some case for the sake of truth [...] correct is also what he said and he hasn't at all fallen outside the proper meaning."
>
> (Maximus the Confessor, *To Thalassius on Various Questions of the Divine Scripture*, Question 35, pp. 227-229, Vol. 14B, Philokalia)

Clothes

It can be pretty obvious that the various clothes that are mentioned in the Scriptures are usually related to what our inner man wears; but they can also indicate our life's "garments".

> "The garments are washed at divine command before he ascends the mountain, the garments representing for us in a figure the outward respectability of life (cf. Exodus 19:10). No one would say that a visible spot on the garments hinders the progress of those ascending to God, but I think that the outward pursuits of life are well named the "garment".

(Gregory of Nyssa, *The Life of Moses*, Book II, p. 77)

Wedding garment

We could say that the necessary wedding garment which must adorn our internal in order for the inner union (marriage) with the Divine can be performed, is self-denial (self-surrendering), to which we are constantly called by the Bridegroom of our soul in order to be united with Him.

"For the true wedding garment is the dispassion

of the deiform soul which has renounced worldly desires."

(Evagrios the Solitary, *on Discrimination in respect of Passions and Thoughts*, 22, p. 52, Vol. 1, Philokalia)

Coats of skin

"Many have removed all their 'coats of skin' (Gen. 3:21) except the last, that of self-esteem. This is cast off only by those who are disgusted with what produces it: their own self-satisfaction."

(St. Ilias the Presbyter, *A Gnomic Anthology*, Part IV, Verse 131, p. 64, Vol. 3, Philokalia)

Girdle

'*Let your loins be girded, and your lamps burning*', says the Lord (Luke 12:35). A good girdle for our loins—one which enables us to be nimble and unhampered—is self-control combined with humility of heart. By self-control I mean abstinence from all the passions. Our spiritual lamp is lit by pure prayer and perfect love."

(St Theodoros the Great Ascetic, *A Century of Spiritual Texts*, Text 98, p. 35, Vol. 2, Philokalia)

High priest's emblems

"The high priest's emblems in the Old Testament are models for purity of heart. They teach us so to give attention to the gold disc of the heart (cf. Exod. 28:22. LXX) that, should we tarnish it through sin, we should cleanse it with tears, repentance and prayer."

(St. Hesychios the Priest, *On Watchfulness and Holiness*, Section 195, p. 197, Vol. 1, Philokalia)

Veil

"If a man, still enmeshed in sin and anger, dares shamelessly to reach out for knowledge of divine things, or even to embark upon immaterial prayer, he deserves the rebuke given by the Apostle; for it is dangerous for him to pray with head bare and uncovered. Such a soul, he says, ought '*to have a veil on her head because of the angels*' who are present (cf. 1 Cor. 11:5-7*)*, and to be clothed in due reverence and humility."

(Evagrios the Solitary, *On Prayer*, *153 Texts*, 145, p. 70, Vol. 1, Philokalia)

Objects

"Scripture says, '*He who has a purse,*' that is, spiritual knowledge, '*let him take it, and his knapsack as well*' (Luke 22:36), that is, the stoic from which he liberally nourishes his soul with virtue. He who does not have a purse and a knapsack, that is, knowledge and virtue, '*let him sell his garment and buy a sword*' *(ibid.).* By this Scripture means: let him give his own flesh willingly to labors in pursuit of virtue, and for the sake of the peace of God let him wisely wage war against passions and demons, that is, let him acquire the skill of discriminating in the word of God between the lower and the higher."

(St Maximos the Confessor, *On Theology and the Incarnate Dispensation of the Son of God*, First Century, Text 78, pp. 129-130, Vol. 2, Philokalia)

"When Scripture speaks of rod and staff (cf. Ps. 23:4), you should take these to signify in the prophetic sense judgment and providence, and in the moral sense psalmody and prayer."

(St Gregory of Sinai, *One Hundred and Thirty-Seven Texts,* Text 16, p. 215, Vol. 4, Philokalia)

'You have prepared a table before me...' (Ps. 23:5). In this passage, 'table' stands for the practice of the virtues, for this has been prepared for us by Christ to use 'against those who afflict' us. The 'oil' anointing the intellect [*nous*] is the contemplation of created things. The 'cup' of God is the knowledge of God. His 'mercy' is His divine Logos."

(St Maximos the Confessor, *Four Hundred Texts on Love,*

Third Century, Text 2, p. 83, Vol. 2, Philokalia)

"A pure soul can truly be called a 'chosen vessel' (Acts 9:15), 'an enclosed garden', 'a sealed fountain' (Song of Solomon 4:12), and 'a throne of perceptiveness' (Prov. 12:23. LXX)."

(St Theodoros the Great Ascetic, *A Century of Spiritual Texts*, Text 36, p. 20, Vol. 2, Philokalia)

"The breast mentioned in Leviticus (cf. Lev. 7:30, 34) indicates the higher form of contemplation. The shoulder (cf. Lev. 7:32, 34) stands for the mental state and activity concordant with the life of ascetic practice."

(St Maximos the Confessor, *Various Texts on Theology, the Divine Economy, and Virtue and Vice*, Second Century, 45, p. 196, Vol. 2, Philokalia)

Materials and precious stones

Various raw or refined materials are referred to the Scriptures which usually don't interest us so much, whilst in reality they contain a lot of important and notable meanings.

"Let us build on the Lord, as though on a foundation of faith, with gold, silver and precious stones, raising a temple of holiness (cf. 1 Cor. 3:12). Let us build, that is to say, with pure undebased theology, with a way of life that is lucid and radiant, with divine thoughts and conceptual images more precious than jewels. Let us not use wood, hay or stubble, that is, idolatry—which is a passionate desire for sensible things—or a meaningless way of life, or thoughts which are impassioned and as empty of wise understanding as straw."

(St Maximos the Confessor, *On Theology and the Incarnate Dispensation of the Son of God*, Second Century, Text 12, p. 140, Vol. 2, Philokalia)

"We must reflect with wonder how the outer part of the temple of the Old Covenant, where the priests performed sacrifices, was an image of the cosmos (cf. 1 Kgs. 8:64), while within there was the Holy of Holies (cf. Exod. 30:10; Heb. 9:3), in which was offered the incense made of four components, fragrant gum, myrrh, balsam and cassia, which represent the four universal virtues."

(St Peter of Damaskos, *Book I – The Difference between Thoughts And Provocations*, p. 209, Vol. 3, Philokalia)

Constructions

Human constructions are often illustrations of our inner efforts (right or wrong) to relate to God; or they might constitute independent symbols which again refer to our internal.

House

"The Holy Scripture says of the midwives who gave life to the sons of the Israelites that, through their fear of God they built themselves houses (Ex. 1:21). Do they mean material houses? What does it mean by saying that these houses have been built through the fear of God? [...] Therefore, it doesn't mean material houses but the house of the soul which a person builds for himself when he keeps the commandments of God."

(Abba Dorotheos, *Practical Teaching on the Christian Life*, Lesson 14, Pgh 149, p. 213)

Tower

It is obvious that the tower symbolizes an inner effort of elevation, whether this is correct (that is, God-inspired) or mistaken, as the eternal symbol of the Tower of Babel indicates (cf. Genesis 11:1-9).

"And so we shall not be able either to treat properly of the effect of prayer, or in a rapid discourse to penetrate to its main end, which is acquired by labouring at all virtues, unless first all those things which for its sake must be either rejected or secured, are singly enumerated and discussed, and, as the Parable in the gospel teaches, (Cf. Luke 14:28) whatever concerns the building of that spiritual and most lofty tower, is reckoned up and carefully considered beforehand. But yet these things when prepared will be of no use nor allow the lofty height of perfection to be properly placed upon them unless a clearance of all faults be first undertaken, and the decayed and dead rubbish of the passions be dug up, and the strong foundations of simplicity and humility be laid on the solid and (so to speak) living soil of our breast, or rather on that rock of the gospel, (Cf. Luke 6:48) and by being built in this way this tower of spiritual virtues will rise, and be able to stand unmoved, and be raised to the utmost heights of heaven in full assurance of its stability."

(John Cassian, *Conferences*, 9, Chapter 2, pp. 387-388)

"Sublime knowledge about God stands in the soul like a tower, fortified with the practice of the commandments. That is the meaning of the text, *'Uzziah built towers in Jerusalem'* (2 Chr. 26:9). A man builds towers in Jerusalem when he is blessed with success in his search for the Lord through contemplation accompanied by the requisite fear, that is, by observing the commandments; for he then establishes the principles of divine knowledge in the undivided and tranquil state of his soul."

(St Maximos the Confessor, *Various Texts on Theology, the Divine Economy, and Virtue and Vice*, Second Century, 63, p. 200, Vol. 2, Philokalia)

Gate

"Like the gates of a city, we have to open the organs of sense-perception in order to satisfy essential needs; but in so doing we must take care not to give access at the same time to warlike tribes that seek to attack us (cf. Ps 68:30)."

(St. Ilias the Presbyter, *A Gnomic Anthology*, Part IV, Verse 126, p. 63, Vol. 3, Philokalia)

Well

"When like the patriarchs we learn to dig wells of virtue and spiritual knowledge within ourselves by means of ascetic practice and contemplation, we will find within us Christ the spring of life (cf. Gen. 26:15-18). Wisdom commands us to drink from this spring, saying, *'Drink water from your own pitchers and from the spring of your own wells'* (Prov. 5:15). If we do this we shall find that the treasures of wisdom truly are within us."

171

(St Maximos the Confessor, *On Theology and the Incarnate Dispensation of the Son of God*, Second Century, Text 40, p. 147, Vol. 2, Philokalia)

Closet (Inner chamber)

"But thou, when thou prayest, enter into thy closet, and when thou hast shut thy door, pray to thy Father, which is in secret (Matt. 6:6). The closet of our soul is our body; our doors are our five senses."

(*On the Necessity of Constant Prayer for all Christians in General*, From The Life of St. Gregory Palamas, by St. Nikodemos of the Holy Mountain)

"He should again return to prayer, however difficult this work may be and however hard he must push himself until the mind learns by experience easily to suppress its wanderings by all-embracing diligence (or undivided attention) to our Lord Jesus Christ, by constant memory of Him, by frequent penetration into the inner chamber (cf. Mathew 6:6) or the hidden region of the heart and firm rooting of attention there. St. Isaac writes: 'Strive to enter within your inner chamber and you will see the chamber of heaven. For the two are the same and one entrance leads to both."

(Callistus and Ignatius of Xanthopoulos, *Directions to Hesychasts*, Chapter 45, p. 220)

Numbers

"The monad signifies the unmixed (pure), number two the diverse."

(Maximus the Confessor, *To Thalassius on Various Questions of the Divine Scripture*, Question 49, Comment 19, p. 355, Vol. 14B, Philokalia)

"Number five signifies the senses."

(Maximus the Confessor, *To Thalassius on Various Questions of the Divine Scripture*, Question 49, p. 341, Vol. 14B, Philokalia)

Hours and days

Night

Night and darkness usually symbolize the darkened mind, ignorance and confusion. That is why Nicodemus, for example, comes to Jesus by *night*, that is, in confusion, *"Now there was a man of the Pharisees whose name was Nicodemus, a ruler of the Jews. This man came to Him by night"* (John 3:1-2, EMTV).

"The night of the passions is the darkness of ignorance. Or alternatively the night is the state which begets the passions."

(St Gregory of Sinai, *One Hundred and Thirty-Seven Texts*, Text 73, p. 225, Vol. 4, Philokalia)

"Holy knowledge is the light of the soul;

bereft of it, '*the fool walks in darkness*' (Eccles. 2:14)."

(St. Thalassios the Libyan, *On Love, Self-Control and Life in Accordance with the Intellect,* First Century, Text 51, p. 310, Vol. 2, Philokalia)

Saturday

"The Sabbath (cf. Exod. 16:23; 20:10) signifies rest from the passions, and from the intellect's [*nous'*] gravitation towards the nature of created beings. It signifies the total quiescence of the passions, a complete cessation of the intellect's [*nous'*] gravitation towards created things, and its total entry into the divine."

(St Maximos the Confessor, *Various Texts on Theology, the Divine Economy, and Virtue and Vice*, Fifth Century, 43, p. 271, Vol. 2, Philokalia)

"The Sabbath signifies the dispassion of the deiform soul that

through practice of the virtues has utterly cast off the marks of sin."

(St Maximos the Confessor, *On Theology and the Incarnate Dispensation of the Son of God*, First Century, Text 37, p. 122, Vol. 2, Philokalia)

Incorporeal beings

The incorporeal beings that are presented in the Scriptures are symbolizing internally the various positive or negative contents of our soul. Angels illustrate the higher meanings and data, whilst the demons our familiar passions; that is why they are mentioned as the demon of gluttony, of vain-glory, of pride, etc.

"He invokes God's mercy by crying out silently and by striving to advance still further in virtue and knowledge; and he receives as an ally, or rather as his salvation, an angel, that is, one of the higher principles of wisdom and knowledge, who cuts off *every mighty man, warrior, leader and commander in the camp*' (2 Chr. 32:21)."

(St Maximos the Confessor, *Various Texts on Theology, the Divine Economy, and Virtue and Vice*, Third Century, 2, p. 210, Vol. 2, Philokalia)

"The cherubim – chastity and gentleness of the soul

(cf. Exodus 25:18-22)."

(Evagrius of Pontus, *Maxims 2*, Maxim 18, p. 231)

Specific terms

Letter of the Law

"Some commandments of the Mosaic Law must be kept both physically and spiritually, others only spiritually. For example, *'You shall not commit adultery, you shall not kill, you shall not steal'* (Exod. 20:13-15) and so on must be kept both physically and spiritually (the spiritual observance is threefold, as explained below). To be circumcised (cf. Lev. 12: 3), to keep the Sabbath (cf. Exod. 31:13), and to slaughter the lamb and eat unleavened bread with bitter herbs (cf. Exod. 12:8; 23:15) and similar injunctions are to be kept only spiritually."

(St Maximos the Confessor, *Four Hundred Texts on Love*, Second Century, Text 86, p. 80, Vol. 2, Philokalia)

"So long as he cleaves to the letter, his inner hunger for spiritual knowledge will not be satisfied; for he has condemned himself like the wily serpent to feed on the earth—that is, on the outward or literal form—of Scripture (cf. Gen. 3:14), and does not, as a true disciple of Christ, feed on heaven—that is, on the spirit and soul of Scripture, in other words, on celestial and angelic bread."

(St Maximos the Confessor, *Various Texts on Theology, the Divine Economy, and Virtue and Vice*, Fifth Century, 35, p. 268, Vol. 2, Philokalia)

"The letter kills" says Scripture, *"but the Spirit gives life"* (2 Cor. 3:6). Consequently, the letter whose nature is to kill must be killed by the life-giving Spirit. For what is material in the Law and what is divine—namely, the letter and the Spirit—cannot coexist, nor can what destroys life be reconciled with that which by nature bestows life.

The Spirit bestows life, the letter destroys it. Thus the letter cannot function at the same time as the Spirit, just as what gives life cannot coexist with what destroys life and the prejudice from which he suffers as a result. This is to show that, thanks to contemplation, the letter of the Law has been killed by spiritual knowledge."

(St Maximos the Confessor, *Various Texts on Theology, the*

Divine Economy, and Virtue and Vice, Fifth Century, 39-40, p. 270, Vol. 2, Philokalia)

"All sacred Scripture can be divided into flesh and spirit as if it were a spiritual man. For the literal sense of Scripture is flesh and its inner meaning is soul or spirit. Clearly someone wise abandons what is corruptible and unites his whole being to what is incorruptible.

The Law is the flesh of the spiritual man who here corresponds to sacred Scripture; the prophets are the senses; the Gospel is the noetic soul that functions through the flesh of the Law and the senses of the prophets, revealing its power in its actions."

(St Maximos the Confessor, *On Theology and the Incarnate Dispensation of the Son of God*, First Century, Texts 91-92, p. 134, Vol. 2, Philokalia)

Enemies

It must be absolutely clear for us, that whenever Scriptures refer to various enemies, and often with pretty harsh words, it is impossible to interpret them literally without attributing to their Inspirer our familiar human passions (wrath, vindictiveness, revengefulness).

"Each one then of the saints when he looks on the destruction of his foes and his own triumphs, exclaims with delight: "*I will follow after mine enemies and overtake them: and I will not turn until they are destroyed. I will break them and they shall not be able to stand: they shall fall under my feet*" (Psalm 17:38-39) and in his prayers against them the same prophet says: "*Judge thou, O Lord, them that wrong me:*

overthrow them that fight against me. Take hold of arms and shield: and rise up to help me. Bring out the sword and shut up the way against them that persecute me: say to my soul, I am thy salvation" (Psalm 34:1-3). And when by subduing and destroying all our passions we have vanquished these, we shall then be permitted to hear those words of blessing: *"Thy hand shall be exalted over thine enemies, and all thine enemies shall perish"* (Micah 5:8). And so when we read or chant all these and such like passages found in holy writ, unless we take them as written against those spiritual wickednesses which lie in wait for us night and day, we shall not only fail to draw from them any edification to make us gentle and patient, but shall actually meet with some dreadful consequence and one that is quite contrary to evangelical perfection. For we shall not only not be taught to pray for or to love our enemies, but actually shall be stirred up to hate them with an implacable hatred, and to curse them and incessantly to pour forth prayers against them. And it is terribly wrong and blasphemous to think that these words were uttered in such a spirit by holy men and friends of God, on whom before the coming of Christ the law was not imposed for the very reason that they went beyond its commands, and chose rather to obey the precepts of the gospel and to aim at apostolical perfection, though they lived before the dispensation of the time."

(John Cassian, *Conferences*, 7, Chapter 21, pp. 369-370)

"The commandment given by God to the first man, Adam, told him to keep watch over the head of the serpent (cf. Gen. 3:15. LXX), that is, over the first inklings of the pernicious thoughts by means of which the serpent tries to creep into our souls. If we do not admit the serpent's head, which is the provocation of the thought, we will not admit the rest of its body—that is, the assent to the sensual pleasure which the thought suggests—and so debase the mind towards the illicit act itself. As it is written, we should 'early in the morning destroy all the wicked of the earth' (Ps. 101:8), distinguishing in the light of divine knowledge our sinful thoughts and then eradicating them completely from the earth—our hearts—in accordance with the teaching of the Lord. While the children of Babylon—by which I mean our wicked thoughts—are still young, we should dash them to the ground and crush them against the rock, which is Christ (cf. Ps. 137:9; 1 Cor. 16:4). If these thoughts grow stronger because we assent to them, we will not be able to overcome them without much pain and labor."

(St. John Cassian, *On the Eight Vices*, pp. 76-77, Vol. 1, Philokalia)

"We must not only put bodily passions to death but also destroy the soul's impassioned thoughts. Hence the psalmist says, *'Early in the morning I destroyed all the wicked of the earth, that I might cut off all evil-doers from the city of the Lord'* (Ps. 101:8)—that is, the passions of the body and the soul's godless thoughts."

(St Maximos the Confessor, *On Theology and the Incarnate Dispensation of the Son of God*, Second Century, Text 97, p. 163, Vol. 2, Philokalia)

Scriptures illustrate certainly very graphically man's inner battle, and sometimes perhaps too graphically, according to our time at least. And it is true that they often have been tragically misinterpreted. Yet, there were always those interpreters who didn't leave any room for misinterpretation for those who seek sincerely their meanings. And this sincere intention constitutes a necessary condition for the understanding of the Scriptures for it is a fact that when we are not sincere in our search, we distort even the most easy to understand meanings let alone the difficult ones.

Hades

'Hades' is the ignorance of the rational nature that arises

as a result of the deprivation of the contemplation of God."

(Evagrius of Pontus, *Thirty-three Chapters*, p. 227)

"Scripture says: 'Hell [Sheol-Hades] and perdition are manifest to the Lord' (Prov. 15:11). This refers to ignorance of heart and forgetfulness. Hell [Sheol-Hades] is ignorance, for both are dark; and perdition is forgetfulness, for both involve extinction."

(St. Mark the Ascetic, *On the Spiritual Law*, Texts 61-62, p. 114, Vol. 1, Philokalia)

Ascension

"Let us go forward with the heart completely attentive and the soul fully conscious. For if attentiveness and prayer are daily joined together, they become like Elijah's fire-bearing chariot (cf. 2 Kgs 2:11), raising us to heaven. What do I mean? A spiritual heaven, with sun, moon and stars, is formed in the blessed heart of one who has reached a state of watchfulness, or who strives to attain it; for such a heart, as a result of mystical contemplation and ascent, is enabled to contain within itself the uncontainable God."

(St Philotheos of Sinai, *Forty Texts on Watchfulness*, Text 27, p. 26, Vol. 3, Philokalia)

Passover

"But what does the "Passover" of Christ mean? The Israelites celebrated the "Fasek" (Passover) when they left the land of Egypt. The Passover that the saint now exhorts us to celebrate is something the soul accomplishes when it escapes from the spiritual Egypt, that is to say, from sin. When the soul passes over from sin to virtue, it celebrates the "Fasek" – the Passover of the Lord, as Evagrius said: "The Passover of the Lord is the passage away from evil."

(Abba Dorotheos, *Practical Teaching on the Christian Life*, Lesson 16, Pgh 166, pp. 235-236)

Promised Land

"The leader of the people of Israel first must flee from Egypt—the actual committing of sin—next must cross over the Red Sea—servitude through attachment—and thirdly must dwell in the desert—the desert lying between the impulses to sin and the outward fulfillment of these impulses. Only then, sending ahead his visual and visionary force, can he spy out the promised land —dispassion (cf. Josh. 2:1)."

(St. Ilias the Presbyter, *A Gnomic Anthology*, Part III, Verse 14, p. 49, Vol. 3, Philokalia)

"Prayer combined with spiritual contemplation constitutes the Promised Land in which there flows, like 'milk and honey' (Exod. 3:8), the spiritual knowledge of the principles of God's providence and judgment. Prayer combined with a certain measure of natural contemplation is Egypt, in which those who pray still encounter the memory of their grosser desires. Simple prayer is manna in the desert (cf. Num. 11:7). Since it is unvarying, this manna does not disclose to the impatient the promised blessings for which they long; but for those who persevere with such restricted food, it imparts most excellent and abiding nourishment."

(St. Ilias the Presbyter, *A Gnomic Anthology*, Part IV, Verse 52, p. 54, Vol. 3, Philokalia)

"The land of the Chaldeans is a way of life dominated by the passions, in which the idols of sins are fashioned and worshipped. Mesopotamia, the land between the rivers, is a way of life that vacillates between opposites. The promised land is a state filled with every blessing. Everyone, then, who like ancient Israel neglects this state, loses the freedom which he has been granted, and allows himself once more to be dragged off into slavery to the passions."

(St Maximos the Confessor, *On Theology and the Incarnate Dispensation of the Son of God*, Second Century, Text 48, p. 149, Vol. 2, Philokalia)

"The land of the gentle (cf. Ps. 37:11) is the kingdom of heaven. Or else it is the theandric state of the Son, which we have attained or are in the process of attaining, having through grace been reborn as sons of God into the new life of the resurrection. Or again, the holy land (cf. Ex. 3:5) is our human nature when it has been divinized or, it may be, the land purified according to the measure of those dwelling in it. Or, according to another interpretation, it is the land granted as an inheritance (cf. Numb. 34:13) to those who are truly saints, the untroubled and divine serenity and the peace that transcends the intellect (cf. Phil. 4:7)—the land wherein the righteous dwell quietly and unmolested."

(St Gregory of Sinai, *One Hundred and Thirty-Seven Texts*, Text 47, p. 221, Vol. 4, Philokalia)

Dead

"The Lord also described those who live in this vain world as 'dead', for when one of His disciples asked to be allowed to go and bury his father, He refused permission, and told him to follow Him, leaving the dead to bury their dead (cf. Matt. 8 : 22). Here, then, the Lord clearly calls those living people 'dead', in the sense that they are dead in soul. As the separation of the soul from the body is the death of the body, so the separation of God from the soul is the death of the soul. And this death of the soul is the true death. This is made clear by the commandment given in paradise, when God said to Adam, '*On whatever day you eat from the forbidden tree you will certainly die*' (cf. Gen. 2:17). And it was indeed Adam's soul that died by becoming through his transgression separated from God; for bodily he continued to live after that time, even for nine hundred and thirty years (cf. Gen. 5:5)."

(St Gregory Palamas, *To the Most Reverend Nun Xenia*, Texts 8-9, pp. 295-296, Vol. 4, Philokalia)

Resurrection

"*And he arose, and came to his father. But when he was yet a great way off, his father saw him, and had compassion, and ran, and fell on his neck, and kissed him. And the son said unto him, "Father, I have sinned against heaven, and in thy sight, and am no more worthy to be called thy son." But the father said to his servants, "Bring forth the best robe, and put it on him; and put a ring on his hand, and shoes on his feet: and bring hither the fatted calf, and kill it; and let us eat, and be merry: For this my son was* dead, *and is* alive again" (Luke 15:20-24).

Since there are *dead* which are related to our internal, it's clear that there will be the corresponding *inner resurrection*. So it becomes obvious that St Paul refers to this inner resurrection and impending salvation, "*Knowing the time, that now it is high time to awake out of* sleep: *for now is our salvation nearer than when we believed*" (Romans 13:11), following the footsteps of Jesus' Teaching who also referred to the imminent Kingdom of Heaven, "*And he said unto them, Verily I say unto you, That there be some of them that stand here, which shall not taste of death, till they have seen the kingdom of God come with power*" (Mark 9:1) and to the immediateness of His Presence, "*Verily I say unto you, This generation shall not pass, till all these things be fulfilled*" (Matthew 24:34).

Unfortunately though, our carnal mind obliges us constantly to turn our attention *outside* and look for everything outside of us, despite of the fact that the words of our Teacher are more than clear, "*And when he was demanded of the Pharisees, when the kingdom of God should come, he answered them and said, "The kingdom of God cometh not with observation: Neither shall they say, Lo here! or, lo there! for, behold, the kingdom of God is within you". And he said unto the disciples, "The days will come, when ye shall desire to see one of the days of the Son of man, and ye shall not see it. And they shall say to you, See here; or, see there: go not after them, nor follow them*" (Luke 17:20-23) and "*Then if any man shall say unto you, Lo, here is Christ, or there; believe it not*" (Matthew 24:23).

> "*Know ye not your own selves,*
> *how that Jesus Christ is in you*" (2 Corinthians 13:5).

So the external misinterpretation which places everything *outside* of us is truly painful and sad to its results, for it deprives us of the treasure which is *near* and *at hand*, and removes it to a vague and uncertain future (usually after death!). It is known historically that this kind of misinterpretation led many people in *tragic-comic* situations where they expected the external end of the world at the *expense* of the fulfillment of their *inner potential*. But what is even stranger is that up today, this kind of misinterpretation is attributed to the most eminent Paul. The majority of scholars believe unquestionably that this great Apostle was mistaken in his judgment and believed that the glorious resurrection of the dead would take place during his lifetime. It is very possible that this kind of (external) misinterpretations were made by the wider circle of followers of the christian teaching, as it happens also in our days, but to attribute this kind of indiscretion to the man who spread the Teaching of Christ to the largest part of the known world of his time, is truly peculiar. Yet, from another view, it shouldn't surprise us so much, since the same mistake has also been attributed to Jesus Himself!

> *"Verily, verily, I say unto you, The hour is coming, and now is, when the dead shall hear the voice of the Son of God: and they that hear shall live"* (John 5:25).

One of the passages of Paul's epistles which has led the scholars to the certain view that the Apostle of the nations (gentiles) waited for the imminent *external fulfillment* of the prophecy concerning the end of the *world* (and the consequent resurrection of the dead) is to be found in the First Epistle to Corinthians (7:17-29) where he urges his brethren to remain to the place (calling) in which they already are, for the time is short.

> *"Let every man abide in the same calling wherein he was called. Art thou called being a servant? Care not for it: but if thou mayest be made free, use it rather. For he that is called in the Lord, being a servant, is the Lord's freeman: likewise also he that is called, being free, is Christ's servant. Ye are bought with a price; be not ye the servants of men. Brethren, let every man, wherein he is called, therein abide with God. [...] This I say, brethren, the time is short"* (1 Corinthians 7:20-24, 29).

Yet, whoever has studied any of the real spiritual traditions, he will know that man is often urged not to change anything from his external conditions, for precisely these conditions are the best for his inner work. And if he performs his *inner* work, "*be not ye the servants of men*", with the urgency that it deserves, "*the time is short*", this might also bring some corresponding external results, "*Art thou called being a servant? Care not for it: but if thou mayest be made free, use it rather.*"

No, it's not in any way reasonable for St Paul not to know the inner interpretation of the resurrection of the dead, which was known by all the real, subsequent Fathers of the Church.

> "The disciple. What is the resurrection of the soul, namely if ye be risen with Christ? (Coloss. 3:1)

> The teacher. This is what is said by the apostle in another place: "*For God who commanded the light to shine out of darkness, hath shined in our hearts*" (2 Cor. 4:6). Resurrection he calls leaving the old state, which in the likeness of Hell hindered him from seeing the light of the Gospel rise, so to say, which is the breath of life in the hope of the resurrection by which the dawn of divine wisdom rises in the heart, so that he now is a new man in whom is nothing of this world. As it has been said: "*A new heart also will I give you; and a new spirit will I put within you*" (Ez. 36:26)."

> (Isaac of Nineveh, *Mystic Treatises*, XXXV, pp. 165-166)

> '*Behold, the kingdom of heaven is within you*' (Luke 17:21). For, as St John of Damaskos says, the kingdom of heaven is not far away, not outside us, but within us. Simply choose to overcome the passions, and you will possess it within you because you live in accordance with God's will. But if you do not choose to do this, you will end up with nothing. For the kingdom of God, say the fathers, is to live in conformity to God; and this is also the meaning of Christ's first and second coming."

(St Peter of Damaskos, *Book I – The Fourth Stage of Contemplation*, p. 126, Vol. 3, Philokalia)

And of course we also know that St Paul was teaching himself the allegorical interpretation of the Scriptures, "*And all these things as* types *did happen to those persons, and they were written for our admonition*" (1 Corinthians 10:11, YLT); "*Which things are an* allegory" (Galatians 4:24). So we can see that this divine Apostle doesn't need our defense since his writings (when they are interpreted from an internal view) make themselves clear his meanings and the correctness of his teaching:

"*For as in Adam all die, even so in Christ shall all be made alive. But every man in his own order: Christ the firstfruits; afterward they that are Christ's at his coming. [...] The last enemy that shall be destroyed is death [...] I die daily [...] Awake to righteousness, and sin not [...] But some man will say, How are the dead raised up? and with what body do they come? Thou fool, that which thou sowest is not quickened, except it die: And that which thou sowest, thou sowest not that body that shall be, but bare grain, it may chance of wheat, or of some other grain: But God giveth it a body as it hath pleased him, and to every seed his own body. All flesh is not the same flesh: but there is one kind of flesh of men, another flesh of beasts, another of fishes, and another of birds. There are also celestial bodies, and bodies terrestrial: but the glory of the celestial is one, and the glory of the terrestrial is another. There is one glory of the sun, and another glory of the moon, and another glory of the stars: for one star differeth from another star in glory.*

So also is the resurrection of the dead. It is sown in corruption; it is raised in incorruption: It is sown in dishonour; it is raised in glory: it is sown in weakness; it is raised in power: It is sown a psychic [ψυχικό] *body; it is raised a spiritual body. There is a* psychic [ψυχικό] *body, and there is a spiritual body. And so it is written, The first man Adam was made a living soul; the last Adam was made a quickening spirit. Howbeit that was not first which is spiritual, but that which is* psychic [ψυχικό]; *and afterward that which is spiritual. The first man is of the earth, earthy: the second man is the Lord from heaven. As is the earthy, such are they also that are earthy: and as is the heavenly, such are they also that are heavenly. And as we have borne the image of the earthy, we shall also bear the image of the heavenly. Now this I say, brethren, that flesh and blood cannot inherit the kingdom of God; neither doth corruption inherit incorruption"* (1 Corinthians 15:22-50).

In these very beautiful and enlightening passages, Paul reveals us all the inner interpretation of the resurrection of the dead, using terms that have been misinterpreted variously during the centuries and of course up to our days. Phrases like, *"flesh and blood cannot inherit the kingdom of God; neither doth corruption inherit incorruption"* and *"so also is the resurrection of the dead. It is sown in corruption; it is raised in incorruption: It is sown in dishonour; it is raised in glory: it is sown in weakness; it is raised in power: It is sown a* psychic [ψυχικό] *body; it is raised a spiritual body. There is a* psychic [ψυχικό] *body, and there is a spiritual body"*, reveal clearly that the great Apostle refers to internal realities that don't leave much room for misinterpretations; yet, our carnal mind, which insists in lowering everything down to its level, keeps misinterpreting them, that is why in most, if not all, the translations of the New Testament, the word "psychic" [*ψυχικό*] is rendered as "natural"!

Still, both the Apostles and of course Jesus Himself, used very specific terms (death, dead, sleep, awakening, resurrection) in order to illustrate the corresponding inner states, that is why we see them being constantly interrelated, *"Awake thou that sleepest, and arise from the dead, and Christ shall give thee light"* (Ephesians 5:14), creating thus a magic Image which keeps slipping us away, until we begin recreating inside us: *"Watch ye therefore: for ye know not when the master of the house cometh, at even, or at midnight, or at the cockcrowing, or in the morning: Lest coming suddenly he find you sleeping. And what I say unto you I say unto all, Watch"* (Mark 13:35-37).

Sleep

"Therefore let us not sleep, as do others;
but let us watch and be sober" (1 Thessalonians 5:6)

In the christian tradition, the physical death is understood as a separation of the soul from the body, whilst, the inner death can be perceived as a separation of the soul from the spirit or as separation of our spirit from God's Spirit. But there is also another inner interpretation of death which refers in dying to our old "self" so we can be (re)born to our Real Self. Yet, in order to die to something, we must first *awake* to it, that is, *realize* it.

"I know thy works, that thou hast a name that thou livest, and art dead.
Be watchful [Wake up], and strengthen the things which remain,
that are ready to die: for I have not found thy works perfect before God"
(Apocalypse 3:1-2).

In the New Testament, the words *wake up* and *watch* are mentioned pretty often and are always given as exhortations. And it's again impressive how the mind of the senses is incapable of perceiving their inner sense and thinks that they refer to physical sleep!

The most impressive misinterpretation of the term *sleep*, is related to one of the most leading moments of the evangelic narrations where Jesus asks from his disciples to be watchful (awake) while He is praying.

"And they came to a place which was named Gethsemane: and he saith to his disciples, "Sit ye here, while I shall pray." And he taketh with him Peter and James and John, and began to be sore amazed, and to be very heavy; And saith unto them, "My soul is exceeding sorrowful unto death: tarry ye here, and watch." And he went forward a little, and fell on the ground, and prayed

that, if it were possible, the hour might pass from him. And he said, "Abba, Father, all things are possible unto thee; take away this cup from me: nevertheless not what I will, but what thou wilt." And he cometh, and findeth them sleeping, and saith unto Peter, "Simon, sleepest thou? Couldest not thou watch one hour? Watch ye and pray, lest ye enter into temptation. The spirit truly is ready, but the flesh is weak." And again he went away, and prayed, and spake the same words. And when he returned, he found them asleep again, for their eyes were heavy, neither wist they what to answer him. And he cometh the third time, and saith unto them, "Sleep on now, and take your rest" (Mark 14:32-41).

The materialistic interpretation wants the disciples to have fallen physically to sleep! And this literal interpretation is repeated through the centuries, often by very serious scholars, who believe that Jesus urged His disciples not to fall asleep so He won't feel loneliness!

Yet, this misinterpretation underestimates both the disciples and Jesus and it is evidently disorienting since the evangelic narration is absolutely clear: *"Watch ye and pray, lest ye enter into temptation."* Jesus urges the disciples to be watchful for their own sake, not His own. And indeed after awhile, Peter who has received a special pointing out, *"Simon, sleepest thou?"* denies Jesus *three times*, that is, *completely*.

This carnal misinterpretation is also due to the famous saying, *"The spirit truly is ready, but the flesh is weak"*, which is considered as a reference to the weak body which falls to sleep! Whilst in essence it refers precisely to our carnal mind which distorts all the spiritual (inner) symbolisms! Despite how ready (willing) is our spirit to be *awake*, our flesh (our carnal mind) is incapable (weak) of *understanding*.

Sleep, is one of the most self-evident inner symbols and it doesn't signify of course the external (physical) sleep but what is taking place during sleep. The basic characteristics of physical sleep are that when we are asleep some of our organs of perception cease to function actively and also we have less control upon our overall being. We do not control the incoming of our impressions;

we do not have control over our thoughts and feelings; and the control of our body becomes entirely instinctive; in general, we are in a more *vulnerable* condition.

The same phenomena can be observed accordingly, when we are asleep internally, psychologically or spiritually. Some of our *organs of perception* are not functioning actively and we have less control over our internal world. So we are in a vulnerable state and thus subjected to all kinds of temptation.

"I laid me down and slept" (Psalm 3:5).

He means the *nous'* sleep, due to which he fell into sin."

(St. Athanasius the Great, *Commentary on the Psalms, Works*, Vol. 5, p. 101)

At the level of the soul, *sleep* refers to ignorance, to lack of self-knowledge; and we can easily observe this kind of sleep, if not in ourselves, certainly in others. We can easily see in others how they might be asleep to some of their obvious traits which everyone else around them knows. And these might be traits that also concern us, but we do not see them, simply because we are equally asleep to them! And in our case, they might even be more inflated and then of course what can be more appropriate than the deep words:

"And why beholdest thou the mote that is in thy brother's eye, but considerest not the beam that is in thine own eye? Or how wilt thou say to thy brother, "Let me pull out the mote out of thine eye" and, behold, a beam is in thine own eye? Thou hypocrite, first cast out the beam out of thine own eye; and then shalt thou see clearly to cast out the mote out of thy brother's eye" (Matthew 7:3-5).

We have heard these words many times, and if we want to be honest, we will have to admit that in a strange way we don't really feel that they concern us particularly. This fact is based on a singular property of *sleep* (external and internal). When we are asleep, we can almost never perceive that we are asleep. If at any moment we realize that we are asleep, then we usually wake up. So the only way in reality to be aware that we are asleep, is to *awake.*

World

"Scripture calls material things 'the world'."

(St Maximos the Confessor, *Four Hundred Texts on Love,* Second Century, Text 53, p. 74, Vol. 2, Philokalia)

"If you wish to see the blessings *'that God has prepared for those who love Him'* (1 Cor. 2:9), then take up your abode in the desert of the renunciation of your own will and flee the world. What world? The world of the lust of the eyes, of your fallen self (cf. 1 John 2:16), the presumptuousness of your own thoughts, the deceit of things visible."

(Nikitas Stithatos, *On the Practice of the Virtues,* One Hundred Texts, 75, pp. 98-99, Vol. 4, Philokalia)

'I have said these things to you, so that in Me you may have peace. In the world you will experience affliction; but have courage, for I have overcome the world' (John 16:33). In other words, 'In Me, the Logos of virtue, you have peace, for you have been released from the swirl and turmoil of material passions and objects; in the world—that is, in a state of attachment to material things—you are afflicted because of the successive changes of these things.'

(St Maximos the Confessor, *On Theology and the Incarnate Dispensation of the Son of God,* Second Century, Text 95, p. 162, Vol. 2, Philokalia)

"The world is bodily behaviour and carnal thoughts."

(Isaac of Nineveh, *Mystic Treatises*, II, p. 13)

Latin, Greek and Hebrew

"The charge made against the Savior in the inscription on the Cross clearly showed that He who was crucified was Lord and king of practical, natural and theological philosophy. For Scripture says that the inscription was written in Latin, Greek and Hebrew (cf. John 19:20). I take Latin to signify the practical branch of philosophy, since according to Daniel (cf. Dan. 2:40) the Roman empire was appointed to be the most resolute and manful of all the kingdoms on earth; for the distinguishing feature of the practice of the virtues, or practical philosophy, is resolution and manfulness, I take Greek to signify natural contemplation, since the Greek nation more than any other people has pursued natural philosophy. I take Hebrew to signify initiation into the mysteries of theology, since this nation was from the beginning clearly consecrated to God through the patriarchs."

(St Maximos the Confessor, *On Theology and the Incarnate Dispensation of the Son of God*, Second Century, 96, pp. 162-163, Vol. 2, Philokalia)

Testament

The *testament* consists of an *agreement* between God and us which has derived from an *experience*. And this experience is a foundation upon which we can build our inner house. If we forget it, we cease to keep our agreement. If we retain it alive, then the correct construction of our soul takes place and so our experience *deepens* and our agreement is automatically *renewed*.

"The law of the Old Testament through practical philosophy cleanses human nature of all defilement. The law of the New Testament, through initiation into the mysteries of contemplation, raises the intellect by means of spiritual knowledge from the sight of material things to the vision of spiritual realities."

(St Maximos the Confessor, *Various Texts on Theology, the Divine Economy, and Virtue and Vice*, First Century, 67, p. 179, Vol. 2, Philokalia)

"The Old Testament makes the body obedient to the intelligence and raises it towards the soul by means of the virtues, preventing the intellect [*nous*] from being dragged down towards the body. The New Testament fires the intellect [*nous*] with love and unites it to God."

(St Maximos the Confessor, *Various Texts on Theology, the Divine Economy, and Virtue and Vice*, Fourth Century, 84, p. 256, Vol. 2, Philokalia)

"Reformation of life, angelic worship, the willing separation of the soul from the body, and the beginning of divine renewal in spirit—these are proclaimed in the veiled language of the New Testament."

(St Maximos the Confessor, *Various Texts on Theology, the Divine Economy, and Virtue and Vice*, First Century, 85, p. 184, Vol. 2, Philokalia)

Son of God

"Created man cannot become a son of God and god by grace through deification, unless he is first through his own free choice begotten in the Spirit."

(St Maximos the Confessor, *Various Texts on Theology, the Divine Economy, and Virtue and Vice*, Fifth Century, 97, p. 284, Vol. 2, Philokalia)

"The faithful man becomes heir of God, joint-heir with Christ (Romans 8:17), a second Christ in a way and partaker of divine nature (2 Peter 1:4)—something which transcends all nous and surpasses all intellect—and thus he becomes clearly son of God and god by grace."

(Callistus Angelikoudis, *Chapters on Prayer*, Chapter 73, p. 200, Vol. 5, Philokalia)

The Life of Jesus

The Life of Jesus constitutes of course the greatest inner symbol and indicates all the stages that we need to go through in order to walk the Path of Love from beginning to end. Its external *historic reality* certainly concerns us, but it concerns us *overall*, as *humanity*, whilst its internal reality concerns us much more *directly* and *personally*. And if we do not experience it in our present, then it is bereaved much of its significance as a past historic event which might *determined* the course of humanity but eventually left *us* indifferent.

"The divine Logos, who once for all was born in the flesh, always in His compassion desires to be born in spirit in those who desire Him. He becomes an infant and moulds Himself in them through the virtues. He reveals as much of Himself as He knows the recipient can accept."

(St Maximos the Confessor, *Various Texts on Theology, the Divine Economy, and Virtue and Vice*, First Century, 8, pp. 165-166, Vol. 2, Philokalia)

"For he who seeks Christ, says St Maximos, should seek him not outside but inside himself.' Like Christ he should become sinless in body and soul, in so far as a human being can do this; and he should guard the testimony of his conscience (cf. 2 Cor. 1:12) with all his strength. In this way, even though in the eyes of the world he is poor and of no consequence, he will rule as a king over his will at all times, rising above it and rejecting it."

(St Peter of Damaskos, *Book I – The Fourth Stage of Contemplation*, p. 126, Vol. 3, Philokalia)

"There are three stages on the spiritual path: the purgative, the illuminative and finally the mystical, through which we are perfected. The first pertains to beginners, the second to those in the intermediate stage, and the third to the perfect. It is through these three consecutive stages that we ascend, growing in stature according to Christ and attaining 'mature manhood, the measure of the stature of the fullness of Christ' (Eph. 4:13)."

(Nikitas Stithatos, *On Spiritual Knowledge, Love and the Perfection of Living*, One Hundred Texts, 41, p. 150, Vol. 4, Philokalia)

"Everyone baptized into Christ should pass progressively through all the stages of Christ's own life, for in baptism he receives the power so to progress, and through the commandments he can discover and learn how to accomplish such progression. To Christ's conception corresponds the foretaste of the gift of the Holy Spirit, to His nativity the actual experience of joyousness, to His baptism the cleansing force of the fire of the Spirit, to His transfiguration the contemplation of divine light, to His crucifixion the dying to all things, to His burial the indwelling of divine love in the heart, to His resurrection the soul's life-quickening resurrection, and to His ascension divine ecstasy and the transport of the intellect [nous] into God. He who fails to pass consciously through these stages is still callow in body and spirit, even though he may be regarded by all as mature and accomplished in the practice of virtue."

(St Gregory of Sinai, Further Texts, Text 1, p. 253, Vol. 4, Philokalia)

"Our spiritual growth corresponds to the different stages in the life of our Lord Jesus Christ. While we are infants in need of milk (cf. Heb. 5:12) we are suckled on the milk of the introductory virtues acquired through bodily discipline; yet this is of but limited profit (cf. 1 Tim. 4:8) to us once we begin to grow in virtue and gradually leave our infancy behind. When we attain adolescence and are nourished by the solid food of the contemplation of the spiritual essences of things—for our soul's organs of perception are now well attuned (cf. Heb. 5:14)—it may be said that we increase in stature and in grace (cf. Luke 2:52), and sit among the elders (cf. Luke 2:46), disclosing to them things hidden in the depths of darkness (cf. Job 12:22). When we have reached 'mature manhood, the measure of the stature of the fullness of Christ' (Eph. 4:13), we proclaim to all the meaning of repentance, teach others about the kingdom of heaven (cf. Matt. 4:17) and press on towards the Passion (cf. Luke 12:50). For this is the ultimate goal of everyone who has reached perfection in the practice of the virtues: after passing through all the different ages of Christ he finally undergoes the trials that Christ suffered on the cross."

(Nikitas Stithatos, *On Spiritual Knowledge, Love and the Perfection of Living*, One Hundred Texts, 50, p. 154, Vol. 4, Philokalia)

Seven Persons

At this point we will attempt an inner interpretation of the roles that might play seven of the most significant persons which are related to the Jesus Christ's drama. We will examine briefly the possible roles of John the Baptist, Virgin Mary, the triad Peter, James, John, St Paul and of the notorious Judas!

John the Baptist

John the Baptist symbolizes internally the initial stage of our spiritual course. We need purgation (baptism), fasting (cutting off the old bonds) and emptying (wilderness) so the new can enter; so that *metanoia* (repentance) is made possible, which prepares the coming of the Divine element, of the Kingdom of Heaven.

That is why Jesus asks from John to baptize Him, despite his protests, *"Then cometh Jesus from Galilee to Jordan unto John, to be baptized of him. But John forbad him, saying, "I have need to be baptized of thee, and comest thou to me?" And Jesus answering said unto him, "Suffer it to be so now: for thus it becometh us to fulfil all righteousness." Then he suffered him."* (Matthew 3:13-15), indicating thus that the stage of John is requisite for the inner growth of man.

And later on when the disciples of John compare, due to their ignorance, their teaching with His, *"Then came to him the disciples of John, saying, Why do we and the Pharisees fast oft, but thy disciples fast not?"* (Matthew 9:14), Jesus takes this chance to indicate again the significance of the purgation which must take precedence, relating the parable of the old and the new wine, *"And Jesus said unto them, Can the children of the bridechamber mourn, as long as the bridegroom is with them? But the days will come, when the bridegroom shall be taken from them, and then shall they fast. No man putteth a piece of new cloth unto an old garment, for that which is put in to fill it up taketh from the garment, and the rent is made worse. Neither do men put new wine into old bottles: else the bottles break, and the wine runneth out, and the bottles perish: but they put new wine into new bottles, and both are preserved*" (Matthew 9:15-17).

Nevertheless, He doesn't omit to warn us that the stage of John, is not but a preparatory stage: it is the highest one in the *human* level but the least in the Divine, "*Verily I say unto you, Among them that are born of women there hath not risen a greater than John the Baptist: notwithstanding he that is least in the kingdom of heaven is greater than he*" (Matthew 11:11). We could say that this stage does not essentially belong in the Divine path but it is *before* the Way (John is the *fore-runner*). Still, it's necessary to pass through it and complete it, so we can be prepared for our entrance into the Divine Way, "*For this is he, of whom it is written, Behold, I send my messenger before Thy face, which shall prepare Thy way before thee*" (Matthew 11:10).

At this stage *before* the way, it's reasonable to doubt from time to time in relation to the Way, "*I am the Way*" (John 14:1) and wonder, "Are You the Way?": "*John Baptist hath sent us unto thee, saying, Art thou he that should come? or look we for another?*" (Luke 7:20), and that is because we are still before the Way; when we will enter into the Way, we will understand more and deeper, "*Jesus answered and said unto them, Go and shew John again those things which ye do hear and see: The blind receive their sight, and the lame walk, the lepers are cleansed, and the deaf hear, the dead are raised up, and the poor have the gospel preached to them*" (Matthew 11:4-5).

So John the Baptist and Forerunner illustrates the necessary preparatory stage of purification (baptism) from which each soul should go through in order to be purified (that is, become virgin: clean, chaste, immaculate) so she can receive the Divine Spirit and conceive the Son of God.

Virgin Mary

Virgin Mary embodies through all the centuries the ultimate model of purity. She receives the Divine Word precisely due to her purity and begets the Son of Love. Internally, she evidently symbolizes for us the chaste soul, the pure soul which can accept the Divine Seed.

"The soul that through the grace of its calling resembles God keeps inviolate within itself the Substance of the blessings bestowed upon it. In souls such as this Christ always desires to be born in a mystical way, becoming incarnate in those who attain salvation, and making the soul that gives birth to Him a Virgin Mother."

(St Maximos the Confessor, *On the Lord's Prayer*, p. 294, Vol. 2, Philokalia)

So Virgin Mary is defined as second Eve and constitutes for humanity the path of return to the Lost Paradise. The first Eve was considered as the cause of loss of Paradise and the second Eve is the cause of salvation. That is to say that the spiritual man turned outward through the soul and thus was cut off from the Spirit inside him, so this is also his way of return.

When our soul is clean and pure, turned to her internal, she hears the (ev)angelic words: "*And the angel came in unto her, and said, "Hail, thou that art highly favoured, the Lord is with thee: blessed art thou among women*" (Luke 1:28) and it's natural then to be "troubled" from this unexpected joyful message, for it's true that we don't really know what to expect upon our return inwards, "*And when she saw him, she was troubled at his saying, and cast in her mind what manner of salutation this should be*" (Luke 1:29). Yet, the assurance that we are on good way comes at once, "*And the angel said unto her, Fear not, Mary: for thou hast found favour with God. And, behold, thou shalt conceive in thy womb, and bring forth a son*" (Luke 1:30-31). If then we give our consent, "*And Mary said, Behold the handmaid of the Lord; be it unto me according to thy word. And the angel departed from her*" (Luke 1:38), the gestation of the Son of Love will begin in us and soon it will lead to the birth of our Real Self; and this of course is only the initial stage of our new course in the Kingdom of God.

"What happened in the stainless Mary when the fullness of the Godhead which was in Christ shone out through her, that happens in every soul that leads by rule the virgin life. No longer indeed does the Master come with bodily presence; *"we know Christ no longer according to the flesh"* (2 Cor. 5:16); but, spiritually, He dwells in us and brings His Father with Him, as the Gospel somewhere tells (see John 14:23)".

(St. Gregory of Nyssa, *On Virginity*, Chapter 2, pp. 344-345)

In this point it would be interesting to examine briefly the role of Joseph in the process of birth of the Son of God by the Virgin Mary. Internally, Joseph symbolizes probably the intellect. The intellect cannot play an *essential* role in the birth of the spirit into the pure heart but still retains a significant part. The intellect must be mature enough in order to understand the truth of the heart, so it won't hinder her in her work, "*Joseph, thou son of David, fear not to take unto thee Mary thy wife: for that which is conceived in her is of the Holy Ghost*" (Matthew 1:20). And also it must support her as well, by being able to receive the practical instructions from the world of the Spirit, which aim in protecting the spiritual birth from all the external and internal enemies, "*The angel of the Lord appeareth to Joseph in a dream, saying, "Arise, and take the young child and his mother, and flee into Egypt, and be thou there until I bring thee word: for Herod will seek the young child to destroy him*" (Matthew 2:13).

Peter, James, John

The triad of Peter, James and John symbolizes in essence the triad of Faith, Hope and Love.

"For those who like Peter have advanced in faith, and like James have been restored in hope, and like John have achieved perfection in love, the Lord ascends the high mountain of theology and is transfigured (cf. Matt. 17:1)."

(Nikitas Stithatos, *On Spiritual Knowledge, Love and the Perfection of Living*, One Hundred Texts, 52, p. 155, Vol. 4, Philokalia)

In the Gospels and the Acts of the Apostles there aren't many clues as to the personalities of these disciples, except perhaps for Peter; yet, it is interesting to note that the New Testament is embellished with their epistles. So either through the personal references to those Apostles or through their so-called epistles, we will try to see how they represent for us this special triad of virtues.

It is pretty known for *Peter* that he embodies the virtue of Faith, "*Simon, Simon, behold, Satan hath desired to have you, that he may sift you as wheat: But I have prayed for thee, that thy faith fail not: and when thou art converted, strengthen thy brethren*" (Luke 22:31-32). And perhaps he is mentioned a lot more than the other disciples in the Gospels, because Faith is the foundation, the rock, upon which all the other virtues are build, with Love of course being the roof of our inner structure.

"Rock was the name given to faith due to stability, immutability, reliability, and the complete immobility of its truth and because it doesn't retreat in any way against the revolts of falsehood."

(Maximus the Confessor, *To Thalassius on Various Questions of the Divine Scripture*, Question 54, Comment 20, p. 49, Vol. 14C, Philokalia)

Peter is renamed from Simon to Peter, that is, rock, and hears the famous words, "*And I say also unto thee, That thou art Peter, and upon this rock I will build my church*" (Matthew 16:18). He hears these words when he declares his faith in Jesus Christ being the Son of God, "*He saith unto them, "But whom say ye that I am?" And Simon Peter answered and said, "Thou art the Christ, the Son of the living God." And Jesus answered and said unto him, "Blessed art thou, Simon Barjona: for flesh and blood hath not revealed it unto thee, but my Father which is in heaven*" (Matthew 16:15-17).

Yet, since Peter embodies the virtue of faith, it's reasonable to be also depicted as having little faith. Jesus often rebukes him, to the point of calling him "Satan", but the clearest depiction of his lack of faith is when he sinks in the waters:

> "*And when the disciples saw Him walking on the sea, they were terrified, and said, "It is a ghost!" And they cried out for fear. But immediately Jesus spoke to them, saying, "Have courage! It is I AM; do not fear." But Peter answered Him and said, "Lord, if it is You, command me to come to You on the waters." So He said, "Come." And stepping down from the boat, Peter walked on the waters to go toward Jesus. But seeing the strong wind, he was afraid, and beginning to sink he cried out, saying, "Lord, save me!" And immediately, Jesus reaching out His hand, laid hold of him, and said to him, "O you of little faith, why did you doubt?"* (Matthew 14:26-31, EMTV).*

The whole story of Peter, culminating in his threefold denial and his instant remorse, illustrates for us the struggle between faith and little faith and shows us the path for the foundation of the first requisite virtue for the constructing of our *inner* Church.

We can be better acquainted with *James*, through his epistle which is special in that it clearly refers to a specific stage of our inner evolution. It refers to the fruitfulness of faith; that is, to hope. For it is true that hope complements faith.

We can believe in something, without hoping into it. But we cannot truly hope in something, without believing into it. Hope means *faith with works* and that is precisely what the epistle of James teaches. Yet, in his epistle he doesn't use directly the word hope but he uses the word patience which entails its meaning:

> "*My brethren, count it all joy when ye fall into divers temptations; Knowing this , that the trying of your faith worketh patience. But let patience have her perfect work, that ye may be perfect and entire, wanting nothing. If any of you lack wisdom, let him ask of God, that giveth to all men liberally, and upbraideth not; and it shall be given*

him. But let him ask in faith, nothing wavering. For he that wavereth is like a wave of the sea driven with the wind and tossed. For let not that man think that he shall receive any thing of the Lord. A double minded [two-souled, YLT] man is unstable in all his ways" (James 1:2-8).

From this passage we can understand that wavering suggests lack of hope, and also that hope is the mother of patience. So James embodies for us, through his epistle, the *practical* faith, *"But be ye doers of the word, and not hearers only, deceiving your own selves"* (James 1:22). And he is so unequivocal in his suggestion, that is, in the example he embodies, *"Even so faith, if it hath not works, is dead"* (James 2:17), that many scholars have claimed that these words contradict St Paul's words, *"For by grace are ye saved through faith; and that not of yourselves: it is the gift of God: Not of works, lest any man should boast"* (Ephesians 2:8-9). And indeed there is a seeming contradiction in these passages which yet disappears when we realize that Paul refers to what we believe as our *own* works—concerning which we are in danger of boasting—and not to the works (fruits) of the *God-given* faith, which is the basis of hope, *"Faith is the substance of things hoped for"* (Hebrews 11:1). That is to say, that when faith is established in us, it brings forth its fruits, its works; and the works of faith are patience which comes from real hope into what we believe. That means that faith is complemented by hope which puts it into practice and these two virtues are completed by the third virtue of the triad, by love, which includes both of them, *"All it believeth, all it hopeth, all it endureth. The Love doth never fail"* (1 Corinthians 13:7, YLT).

And thus we come to *John* who is the third disciple of the elect triad and is known as the *beloved* disciple of Jesus. Now, his three epistles embody completely the reality of Love. Besides, John is the one who reveals us that *"God is Love"* (1 John 4:8, 16). In his three epistles there are some of the most beautiful and profound passages in relation to love which reveal at the same time her meaning. They reveal that *Love means Unity*, with God and our neighbor.

"Whoever may keep his word, truly in him the love of God hath been perfected; in this we know that in him we are. He who is saying in him he doth remain, ought according as he walked also himself so to walk"
(1 John 2:5-6).

"See ye what love the Father hath given to us,
that children of God we may be called" (1 John 3:1).

"Because this is the message that ye did hear from the beginning,
that we may love one another" (1 John 3:11).

"In this we have known the love, because he for us his life did lay down, and we ought for the brethren the lives [souls] to lay down" (1 John 3:16).

"Beloved, let us love one another: for love is of God; and every one that loveth is born of God, and knoweth God. He that loveth not knoweth not God; for God is love. In this was manifested the love of God toward us, because that God sent his only begotten Son into the world, that we might live through him. Herein is love, not that we loved God, but that he loved us, and sent his Son to be the propitiation for our sins. Beloved, if God so loved us, we ought also to love one another. No man hath seen God at any time. If we love one another, God dwelleth in us, and his love is perfected in us. Hereby know we that we dwell in him, and he in us, because he hath given us of his Spirit. And we have seen and do testify that the Father sent the Son to be the Saviour of the world. Whosoever shall confess that Jesus is the Son of God, God dwelleth in him, and he in God. And we have known and believed the love that God hath to us. God is love; and he that dwelleth in love dwelleth in God, and God in him. Herein is our love made perfect, that we may have boldness in the day of judgment: because as he is, so are we in this world. There is no fear in love; but perfect love casteth out fear: because fear hath torment. He that feareth is not made

perfect in love. We love him, because he first loved us. If a man say, I love God, and hateth his brother, he is a liar: for he that loveth not his brother whom he hath seen, how can he love God whom he hath not seen? And this commandment have we from him, That he who loveth God love his brother also" (1 John 4:7-21).

"By this we know that we love the children of God, when we love God, and keep his commandments. For this is the love of God, that we keep his commandments: and his commandments are not grievous" (1 John 5:2-3).

So we can clearly see that John has been rightfully named "the apostle of Love" since it's true that his epistles brim over with love, *"The elder unto the wellbeloved Gaius, whom I love in the truth"* (3 John 1:1) and give us the feeling that Love is indeed the Reality for the *beloved* disciple of Jesus, *"The elder unto the elect lady and her children, whom I love in the truth [...]And now I beseech thee, lady, not as though I wrote a new commandment unto thee, but that which we had from the beginning, that we love one another"* (2 John 1:1, 5).

Thus John completing the elect triad of the disciples and apostles of Jesus, completes the elect triad of virtues, personifying for us the Truth of Love.

St Paul

St Paul embodies completely the notion of *practical metanoia*. He truly represents the inner restoration (*metamorphosis*) of Love; from being a persecutor (as Saul) of Love, he is completely conversed and begins (as Paul) to pursue Her!

"This is a faithful saying, and worthy of all acceptation, that Christ Jesus came into the world to save sinners; of whom I am chief. Howbeit for this cause I obtained mercy, that in me first Jesus Christ might shew forth all longsuffering, for a pattern to them which should hereafter believe on him to life everlasting" (1 Timothy 1:15-16).

The chapter "St Paul" both as an internal symbol and as an external reality cannot be exhausted of course in a few lines. Here we only attempt a very brief inner interpretation of this great personality which constitutes the perfect pattern for all those who did not know Jesus Christ during his Incarnation but are trying to embody Him within them, *"Not I, but Christ liveth in me"* (Galatians 2:20). Despite of the fact that he had never been personally a disciple of Christ, we could say, symbolically at least, that his apostolic work surpassed even the one of the first Apostles. He became a super Apostle. That is to say, he undertook a mission which transcended the known limits of such a work. He became the Apostle of the nations (gentiles); and the nations symbolize those sides of ours who don't really know anything about the real God, in contrast to those more pious sides of ours which only need to be revitalized. He symbolizes this side of ours which once persecuted Truth and now pursues Her whole-heartedly, having truly understood. While he is on the way of persecution (of *others*) he is completely conversed and follows the Way of Sacrifice (of *himself*).

Many of us might have truly lived the course of Paul but certainly all of us contain certain sides like these who are opposed to the Truth simply due to ignorance, due to mistaken perceptions. These sides are not destined to be put to death, that is, to be eradicated, but to be reversed, in order to *see*, *"Something like scales fell from his eyes, and he could see again"* (Acts 9:18, EMTV). So Paul consists of the ultimate example of true *metanoia*, of *practical conversion*.

Judas Iscariot

Judas takes the last place in this attempt of interpreting the roles that are personified by seven of the most significant persons of the New Testament, and it was kept according to the narrative of the Gospels for the last twelfth disciple.
It's interesting to note the fact that the epistles which are contained in the New Testament and contain further explanations regarding the four Gospels are attributed to Paul; to Peter, James and John; and to... Judas! Not of course to the widely known Judas the

Iscariot but to the less known Judas the brother of James, *"Judas, a servant of Jesus Christ and a brother of James"* (Judas 1:1). [*Jude,* in its English rendering, probably so it won't be reminiscent of the "bad" Judas; but in reality the ancient Greek name is indeed *Judas* (*Yehouda*), precisely the same with the name of Judas the Iscariot.] Nevertheless, perhaps it's not accidental that one of the epistles that embellish the Gospel of Love carries the name of the famous betrayer… and is dedicated exclusively to the eternal problem of the false-teachers! And thus it refers, in one sense, to betrayers, *"For there are certain men crept in unawares, who were before of old ordained to this condemnation, ungodly men, turning the grace of our God into lasciviousness, and* denying *the only Lord God, and our Lord Jesus Christ"* (Judas 1:4).

Now, the drama of Jesus' Story along with all of its protagonists has been engraved indelibly into humanity's consciousness as an experience it once lived. Humanity could never be the same after this experience.

All of the disciples, and Jesus Christ Himself, represent human types, and mostly states of consciousness. The roles they have been shouldered, symbolize aspects of ourselves, such as, disbelief, unbelief, doubting and questioning, ignorance, lack of understanding, vanity, self-assertion, antagonism, negligence, insensitivity, fear, aggression but also faith, strength, wisdom, maturity, discernment, self-sacrifice, Love.

So Judas is shouldered with the most difficult perhaps role (after the one of Jesus), the one of absolute denial, absolute betrayal of Love; the role of absolute darkness; the role of the devil. He accepts to be taken over completely by the devil (egoism), manifesting thus our darkest side. By playing this role he shows us what we all of us contain potentially and engraves in the collective subconscious, the dimension and significance of this side of ours; its experience and consequences. After him, no man would ever want to be in his place; no one would even dare to think of BEING Judas. Thus by playing this role, Judas suffers and learns for the sake of humanity the lesson of this experience, *the pain of the absolute negation of Love.*

Now, the evidences that make out a case for Judas playing consciously his part, are plenty. First of all, it is obvious that the whole Drama of Jesus Christ was premeditated and prophesized, since there are constant references which testify to this fact, "*And now I am no more in the world, but these are in the world, and I come to thee. Holy Father, keep through thine own name those whom thou hast given me, that they may be one, as we are. While I was with them in the world, I kept them in thy name: those that thou gavest me I have kept, and none of them is lost, but the son of perdition; that the scripture might be fulfilled*" (John 17:11-12).

Judas was lost, that the scripture might be fulfilled. If we do not interpret this loss as conscious, then we are in danger of falling to an interpretation which almost offends God who conceived this Plan.

It is self-evident that Jesus didn't need any "help" to be handed over to His persecutors; one of His public provoking appearances was enough to arrest Him at once, "*Are ye come out, as against a thief, with swords and with staves to take me? I was daily with you in the temple teaching, and ye took me not: but the scriptures must be fulfilled*" (Mark 48-49).

And it is certainly blasphemous the idea that God used a "pawn" in an extremely crude way in order to fulfill his Plan. For even if Judas was the worst of all, which one of us the little ones, with the whit of Love inside us, would choose him, giving him a part beyond his strength, which would put so much pressure on him, exhorting him to bring the worst out of him? Which one of us would accept knowingly for such a drama to be conducted, which would result not only in the devastating destruction of a weak being but also in his eternal damnation by himself, by men and by God? If we would not be able for such an atrocious and criminal choice, due to the whit of Goodness within our heart, let alone Love Herself!

And of course, this kind of interpretation of the role of Judas, insults inconceivably the Teacher of Love (who is constantly referred as knowing the thoughts in His disciples' hearts) considering Him as either naïve or a criminal. And so brings forth the unanswerable question: "If Jesus knew that Judas was going to betray Him, why did He choose him?"

But also the rest evidences of these evangelic narrations, testify clearly to the inadequacy of this interpretation. The money that Judas receives is very little and the realization of his "mistake" is very prompt, so the reasonable questions appear: "How foolish was Judas to receive just a very little money in order to betray the very Son of God? And hadn't he understood anything of His greatness all this time? And why did he betray Him for an insignificant amount of money which he returned at once, with the only result of self-condemning?"

When Jesus says that someone will deliver Him up, *everyone* wonders *who* that might be, *"And while they are eating, he said, "Verily I say to you, that one of you shall deliver me up." And being grieved exceedingly, they began to say to him, each of them, "Is it I, Sir?"* (Matthew 26:21-22, YLT). Were they all so inadequate and so capable of betraying their Teacher, whilst at the same time they had enough self-knowledge to recognize that? When Jesus said to Peter that he will deny Him three times, Peter doubted Him! *"And Jesus saith unto him, "Verily I say unto thee, That this day, even in this night, before the cock crow twice, thou shalt deny me thrice." But he spake the more vehemently, "If I should die with thee, I will not deny thee in any wise."* Likewise also said they all." (Mark 14:30-31). The disciples are in reality wondering *who might play that part*; to whom shall this role might be given, *"Therefore the disciples were looking at one another, perplexed about whom He was speaking"* (John 13:22, EMTV). And the only one who seems to know the answer, is the one who has already been shouldered with this role and at this moment he accepts it also openly, *"And Judas, he who delivered him up, answering said, "Is it I Rabbi?" He saith to him, "Thou hast said."* (Matthew 26:25, YLT), that is, *you* chose it.

Jesus says that someone will deliver Him up, and at the question of His disciples, who will play this part, *"Lord, who is it?"* (John 13:25), Jesus answers, *"It is the one to whom I shall give a piece of bread when I have dipped it"* (John 13:26, EMTV), and so Judas is the first who receives the Holy Communion of the blood and flesh of Jesus Christ, that is, he participates in His self-denial and self-sacrifice by playing his own unique role, *"And after the piece of bread, then Satan entered him. Therefore Jesus said to him, "What you do, do quickly"* (John 13:27, EMTV).

And there are of course plenty more questions that result if we want to interpret the betrayal of Judas as unconscious, such as: What did Judas do long before the Last Supper, when Jesus sends His disciples to teach, heal and *raise the dead*?

"And when he had called unto him his twelve disciples, he gave them power *against unclean spirits, to cast them out, and to heal all manner of sickness and all manner of disease. Now the names of the twelve apostles are these; The first, Simon, who is called Peter, and Andrew his brother; James the son of Zebedee, and John his brother; Philip, and Bartholomew; Thomas, and Matthew the publican; James the son of Alphaeus, and Lebbaeus, whose surname was Thaddaeus; Simon the Canaanite, and* Judas Iscariot, *who also betrayed him [deliver Him up, YLT]. These twelve Jesus sent forth, and commanded them, saying, "Go not into the way of the Gentiles, and into any city of the Samaritans enter ye not: But go rather to the lost sheep of the house of Israel. And as ye go, preach, saying, The kingdom of heaven is at hand. Heal the sick, cleanse the lepers, raise the dead, cast out devils: freely ye have received, freely give"* (Matthew 10:1-8).

Judas is clearly included in the Twelve Disciples and he is also been given the power to heal and resurrect. There is not any reference excluding him. So is the Scripture mistaken in including him clearly to the Twelve Disciples who perform all these miracles? But even if in some way he didn't participate in the disciples' miracles, how could he remain unaffected by all he sees? And even if he did not believe anything from what he was seeing, why did he keep on *following* Jesus in His *laborious* course?

There have been many attempts to fill these intentionally created gaps of the story of Judas, by saying that Judas might thought that Jesus would create an earthly kingdom and when he realized that He talked about a heavenly, spiritual kingdom, he got frustrated and betrayed Him. But something like this could be true only for the outer circle of Jesus' disciples, for some unknown person from the crowds, and not for one of the Twelve. For Jesus often takes them to the side and teaches them openly the Truth. What did Judas do then? They simply dragged him along, whilst he didn't understand anything?

This interpretation presents Jesus choosing for His closest circle of disciples one of the most incapable and weak men He could possibly find, giving him a part which he certainly wouldn't endure, having at the same time full awareness of the consequences of His choice.

So we attribute unconsciously and thoughtlessly this atrocious action to the Son of Love who sacrificed Himself for all humanity to be saved, thinking that it's possible for the "son of perdition" to have been also sacrificed (without his conscious consent) along His Way. One of those that His Father had given Him to keep them was lost so *"that the Scripture might be fulfilled"*, a phrase that remains completely incomprehensible to us.

Thus the only reasonable, and perhaps obvious, interpretation of the enigmatic story of Judas is the one that sees him as undertaking consciously the role of the "son of perdition". And this interpretation not only doesn't offend both our understanding and the protagonists of this staggering Story, but comes in no contradiction with the teaching of Jesus, since this role of the "son of perdition" is a painful and difficult *self-sacrificing* part of the highest importance and necessity.

The fulfillment of the Scriptures meant the full illustration and actualization of the metamorphosis from egocentrism to Love. That is why we cannot really claim that Judas didn't betray Jesus; yes, he did betray Him but he *accepted* to betray Him (deliver Him up). He *consented* in the Light of Jesus' Love being removed from his heart and thus being filled by the devil's darkness, personifying thus the most unfortunate and at the same time abhorrent personality that has ever been recorded by human history. In essence, Judas is the most wretched figure of the Gospels, for even Jesus after He experiences His Passion, at the end He triumphs and glorifies Love. Judas on the contrary, has a miserable ending through a relentless *self-condemnation*. And he gains instead of the eternal Glory, the eternal *aversion*.

It is self-evident of course that the most painful and difficult role of self-sacrifice was the one of Jesus Himself; but for Paul too who was self-sacrificed playing the role of the "Apostle of the nations" his role was a difficult one, as well as for Peter who was self-sacrificed in order to play the role of the "Rock of the Church".

In one way or the other, *all* the disciples, following the example of their Teacher, played roles of self-sacrifice, according to their strength and understanding. The tradition presents all the disciples, with the exception perhaps of John, to have experienced the death of a martyr, as did Jesus Himself.

So it is obvious that when the Son of Love called them to follow Him, He knew what He was doing and didn't lead them to their perdition (even if that was one of the roles they had to play, according to the Scriptures) but to their real Glory before God and not necessarily before men.

He chose people to whom He had foreseen their potential; He had foreseen what fruits they could bring forth and with the elaborate accuracy of a merited (farmer) teacher, He led (cultivated) them to their fruitfulness. He showed them and opened for them, the Path of Self-Sacrifice, walking it Himself, and so led them safely to the Glory of God, that is, to self-denial for the sake of Love.

The fact that the chapter of "Judas" rouses our interest is not surprising, nor the attempts of restoring his honor are irrational, since they originate from our fundamental, Divine tendencies of human solidarity. Humanity was always interested in Judas and was seeking for interpretations that would advocate to his innocence or to his forgiveness; and that was so to the extent that she was related to the Divine Love inside her. When she is removed away from Love, she hastens to condemn the person of Judas, ensuring him the worst possible fate.

Yet, we should be careful in our attempt of understanding the person of Judas and discern between himself and his role. His role, that is, the inner state of the "son of perdition" is truly disgraceful, reprehensible and hideous, and that is what his living example teaches us: "Beware, not to become sons of perdition by betraying Love within you, for there is no worse fate than this! The outcome of this dark betrayal will be the most dishonorable *self-condemnation*."

So when we desire to restore the "fame" of Judas, we are surely induced by the rudimentary sense of Love we all have inside us, which doesn't let us to rest in the thinking of the tragic fate of any being, whatever it seems to have committed. But we need to be careful so we won't abrogate the very work of Judas and render unconsciously his role and sacrifice vain. Since his absolute dishonoring, from then up today, was part of his self-sacrifice. For however we interpret the role of Judas, as long as humanity exists (or perhaps until she reaches to her overall metamorphosis) Judas will remain recorded in her soul as the abhorrent betrayer of Love. In this way we are meant to remember him and this is completely reasonable since that was the role he was called to play and *experience* for the sake of humanity, symbolizing thus forever the tragic consequence of the negation of Love which is a cruel *self-condemnation*.

In this point we could perhaps try to understand another important symbolic element of this narrative: the kiss of Judas, *"And he who did deliver him up did give them a sign, saying, "Whomsoever I will kiss, it is he: lay hold on him;" and immediately, having come to Jesus, he said, "Hail, Rabbi," and kissed him"* (Matthew 26:48-49, YLT). This act of Judas has been considered as the ultimate proof of his unworthiness since he used as symbol of love (kiss) to betray Love. Yet, the kiss of Judas could also be an indication of his deep love for Jesus and might consisted of a tragic last kiss before the summit of His Passion. Besides, Judas is the only one mentioned in the Gospels kissing Jesus! Now, Jesus poses the question, *"Judas, with a kiss the Son of Man dost thou deliver up?"* (Luke 22:48, YLT) which initially seems to indicate either surprise or reproach, but if we look deeper it seems to contain a hidden Truth: In Reality there isn't any opposed force to Love which can fight Her, but only the lack of understanding Her. So the only way to betray Love is through Her distortion, through a "kiss" which means that every act of evil is in essence an act of distorted "love". That means that even the negation of Love takes place within Her boundaries! So we are taught that *behind everything Love is hidden*, for *nothing* can exist outside of Her!

Concluding, all the persons of the Evangelic Drama constitute *aspects of our psychology*. The History of Jesus illustrates the journey of our soul and spirit which is complemented thoroughly by the various side-stories of all the rest persons who illustrate our different aspects both personally and collectively. Every experience of a human-cell of humanity is recorded to her collective subconscious (and conscious), and the deeper it is, the more indelibly is engraved inside her and carves her potential paths. So next we will examine the primordial original sin and the subsequent Fall of the first man, searching again for its inner interpretation, that is, the interpretation which concerns mainly *our very selves*.

Fall

The allegorical story of the Fall refers to the fall from Unity to duality (disunity), which begets multiplicity. The tree of the knowledge of good and evil, is the symbol of duality. The Tree of Life is the symbol of Unity, of Love.

"The tree of life is the divine love which Adam lost by his fall, after which he worked and wearied himself (cf. Genesis 3:23). Those who are bereft of divine love are still eating the bread that is won by the sweat of their labour, even though they work righteousness, as was commanded to the head of our race when he lost it by his fall (cf. Genesis 3:19). Until we find love, we work in the earth with her thorns. Among thorns we sow and reap, even if we sow the seed of righteousness. Perpetually we are pricked by them, even if we are justified, and live with sweat on our faces."

(Isaac of Nineveh, *Mystic Treatises*, XLIII, p. 211)

This fall is taking place inside us (and in humanity) when we fall from the spiritual level to the psychological and from the psychological to the physical (material).

Adam, who receives the breath (spirit) of God, symbolizes the spiritual man, our spirit. Eve, who is created from Adam's ribs, symbolizes the psychological man, our soul. The serpent is a symbol of our materialistic mind, of the mind of the senses, which leads our soul (Eve) into temptation and calls her to taste the fruits of its (egoistic) perception. Now, the perception of the serpent (materialistic mind) is not simple (single), it is *cunning*, that is, *dual*. The mind of the senses doesn't perceive the Unity, it believes instead firmly to multiplicity. It sees many things which conceives them all as separated. For the eyes of the senses everything that exists is cut off from all else. And thus it is produced, for our materialistic mind, the *good* and *evil*; the *yes* and *no*; which conflict with each other and are perceived as *opposite*. And of course they are changeable and sometimes mixed. That is, what seems to be good might be evil, and reversely.

This is the perception of the cunning (evil) eye which cannot grasp that all is One, Good, and without any conflict in between them, whether they are expressed as Yes or as No. That is why Jesus says to His disciples, *"But let your word be "Yes", "yes"; or "No", "no." For whatever is more than these is from the cunning [evil] one"* (Matthew 5:17, EMTV), and elsewhere urges them for their eye (inner perception) to be *single (simple)* and not *cunning,* *"The light of the body is the eye: if therefore thine eye be single, thy whole body shall be full of light. But if thine eye be cunning [evil], thy whole body shall be full of darkness. If therefore the light that is in thee be darkness, how great is that darkness"* (Matthew 6:22-23).

Unfortunately, in the English language the meaning of the "cunning one" [ponirós] has been essentially lost, since it's always rendered as the "evil" or the "wicked" one. Some relative examples would be:

"And lead us not into temptation, but deliver us from evil [cunning]" (Matthew 6:13).

"O generation of vipers, how can ye, being evil [cunning ones], speak good things? For out of the abundance of the heart the mouth speaketh. A good man out of the good treasure of the heart bringeth forth good things: and an evil [cunning] man out of the evil [cunning] treasure bringeth forth evil [cunning] things" (Matthew 12:34-35).

"When any one heareth the word of the kingdom, and understandeth it not, then cometh the wicked [cunning] one, and catcheth away that which was sown in his heart" (Matthew 13:39)

"We know that whosoever is born of God sinneth not; but he that is begotten of God keepeth himself, and that wicked [cunning] one toucheth him not" (1 John 5:18).

"We know that we are from God, and the whole world lies under the sway of the evil [cunning] one" (1 John 5:19, EMTV).

"I pray not that thou shouldest take them out of the world, but that thou shouldest keep them from the evil [cunning]" (John 17:15).

"Of the tree of the knowledge of good and evil [cunning], of it ye shall not eat" (Genesis 2:17, LXX).

Now, Man is a Unified psycho-somatic and psycho-spiritual entity which is nevertheless "divided" in levels, with the psyche (soul) constituting, as we can see, the intermediate level. We could liken Man to a three-storied house where the body consists of the first floor (level), the soul is the second floor (level) and the spirit is the third floor (level). When Man is in order then the spirit, as the highest level, has the control of the other levels. When he is in disorder (*fall*), the control is assumed by the lowest level, the body, which orders about the soul and cuts off completely the spirit from any contact, condemning it thus to *death*. That was the death—a *spiritual* death—that the first man (and every man) experienced when he was carried away by his soul (his human self) which was carried away by his materialistic mind (his animal self) and thus turned *out* of Himself (his Divine Self) and lost the Kingdom of God, *"For the wages of sin is death"* (Romans 6:23).

The Kingdom of God signifies an internal state, *"The kingdom of God is within you"* (Luke 17:21) in which the Lord within us, the *King*, is God and we are in an indissoluble communication and connection with Him. So when he *get out of ourselves*, we lose the taste of Reality; we cease to be fed from the Tree of Life, and we are fed by the fruits of non-reality, of the tree of knowledge of good and evil.

We are called to seek first the Kingdom of God and then everything else, *"Seek ye first the kingdom of God, and his righteousness; and all these things shall be added unto you"* (Matthew 6:33). That means that to be in order, to stand onto our *height*, we must be stable in our *depth*, and from *in there* look at the world outside us. For within us is the Real Source of Life from which we are fed and Live.

Otherwise, when we get out of our Self, and seek Life outside of us, indeed we find *many* sources of life; good ones (life) and evil ones ("life"). But in that way we fall from our internal height and are cut off from our internal Paradise, from our internal feeding. And so we *reverse* the right order of things and see them upside down, that is, from outside to inside. What does this mean? It means that everything that happens is affecting us. We do not have internal integrity, internal *simplicity* (singleness) and thus we become prays of multiplicity. If things go well, we are well; if things get bad, we are bad. And every source of happiness is to be found *out* there: love, relations, nature, wealth, learning, prosperity, life itself after all is for us outside and around us.

> "We have miserably fallen from the unified and *noetic* spiritual life and from the ability to contemplate the face of God and to be glorified as we would be altered by the rays of divine beauty, and we found ourselves, as we shouldn't have, separated and divided into many, enjoying inappropriately the divided life and its otherness. [...]

> We've lost the principal One and the unified life and order, and we got torn apart into many and diverse, and our *noetic* power and force, or rather elevation, to say it more appropriately, was lost, not unjustifiably, and we reached to the bottom of no less evil; we, the images of God, worthy of the higher and heavenly life, we chose unwisely to care for the lower things."

> (Callistus Katafygiotis, *On Union with God, and Life of Theoria*, Chapter 76, p. 259, Vol. 5, Philokalia)

Traditionally, man represents usually the spirit and woman represents the soul. This is based probably in the fact that man, as the male principle, represents activity, whilst, woman, as the female principle, represents "passivity", that is, receptivity.

> "Wise men of old gave the soul a feminine name. Indeed she is

> female in her nature as well. She even has her womb."

(*The Exegesis on the Soul*, The Nag Hammadi Library)

And this is the relationship which should exist between our spirit and soul. The spirit is our Real Self, our Real I; it is the Son of God inside us, our Divine Self. The soul is our human self, our subjective I, the son of man inside us, and should have a relation of receptivity with the spirit; the same relationship that our spirit has with the Spirit of God.

In our correct order, that means when our *spirit* (our *nous*, according to the Fathers which doesn't denote the intellect in its ordinary sense) is *united* with our soul and leads her, it becomes a carrier of the spiritual Divine Meanings which are begotten in the soul and constitute eventually our virtuous ideas and feelings.

"Woman symbolizes the soul engaged in ascetic practice;

through union with it the intellect [*nous*] begets the virtues."

(St. Thalassios the Libyan, *On Love, Self-Control and Life in Accordance with the Intellect*, Second Century, Text 27, p. 314, Vol. 2, Philokalia)

The offspring (intellectual and emotional ones) of the soul are born easily and smoothly when there is within us the right order. Otherwise, the soul becomes barren and begets with pain and difficulty her *meanings*, *"I will greatly multiply thy sorrow and thy conception; in sorrow thou shalt bring forth children; and thy desire shall be to thy husband, and he shall rule over thee"* (Genesis 3:16). So we see many women (souls) in the Scriptures being *barren* (cf. Genesis 25:21, 29:31)

"An elder said, "The Shunamite woman took in Elisha (and she conceived and bore a child thanks to the coming of Elisha) despite the fact that she had not relations with any of the men (see 2 Kgs 4:8-37). It is said that the Shunamite woman represents the soul, Elisha the Holy Spirit. At whatever time the soul withdraws from the disturbance and trouble of the world, the Spirit of God comes upon it, at which point it is enabled to bear fruit though it is widowed [*barren* (*steira*), according to the Greek text, PG 65:248A].

(Abba Cronios, *The Book of the Elders*, p. 329)

And only after man (the spirit) restores his relationship with God (the Spirit) can his wife *conceive (bear children)*: *"The name of Abram's wife was Sarai [...] But Sarai was barren; she had no child. [...] The Lord appeared to Abram, and said unto him, "I am the Almighty God; walk before me, and be thou perfect. And I will make my covenant between me and thee, and will multiply thee exceedingly." And Abram fell on his face: and God talked with him, saying, "As for me, behold, my covenant is with thee, and thou shalt be a father of many nations. Neither shall thy name any more be called Abram, but thy name shall be Abraham; for a father of many nations have I made thee. And I will make thee exceeding fruitful, and I will make nations of thee, and kings shall come out of thee. And I will establish my covenant between me and thee and thy seed after thee in their generations for an everlasting covenant, to be a God unto thee, and to thy seed after thee." [...] And God said unto Abraham, "As for Sarai thy wife, thou shalt not call her name Sarai, but Sarah shall her name be. And I will bless her, and give thee a son also of her: yea, I will bless her, and she shall be a mother of nations; kings of people shall be of her"* (Genesis 11:29-30, 17:1-7, 15-16).

In the allegory of Genesis, God creates man, male and female, *"So God created man in his own image, in the image of God created he him; male and female created he them"* (Genesis 1:27) and *later on* He breaths into him his spirit, *"And breathed into his nostrils the breath of life; and man became a living soul"* (Genesis 2:7) and still *afterwards* He makes Eve (his soul) which consists of a result-emanation of the spirit (Adam), *"And the Lord God caused a deep sleep to fall upon Adam, and he slept: and he took one of his ribs, and closed up the flesh instead thereof; and the rib, which the Lord God had taken from man, made he a woman, and brought her unto the man. And Adam said, "This is now bone of my bones, and flesh of my flesh: she shall be called woman, because she was taken out of man"* (Genesis 2:21-23). That is why God commands Adam (the spirit) not to eat from the tree of duality, *"And the Lord God commanded Adam [the man], saying, "Of every tree of the garden thou mayest freely eat: But of the tree of the knowledge of good and evil [cunning], thou shalt not eat of it: for in the day that thou eatest thereof thou shalt surely die"* (Genesis 2:16-17), *before* He made Eve (the soul).

Eve (the soul) never hears directly this commandment from God! For she has only an indirect relationship with Him; she communicates with Him only through her spirit. And therefore she evidently hears the commandment from the spirit and this is who she *disobeys*. Our soul is not essentially in a direct communication with God. In the Scriptures, it is *usually* the angels who bring God's messages to women (soul), whilst men (spirit) can talk directly to God. Our spirit can be in direct contact with Him, because it is created by Him. The soul on the other hand is something like an organ of the spirit; it is its human manifestation. That is why when man listens to his soul, instead of his soul obeying to his spirit, he dies spiritually and becomes a psychic (psychological) man, instead of being a spiritual man (cf. 1 Corinthians 2:14-15).

So in the allegory of the Fall, it is Eve (soul) the one who is tempted by the serpent (the materialistic mind) since she is closer to it, consisting of an intermediate part of our overall being; and she is the one who tempts in her turn Adam (spirit), *"For Adam was first formed, then Eve. And Adam was not deceived, but the woman being deceived was in the transgression"* (1 Timothy 2:13-14).

When of course this narration is perceived literally, it leads to tragic misinterpretations that depict woman as having a greater responsibility than man regarding the fall of humanity. And even though Virgin Mary, as second Eve and of course as woman, is presented as the carrier of humanity's salvation, this misinterpretation resulted historically in the woman being accused first and foremost for the original sin, something which made even more difficult her already difficult position.

The first Even personifies the model of *disobedience* and the second Eve, the model of *obedience*, but both these models illustrate attitudes of our soul. Now, how all this allegory is applied to humanity, is another difficult matter. It is clear that both man and woman play the same role in humanity, since this allegory concerns them equally (both sexes contain within them Adam, Eve, the serpent and Paradise). But when did this Fall really happen and what were its consequences for humanity as a whole; it's so difficult to be grasped as difficult it's to grasp, for example, the age of humanity. What is the objective age of humanity? Is she an infant who just now begins to crawl? Is she a rebel teenager who doesn't really know what he is doing but soon will find his way? Is she a mature grown-up who is ready to give an essential direction to his life? Or an old man who reaches to his last days, unwilling to acknowledge his mistakes and to repent for them? It is very hard to answer this kind of question, because we are deprived of the high perspective which could answer it. But what we can relatively easily perceive is that humanity doesn't stand up to her height. When she fell from this height, doesn't matter so much for us; what matters is that humanity remains in fall. And what should really trouble us is that *we ourselves* are in *fall*.

And regarding to ourselves is far easier to ascertain the course of this fall. We are born in an initial Paradise. That is to say, that from the moment of our conception until our very first years, we are a clean *spirit* in direct communication with anything Divine. As we grow, the powers of our body and soul are developing, and it is then that, due to ignorance and lack of Education, we begin turn outwards, completely forgetting our initial inner purity and the taste of innocence. We begin seeking for meaning and happiness outside us: in games, in amusements, in our needs, in people, but mostly we start wanting… wanting and wanting our *own*. The world of multiplicity becomes our sole reality, and good and evil our guides. Good is what we want, evil what we don't want. Our egoism, that is, our *distorted* perception, is born, and from then on it is unknown when and if we will seek again our lost innocence; our lost inner Paradise; the return to our Father's House.

If we become tired, as the prodigal son, to be fed by the food of the swine, "*And he would fain have filled his belly with the husks that the swine did eat: and no man gave unto him*" (Luke

15:16), we might decide to come to our Self, that is, to turn into our inner world, so we can return to our Father's House where we can be fed abundantly, *"And when he came to himself, he said, "How many hired servants of my father's have bread enough and to spare, and I perish with hunger. I will arise and go to my father, and will say unto him, Father, I have sinned against heaven, and before thee, and am no more worthy to be called thy son: make me as one of thy hired servants." And he arose, and came to his father"* (Luke 15:17-20). Yet, in the parable of the prodigal son, are illustrated only our outward state and its consequences, as well as the decision to turn inwards and its result; it is not depicted the *path of return* which is more difficult than we think and easier than it seems.

And here arises one basic question: What is the reason for all this labor and pain?

Why did God create thus man, with the ability of sin (missing of the Mark)? And why since He knew that man would sin (miss the Mark), didn't He prevent him? Why did he give him a commandment which He knew he would disobey and why did He inflict him with such a hard to bear punishment? Where is the love? The omniscience? The omnipotence?

> "And the diseases of the present creation, and the fact that he have been placed, for the time being, to a lower level than the one of angels, and furthermore our place and learning in the present world, in this first stage of the course of creation, but also the cunning (evil) inclination inside us; all these have an aim. Perhaps God used all these things, both the dreadful and the glorious, as motives to realize the plan of His Economy for us, from the beginning of creation until today. So through all these, His infinite mercy shall be revealed, and His infinite dashing strength. And this is known by all intelligent men. Yet, most people don't know this; they don't know this the ones, who ask the Creator persistently, "Why didn't you create us from the beginning similar to the angels? Why didn't you place us straight away to the future glory?" These people do not know what they say, nor do they know the higher reasons of

the economy of these weaknesses. They do not know that through the things of this world, the sweetness of the Kingdom of Heaven should become more intense."

(Isaac the Syrian, *Ascetical Writings*, from the Second Part, 3rd treatise, 4th century of Gnostic Chapters, Chapter 88, Vol. 2b, pp. 124-125)

It is self-evident than when we take literally an allegorical narration, all kinds of *irrationalities* are brought forth and thus all the *reasonable* questions. This allegorical story was distorted by "christianity" which burdened humanity with the feeling of a heavy guilt for the "crime" of disobedience she committed against an intolerant, retributive "God".

Humanity, either as Adam (and Eve) or as the prodigal son (in the parable of the prodigal son there isn't any kind of hint of punishment on the part of the Father, what is revealed instead is His *infinite* mercy), is a being who evolves and this evolution is taking place through mistakes and straying. And the same is true for us personally and of course for our children. For only in this way does man *matures*.

"This dynamic aspect of human personhood is sometimes expressed by making a distinction between the *image* and the *likeness* of God. The original author of Genesis 1:26, when he wrote the words 'in our image, after our likeness', had probably no intention of marking a contrast between the two terms; they were simply understood as parallel. But many of the Greek Fathers — most notably St Irenaeus, Origen, St Maximus the Confessor and St John of Damascus - treat them as different in meaning. The 'image', on their exegesis, signifies that which the human being posseses from the start and which, despite the Fall, he never entirely loses, whereas the 'likeness' signifies our ultimate objective, the fullness of our sanctification and life in God, our *theosis* or 'deification'. The image is the initial endowment conferred on man at creation, the likeness is his final aim to be attained through the correct exercise of human freedom, aided always by God's grace. Image is to likeness as potentiality to realization, or as starting-point to end-point. The image is not self-sufficient but forward-looking, directed always to its fulfilment in the likeness. Man the traveller, *homo viator*, is throughout his life on a journey from the image to the likeness.

Christian writers have sometimes spoken about an 'original perfection' of the human race in Paradise: Adam at his creation, on such a view, was endowed with all possible fullness of sanctity and knowledge. For us today it is extremely difficult to give any meaning to such a notion. It is therefore important to realize that this is not in fact the only way in which man's unfallen state is envisaged within the early Christian tradition. There is another approach, found for example in such second-century authors as Theophilus of Antioch and Irenaeus, which fits far better with the dynamic distinction that we have drawn between image and likeness. Man at his first creation, so these authors suggest, was like an infant — perfect not so much in an actual as in a potential sense. He was not invested with a realized plenitude of wisdom and righteousness, but was merely in a state of simplicity and innocence. 'He was a child, not yet having his understanding perfected', states Irenaeus. 'It was necessary that he should grow and so come to his perfection'. God the Creator set Adam's feet upon the right path, but Adam had in front of him a long road to traverse between reaching his journey's end."

(Kallistos Ware, *The Mystery of the Human Person*, pp. 68-69)

God didn't give any "command" nor of course did He inflict any kind of punishment. God created, and creates, a being with certain specific possibilities which it can fulfill or not. And the fulfillment of these possibilities has at the same time a determined but not limited character. God doesn't obviously expect from us to do what He wants, or else… we will suffer the consequences. In the Divine Plan of His Love, He has appointed various possibilities (and impossibilities) for His beings, which are free to discover and thus fulfill them.

"Our present lacks are completely necessary for the aim of our ultimate perfection to be realized. For thanks to these lacks the fulfillment of the Divine Economy was completed. So our lacks constitute advantages."

(Isaac the Syrian, *Ascetical Writings*, from the Second Part, 3rd treatise, 4th century of Gnostic Chapters, Chapter 87, Vol. 2b, p. 123)

Our human parents give us life; they create us (physically) and provide us with certain possibilities which they expect us to realize gradually so we can fulfill them. They provide us with an initial (human) paradise of security, feeding, joy and happiness, whilst they know that at some point we will question it and reject it (one way or the other), since this consists of a necessary stage in our *maturing*. They naturally expect that the stage of our "disobedience" will be as smooth as possible, but since they *love* us, they forgive our trespasses even before we commit them and they only want the best for us and *from us*.

Being of course human, we have plenty examples of parents who "love" exceedingly their children and thus imprison them in their "love", rendering them incapable of growing and maturing. Clearly God, as Love, doesn't offer us such a "love"-prison, but endows us instead with our freedom. A freedom which is not negotiable; He doesn't tell us, "I grant you free will to choose your way, but if you do not choose correctly, you shall be condemned eternally to hell." The freedom is absolute. In the sense that we can choose freely either the Way which leads to the Mount, or the "way" which leads to the precipice, and of course we will reap what we sow, but we certainly won't be condemned for our mistake. From ourselves, yes, we will *self-condemn*, when we will realize what possibilities we had and what impossibilities we chose; but from God we will be forgiven and we will be given a new opportunity, if again we want to make use of it.

And if someone asks, "But how many opportunities can we be given?" Regarding ourselves, the answer is, "As much as we can take". Regarding God, the answer is, "As many as His mercy... unlimited."

> *"Then came Peter to him, and said, "Lord, how oft shall my brother sin against me, and I forgive him? Till seven times?" Jesus saith unto him, "I say not unto thee, until seven times: but, until seventy times seven"* (Matthew 18:21-22).

The Restoration of Love (Unity)

The word hell [*kolasis*] is not mentioned anywhere in the Old Testament and in the New Testament is used only *two times*. In an allegorical description of the Judgment Day:

"And whenever the Son of Man may come in his glory, and all the holy messengers with him, then he shall sit upon a throne of his glory; and gathered together before him shall be all the nations, and he shall separate them from one another, as the shepherd doth separate the sheep from the goats, and he shall set the sheep indeed on his right hand, and the goats on the left. Then shall the king say to those on his right hand, "Come ye, the blessed of my Father, inherit the reign that hath been prepared for you from the foundation of the world; for I did hunger, and ye gave me to eat; I did thirst, and ye gave me to drink; I was a stranger, and ye received me; naked, and ye put around me; I was infirm, and ye looked after me; in prison I was, and ye came unto me." Then shall the righteous answer him, saying, "Lord, when did we see thee hungering, and we nourished? Or thirsting, and we gave to drink? And when did we see thee a stranger, and we received? Or naked, and we put around? And when did we see thee infirm, or in prison, and we came unto thee?" And the king answering, shall say to them, "Verily I say to you, Inasmuch as ye did it to one of these my brethren—the least—to me ye did it." Then shall he say also to those on the left hand, "Go ye from me, the cursed, to the fire, the age-during, that hath been prepared for the Devil and his messengers; for I did hunger, and ye gave me not to eat; I did thirst, and ye gave me not to drink; a stranger I was, and ye did not receive me; naked, and ye put not around me; infirm, and in prison, and ye did not look after me." Then shall they answer, they also, saying, "Lord, when did we see thee hungering, or thirsting, or a stranger, or

naked, or infirm, or in prison, and we did not minister to thee?" Then shall he answer them, saying, "Verily I say to you, Inasmuch as ye did it not to one of these, the least, ye did it not to me." And these shall go away to punishment [hell-kolasis] *age-during, but the righteous to life age-during"* (Matthew 25:31-46, YLT)

And it is used once more by the disciple of Love, who reveals us in a sense its essential meaning:

"And we—we have known and believed the love, that God hath in us; God is love, and he who is remaining in the love, in God he doth remain, and God in him. In this made perfect hath been the love with us, that boldness we may have in the day of the judgment, because even as He is, we—we also are in this world; fear is not in the love, but the perfect love doth cast out the fear, because the fear hath punishment [hell-kolasis], *and he who is fearing hath not been made perfect in the love"* (1 John 4:16-18).

It's very interesting to note that in these two cases the word "hell" [kolasis] is rendered as "punishment". Whilst in many other cases where other words are used, such as "Gehenna" or "Hades" they are rendered as "hell". Yet, Gehenna was a place out of Jerusalem where they burned its waste in a fire that was never extinguished, hence, the "unquenchable fire". So all these terms have different meanings (Gehenna, Hades, hell, unquenchable fire, *outer* darkness) but even if we consider them as identical, still they cannot be understood as *opposite* to Paradise, or to the Kingdom of Heaven.

The Kingdom of Heaven is not subjected to duality, to good and evil; so it has no opposite. There is Reality and its negation, or more correctly, its *ab-sence*. Like darkness is not the opposite of the light but its absence. So when we refer both to Paradise and hell comparing them, in a certain sense, we are mistaken, unless we mean the latter as the absence of the former.

The Kingdom of God suggests an inner state of union with God, and its absence—however we name it—clearly suggests a state of disunion, disconnection and separation. And if we name the first state Life, inevitably we will name the second one death, that is, absence of Life.

So if we consider that the word "hell" suggests the absence of Paradise, of the Kingdom of Heaven, then we see that it doesn't refer in any way to any "punishment" of God, but only to an internal state, which sadly is very familiar to all of us and has to do with a sense of alienation and isolation. In its utmost degree, "hell" refers to the sense of absolute loneliness which is indeed the worst possible state for any being since it's in full contradiction with Reality, with Unity.

Yet, we can easily understand that this is not a real state—since it contradicts with Reality—but only an *illusory* state, created by *our very selves*. So it's unreasonable to consider the notion of "hell" (the *illusion* of the absence of Love) as some *punishment* (in its ordinary sense) of God. Certainly this view comes from our closed heart and is due precisely to this closing towards His Love.

> "As for me I say that those who are tormented in hell are tormented by the invasion of love. What is there more bitter and violent than the pains of love? Those who feel they have sinned against love bear in themselves a damnation much heavier than the most dreaded punishments. The suffering with which sinning against love afflicts the heart is more keenly felt than any other torment. It is absurd to assume that the sinners in hell are deprived of God's love. [...] That is what the torment of hell is in my opinion: remorse."
>
> (Isaac of Nineveh (the Syrian), from *The Spiritual World of Isaac the Syrian*, Bp. Hilarion Alfeyev, publ. by Cistercian Publications)

A more profound perspective is the one which understands "hell" as a spiritual state according which man feels the Divine Light as a *"consuming fire"* (cf. Hebrews 12:29). That is, instead of feeling that the Light of God warms us; we feel that it burns us due to our uncleanness. And that is what happens. God's Light is intended, before being able to warm us, to burn all our uncleanness so that the light of our spirit will be able to be reunited with the Light of the Spirit. The Divine Fire has a pedagogic character and not a vindictive one; it is not meant to doom but to save, "*Every man's work shall be made manifest: for the day shall declare it, because it shall be revealed by fire; and the fire shall try every man's work of what sort it is. If any man's work abide which he hath built thereupon, he shall receive a reward. If any man's work shall be burned, he shall suffer loss: but* he himself shall be saved; *yet so as by fire*" (1 Corinthians 3:13-15).

And here arises the *burning* question of the *duration* of this *sense of fire*.

In our days, the world "eternal" is basically connected with the notion of *eternity* which indicates a state of endless time or a time-less state. Yet, in the New Testament, and in its days, the world "eternal" [*aionios*, that is, age-during] was mostly connected with the word "age" which had various meanings and could refer to a life period, to a certain time interval or to a very long time-period. Generally, the use of words "aionios" (eternal, age-during) and "aion" (age-century) were mostly related to definate, but often undefined from man, time-periods, unless they referred to God (cf. Romans 16:26). Besides, in our days as well, the word *age* signifies, among other things, the period of a hundred years. So that means, according to some scholars (see, John Wesley Hanson, *Aión-Aiónios*), that the word "aionios" (eternal) acquired only after five centuries from the time of Jesus, the sense of *endless* (everlasting) duration.

So when Jesus refers to an "aionios kolasis" (age-during hell), He refers in essence to a pedagogic experience of a definite time duration, since the very word "hell" derives its meaning from the Greek "kolazein" which means "cut off" but also "control, correct" as well as "punish".

"The word for punishment is *kolasis*. The word was originally a gardening word, and its original meaning was *pruning trees*. In Greek there are two words for punishment, *timoria* and *kolasis*, and there is a quite definite distinction between them. Aristotle defines the difference; *kolasis* is for the sake of the one who suffers it; *timoria* is for the sake of the one who inflicts it (*Rhetoric* 1.10). Plato says that no one punishes (*kolazei*) a wrong-doer simply because he has done wrong – that would be to take unreasonable vengeance (*timoreitai*). We punish (*kolazei*) a wrong-doer in order that he may not do wrong again (*Protagoras* 323 E). Clement of Alexandria (*Stromateis* 4.24; 7.16) defines *kolasis* as pure *discipline*, and *timoria* as the return of evil for evil. Aulus Gellius says that *kolasis* is given that a man may be corrected; *timoria* is given that dignity and authority may be vindicated (*The Attic Nights* 7.14). The difference is quite clear in Greek and it is always observed. *Timoria* is retributive punishment; *kolasis* is remedial discipline. *Kolasis* is always given to amend and to cure."

(William Barclay, *The Apostles' Creed*, p. 189, publ. by Westminster John Knox Press)

"[324a] For if you will consider punishment [kolazein], Socrates, and what control it has over wrong-doers, the facts will inform you that men agree in regarding virtue as procured. No one punishes a wrong-doer from the mere contemplation [324b] or on account of his wrong-doing, unless one takes unreasoning vengeance like a wild beast. But he who undertakes to punish with reason does not avenge himself for the past offence, since he cannot make what was done as though it had not come to pass; he looks rather to the future, and aims at preventing that particular person and others who see him punished from doing wrong again. And being so minded he must have in mind that virtue comes by training: for you observe that he punishes to deter."

(Plato, *Protagoras*, Plato in Twelve Volumes, Vol. 3, translated by W.R.M. Lamb, Harvard University Press, 1967)

What point would there be in a "hell" of an endless duration, without any possibility of purification or atonement? In such a case there would be only a relentless vengeance which wouldn't aim in anything constructive but only to a ferocious *vain pain*.

And even if the world "aionios" refers indeed to an endless time duration or to a time-less state, it's still a fact that we ignore the *very meaning* of the terms "eternal" and "eternity". These realities are incomprehensible for the human mind and it's not of any use to talk about them *as if* we can understand in any way to what exactly do they refer to. The only possible approach of the human mind regarding the notion of eternity is connected with the *perpetuating* of a situation which is based on a simple Law: Our present is due to our past, so our future, *if we do not change our present*, will be like our past.

So after we realize our ignorance in relation to the very meaning of the notion of eternity, we will have to face our ignorance concerning the *potential growth* in this state of existence.

Eternity is simplistically presented as a state of being where nothing changes, nothing is altered. Nevertheless, the Scriptures refer to fallen angels, that is, to immortal and eternal beings that their inner state was altered; and is being said also that in the future life, the perfection of the saints will be endless and their progress ceaseless.

In any case, what we should rather examine are those really peculiar "human" views of ours, which *find satisfaction* in the dangerously persistent talk of an eternal, unalterable damnation in hell. Whilst at the same time they accept the possibility of an eternal bliss state being altered (fallen angels), they deny tenaciously the possibility of an eternal damned state being changed (their restoration). It's really weird our "human" claim that *wants* an angel to be capable of falling, yet, without ever being able to rise again. It accepts for the saint the after death progress but denies to the sinner the after death *metanoia*.

So we should really be troubled by the persistence which denies categorically, to the point of excommunication and dethronement, any talk about the restoration (rising) of the fallen souls, and doesn't revolt whole-heartedly against inhuman ideas about eternal damnation to endless, hideous and unheard of torments.

This the *potential* future that Love has in store for Her stray children? Human parents forgive their children, through their whit of Love, even if they are unrepentant criminals. Even if no one else forgives them, we all can understand the forgiveness of the Mother and the Father, and deep down we expect it; and if it is not there, we might even accuse them of being stone-hearted parents.

Yet, we easily attribute this harshness to Love and believe that She has in store for Her very children (even by allowing it) such a sinister future that not even the cruelest "human" heart can conceive. A *potential* future that derives its terror mostly from the fact that it is presented as *endless* and *unchangeable*, properties which belong only to God and only He can endow them (*by grace...*) to any being or state.

And not only do we believe in these "holy" and "divine" revelations, but we also consider as ill intended and impious whoever dares to question them. So stone-hearted have we become that the idea of an everlasting, tormenting and diabolical hell, simply *doesn't touch us*. What can we do? If that's the way it is, so be it: eternal torments for the other religions, for the atheists, the heretics, the sinners, that is, for most humanity, and so for plenty of our beloved ones...

Fortunately though, these views are only human inventions or interpretations which were probably propagated for certain reasons. These coarse images of eternal bliss and eternal punishment, hell and unspeakable torments, are intended for the mass of humanity, when she is in an infant (spiritual) age and needs her own "bugbear" so she won't fall from the cliff or put her hand into the fire.

And of course these imaginative threats can also be used individually when man is in an early stage of spiritual immaturity and so in order to find the *strength* to cut off from ways of life that *he himself* has acknowledged as harmful, he derives *energy* and courage out of *fear* (which has *hell*). Yet, this is a very early spiritual stage which soon will be overcome in a normal spiritual progress and thus fear will be abandoned and be replaced as a source of strength from Love. Fear however can always be used as a safety net when the spiritual fighter will tend to deviate from his course and thus tumble. In such cases, fear can again constitute a *provisional* urging so we can come out of our state of weakness.

This is the exclusive use of the various spiritual threats and "punishments" which are often used as *swords* that will cut off our bonds. And this means is usually useful for humanity as a whole, since the mass of humanity is generally delayed in its progress. So the Divine Revelations are always interpreted according to our present level both individually and collectively.

Yet, the real problem is traced to the extent that these "ideas" of eternal, hellish and inexorable torments are not inevitable, due to our level, simplified human interpretations, but misinterpretations of hard-hearted "men". And the thing gets worse when these hard-hearted misinterpretations attract and captivate other cruel hearts which hasten to declare even as "saints" those "theologians" who try with various *intellectual* arguments to *prove* the impossible.

In the first centuries of christianity, but also in the subsequent ones, people were killing each other for insignificant reasons and the death penalty was something very ordinary and acceptable. So it's logical to assume that these *threats* aimed in shocking truly tough-skinned "men" who couldn't be easily shaken out of their internal state. They needed strong shocks which fear can always produce, especially in relation to things that man by definition ignores and consequently is afraid of; as it is with death, afterlife, eternity, even God Himself.

> "It is as St John Chrysostom says about Gehenna: it is almost of greater benefit to us than the kingdom of heaven, since because of it many enter into the kingdom of heaven, while few enter for the sake of the kingdom itself; and if they do enter it, it is by virtue of God's compassion. Gehenna pursues us with fear, the kingdom embraces us with love, and through them both we are saved by Christ's grace."
>
> (St Peter of Damaskos, *Book I – That We Should Not Despair Even If We Sin Many Times,* p. 160, Vol. 3, Philokalia)

Yet, in our time, that we value human life (in theory at least) more than anything, and we have developed a human sensitivity (again in theory) for the sufferings and also the rights of our fellow-men, these threats have lost their meaning and the persistent dogmatic attachment to them, makes them look comical, since they end up being connected with things such as, "If I lie, I will be doomed eternally in hell?" "If I cheat on my husband or wife, I will suffer eternal torments in hell?"

So if we assume that in our days, humanity is even a little more mature and doesn't need any more a fearsome "bugbear" so she won't fall from the cliff, we ought to penetrate deeper (that is, to open to Divine Inspiration and Revelation) into the interpretations of dogmas such as heaven and hell, and others as well, instead of showing a persistent and very odd insistence in interpretations that served other times.

Otherwise, with our persistence in the often limited interpretations of the past, we prove that our relationship with God and so our Divine Inspiration is only theoretical and therefore imaginary, since we have nothing new to be fed, none spiritual food at all. And therefore we chew over old, assimilated foods that are deprived of all nutritive.

And of course, in the unpleasant case that these cruel interpretations are *welcomed* by our heart, then we should wonder seriously about our relationship with Love: how do we conceive Her, and more specifically, *how* do we experience Her?

In this point we should point out that Christianity taught from the start the exactly opposite idea of the one of endless hell. And it didn't taught it simply as a potential future but as a (pre)determined Reality (both for humanity and all creation) which doesn't abolish in any way the *free* will (but certainly abolishes, that is, heals, the *false, enslaved to egoism,* "will"), since the Will of God is *identical* to the will of our Real Self:

> "*One God and Father of all, who is above all, and through all, and in you all*" (Ephesians 4:6) "*who* will have all men to be saved, and to come unto the knowledge of the truth*" (1 Timothy 2:4) "*wherefore God also hath highly exalted him, and given him a name which is above every name: That at the name of Jesus every knee should*

bow, of things in heaven, and things in earth, and things under the earth" (Philippians 2:9-10) *"for it pleased the Father that in him should all fulness dwell; And, having made peace through the blood of his cross, by him to reconcile all things unto himself; by him, I say, whether they be things in earth, or things in heaven"* (Colossians 1:19-20) *"and when all things shall be subdued unto him, then shall the Son also himself be subject unto him that put all things under him, that God may be all in all"* (1 Corinthians 15:28).

Besides, as Christianity teaches, *evil* is *non-existent*, which means that it is *not created*, nor has any real substance; there is only as a *lack* of Good. So how is it possible for something that doesn't exist *in essence*, to exist forever?

"Evil is corruptible because corruption is the nature of evil, which does not possess any true existence whatsoever. Goodness is incorruptible because it exists eternally and never ceases to be, and watches over everything in which it dwells."

(St Maximos the Confessor, *Various Texts on Theology, the Divine Economy, and Virtue and Vice*, Third Century, 57, p. 224, Vol. 2, Philokalia)

Sadly though, this Idea which was named *Restoration (Apokatastasis) of All* (cf. Acts 3:21) remained least known and mostly through its condemnation!

But what exactly does this Idea teach and is it truly compatible with *Ortho-doxy (correct belief-perspective)*? In order to make clearer this notion of the Restoration of Love, we will cite some passages from the great Church Father, Issac the Syrian:

"Just because (the terms) wrath, anger, hatred, and the rest are used of the Creator, we should not imagine that He (actually) does anything in anger or hatred or zeal. Many figurative terms are employed in the Scriptures of God, terms which are far removed from His (true) nature. And just as (our) rational nature has (already) become gradually more illumined and wise in a holy understand of the mysteries which are hidden in (Scripture's) discourse about God – that we should not understand everything (literally) as it is written, but rather that we should see, (concealed) inside the bodily exterior of the narratives, the hidden providence and eternal knowledge which guides all – so too we shall in the future come to know and be aware of many things for which our present understanding will be seen as contrary to what it will be then; and the whole ordering of things yonder will undo any precise opinion we possess now in (our) supposition about Truth. For there are many, indeed endless, things which do not even enter our minds here, not even as promises of any kind.

Accordingly we say that, even in the matter of the afflictions and sentence of Gehenna, there is some (hidden) mystery, whereby the wise Maker has taken as a starting point for its future outcome the wickedness of our actions and willfulness, using it as a way of bringing to perfection His dispensation wherein lies the teaching which makes wise, and the advantage beyond description, hidden from both angels and human beings, (hidden) too from those who are being chastised, whether they be demons or human beings, (hidden) for as long as the ordained period of time holds sway."

(Isaac of Nineveh (Isaac the Syrian), *The Second Part, Chapters IV-XLI*, p. 171)

"If the Kingdom and Gehenna had not been foreseen in the purpose of our good God, as a result of the coming into being of good and evil actions, (then God's) thoughts concerning these would not be eternal; but righteousness and sin were known by

Him before they revealed themselves. Accordingly the Kingdom and Gehenna are matters belonging to mercy, which were conceived of in their essence by God as a result of His eternal goodness. It was not a matter of requiting, even though He gave them the name of requital.

That we should further say or think that the matter is not full of love and mingled with compassion would be an opinion full of blasphemy and insult to our Lord God. (By saying) that He will even hand us over to burning for the sake of sufferings, torment and all sorts of ills, we are attributing to the divine Nature an enmity towards the very rational beings which He created through grace; (the same is true if we say) that He acts or thinks with spite and a vengeful purpose, as though He was avenging Himself.

Among all His actions there is none which is not entirely a matter of mercy, love and compassion: this constitutes the beginning and the end of His dealings with us."

(Isaac the Syrian, *The Second Part, Chapters IV-XLI*, p. 172)

"In love did He bring the world into existence; in love does He guide it during this its temporal existence; in love is He going to bring it to that wondrous transformed state, and in love will the world be swallowed up in the great mystery of Him who has performed all these things; in love will the whole course of the governance of creation be finally comprised. And since in the New World the Creator's love rules over all rational nature, the wonder at His mysteries that will be revealed (then) will captivate to itself the intellect of (all) rational beings whom He has created so that they might have delight in Him, whether they be evil or whether they be just. With this design did He bring them into existence, even though they among themselves have made, after their coming into being, this distinction between the just and the wicked. Even though this is so, nevertheless in the Creator's design there is none, from among all who were created and who have come into being – (that is,) every rational nature – who is to the front or to the back of (God's) love. Rather, He has a single equal love which covers the whole extent of rational creation, all things whether visible or invisible: there is no first place or last place with Him in (this) love for any single one of them, as I have said.

And just as there is not a single nature who is in the first place or last place in creation in the Creator's knowledge – (I refer here to this knowledge) which was set in His purpose eternally, that He would bring them into being: it was not the case of His knowing one before or after another, but all of them equally without any before or after, in a twinkling of an eye – similarly there is not before or after in His love towards them: no greater or lesser amount (of love) is to be found with Him at all. Rather, just like the continual equality of His knowledge, so too is the continual equality of His love; for He knew them (all) before they (ever) became just or sinners. The Creator and His love did not change because they underwent change after He had brought them into being, nor does His purpose which exists eternally (change). And if it were otherwise, He would be subject to change just as created beings are – a shocking idea.

My brethren, if there is anyone to whom these things are difficult to believe, he should be careful lest, by running away from one (element in the argument) he fall into blasphemy at another: imagining that he is spurning the words of a fellow human being, he may find himself arming himself against what concerns the divine Nature, being forced (by the logic of his case) to reduce the glorious Nature of His Creator to weakness and change.

But we know that everyone is agreed on this, that there is

no change, or any earlier and later intentions, with the Creator: there is no hatred or resentment in His nature, no greater or lesser (place) in His love, no before or after in His knowledge. For it is believed by everyone that the creation came into existence as a result of the Creator's goodness and love, (then) we know that this (original) cause does not ever diminish or change in the Creator's nature as a result of the disordered course of creation."

(Isaac the Syrian, *The Second Part, Chapters IV-XLI*, pp. 160-161)

"That we should imagine that anger, wrath, jealousy or the such like have anything to do with the divine Nature is something utterly abhorrent for us: no one in their right mind, no one who has any understanding (at all) can possibly come to such madness as to think anything of the sort about God. Nor again can we possibly say that He acts thus out of retribution, even though the Scriptures may on the outer surface posit this. Even to think this of God and to suppose that retribution for evil acts is to be found with Him is abominable. By implying that He makes use of such a great and difficult thing out of retribution we are attributing a weakness to the (divine) Nature. We cannot even believe such a thing can be found in those human beings who live a virtuous and upright life and whose thoughts are entirely in accord with the divine will – let alone (believe it) of God, that He has done something out of retribution for anticipated evil acts in connection with those whose nature He had brought into being with honour and great love. Knowing them and all their conduct, the flow of His grace did not dry up from them: not even after they (started) living amid many evil deeds did He withhold His care for them, even for a moment.

If someone says that He has put up with them here (on earth) in order that His patience may be known – with the idea that He would punish them there mercilessly, such a person thinks in an unspeakably blasphemous way about God, due to his infantile way of thinking: he is removing from God His kindness, goodness and compassion, (all) the things because of which He truly bears with sinners and wicked men. Such a person is attributing to (God) enslavement to passion, (supposing) that He has not consented to their being chastised here, seeing that He has prepared them for a much greater misfortune, in exchange for a short-lived patience. Not only does such a person fail to attribute something praiseworthy to God, but he also calumniates Him.

A right way of thinking about God would be the following: the kind Lord, who in everything He does looks to ways of assisting rational beings, directs thought concerning judgement to the advantage of those who accept this difficult matter. For it would be most odious and utterly blasphemous to think that hate or resentment exists with God, even against demonic beings; or to imagine any other weakness, or possibility, or whatever else might be involved in the course of retribution of good or bad as applying, in a retributive way, to that glorious (divine) Nature. Rather, He acts towards us in ways He knows will be advantageous to us, whether by way of things that cause suffering, or by way of things that cause relief, whether they cause joy or grief, whether they are insignificant or glorious: all are directed towards the single eternal good, whether each receives judgement or something of glory from Him – not by way of retribution, far from it! – but with a view to the advantage that is going to come from all these things."

(Isaac the Syrian, *The Second Part, Chapters IV-XLI*, pp. 162-164)

"Lest any of those who zealously imagine that they are being zealous for the cause of truth should imagine that we are introducing something novel of our own accord, things of which our former orthodox Fathers never spoke, as though we were bursting out with an opinion which did not accord with truth, anyone who likes can turn to the writings of the blessed Interpreter, a man who had his sufficient fill of the gifts of grace, who was entrusted with the hidden mysteries of the Scriptures, (enabling him) to instruct on the path to truth the whole community of the Church; who, above all, has illumined us orientals with wisdom – nor is our mind's vision capable enough (to bear) the brilliancy of his compositions, inspired by the divine Spirit.

For we are not rejecting his words – far from it! Rather, we accept (him) like one of the apostles, and anyone who opposes his words, introduces doubt into his interpretations, or shows hesitation at his words, (such a person) we hold to be alien to the community of the Church and someone who is erring from the Truth. Therefore, although we could demonstrate (our point) from many passages in a great number of his volumes, nevertheless he makes the point especially clearly at the end of the first volume which he composed against those who say that sin is present by nature.

From the blessed Theodore, the Interpreter. After other luminous statements he says:

'In the world to come, those who have chosen here what is good, will receive the felicity of good things along with praise; whereas the wicked, who all their life have turned aside to evil deeds, once they have been set in order in their minds by punishments and the fear of them, choose the good, having come to learn how much they have sinned, and that they have persevered in doing evil things and not good; by means of all this they received a knowledge of religion's excellent teaching,

246

and are educated so as to hold on to it with a good will, (and so eventually) they are held worthy of the felicity of divine munificence. For (Christ) would never have said 'Until you pay the last farthing' (cf. Matt. 5:26, Luke 12:59) unless it had been possible for us to be freed from our sins once we had recompensed for them through punishments. Nor would He have said 'He will be beaten with many stripes' and 'He will be beaten with few stripes' (cf. Luke 12:47-48) if it were not (the case) that the punishments, measured out in correspondence to the sins, were finally going to have an end'.

These words, and others similar to them are what the blessed Theodore has handed down in his books, clearly and without concealment, openly using straightforward words that are not obscure for (the benefit of) the understanding and instruction of lovers of truth, (showing) what opinions it is appropriate that we should hold concerning God, the Creator of all, and concerning His chastisements and concerning the judgement to come.

Since, according to our Lord's (own) words, the testimony of two men is true – and especially so in the case of people who are wondrously and divinely illumined, let us confirm what we have said with the help of another witness who is trustworthy like (our) first witness, (someone) from whose fountain the clear-sounding Theodore himself drank, a person of high intelligence, (namely) Diodore, the great Teacher of the Church.

By the holy Diodore, bishop of Tarsus.

The blessed Diodore, wonderful among teachers and instructor of (Theodore) concurs with (this) opinion, and he sets it out in an authoritative way in Discource V of (his) book on Providence, saying as follows:

'A reward for labours is reserved for the good, one that is

worthy of the righteousness of the Maker, but stripes for the wicked are not for eternity. Thus, not even in their case is the future condition of immortality of no profit: if they are tormented as they deserve just for a short time, commensurate with their evil and their wickedness, receiving reward in accordance with the measure of their actions, experiencing suffering during a short while, nevertheless (for them) delight in immortality is for ever.'

He comes back to what he is saying (here) with greater precision, as follows: 'If the reward for labours is so great, how much greater is the time of immortality than the time of contests, that is, than this world; whereas the punishments are (far) less than the magnitude and number of sins. The resurrection from the dead should not be considered as belonging only to the good, but it also takes place for the wicked (as well). For God's goodness is greatly to be held in honour: it chastises sparingly'.

These are the words and the opinion of the blessed Diodore. But later on he also says in Discourse VI as follows:

'For God, by means of good rewards, conceals the measure of labours; but in the greatness of grace He diminishes the punishment of those who are chastised and He shortens its length. But He does not let the torment go on for as much time as the time of wrongdoing warrants. Although He requites them with less than they deserve – just as with the good He extends their felicity beyond (its due) measure and time, seeing that the reward has no end – it cannot be known, as I have already said, if God's goodness will always endure retaining the evils (consequent) on guiltiness and causing hurt to those at fault'.

Then, reiterating his words, he says, 'The decree of judgement and of torment is not to the same extent as the felicity of the Kingdom which will obtain then'. And (he has) other similar words with the same opinion and expressing the same view. He also introduces into discussion the case of the demons and their great inclination to evil, saying that 'not even their immense wickedness can overcome the measure of God's goodness'.

These and similar astonishing insights and opinions, leading (us) on to love of, and wonder at, the Creator, belong to these very pillars of the Church: dealing with (God's) dispensation and the divine judgement to come, they concern the immensity of God's mercy, which in its abundance passes beyond and overcomes the evils done by created beings. Such opinions will caste out from our way of thinking the childish opinion of God expressed by those who introduce evil and possibility into His nature, saying that He is changed by circumstances and times. At the same time these opinions (of Theodore and Diodore) will teach us about (the nature of) His chastisements and punishments, whether here or there, (instructing us) concerning what sort of compassionate intentions and purpose He has in allowing (these) to come upon us, what are the excellent outcomes resulting from them, how it is not a matter of our being destroyed by them or enduring the same for eternity, how He allows them to come in a fatherly way, and not vengefully – which would be a sign of hatred. (Their purpose was) that, by thinking in this way we might (come to) know about God, and wonder at Him would draws us on to love of Him, and as a result of that (love) we might feel ashamed at ourselves and set aright the conduct of our lives here."

(Isaac the Syrian, *The Second Part, Chapters IV-XLI*, pp. 165-169)

In addition to these truly exceptional and absolutely clear passages, there were many other great Fathers and Mothers of the Church who taught this Reality. Great teachers such as Clement of Alexandria, Origen, St Macrina, Gregory of Nyssa, Didymus the Blind and Maximus the Confessor, knew the Truth.

"Macrina: If a clay of the more tenacious kind is deeply plastered round a rope, and then the end of the rope is put through a narrow hole, and then some one on the further side violently pulls it by that end, the result must be that, while the rope itself obeys the force exerted, the clay that has been plastered upon it is scraped off it with this violent pulling and is left outside the hole, and, moreover, is the cause why the rope does not run easily through the passage, but has to undergo a violent tension at the hands of the puller. In such a manner, I think, we may figure to ourselves the agonized struggle of that soul which has wrapped itself up in earthy material passions, when God is drawing it, His own one, to Himself, and the foreign matter, which has somehow grown into its substance, has to be scraped from it by main force, and so occasions it that keen intolerable anguish.

Gregory: Then it seems, I said, that it is not punishment chiefly and principally that the Deity, as Judge, afflicts sinners with; but He operates, as your argument has shown, only to get the good separated from the evil and to attract it into the communion of blessedness.

Macrina: That, said the Teacher, is my meaning; and also that the agony will be measured by the amount of evil there is in each individual. For it would not be reasonable to think that the man who has remained so long as we have supposed in evil known to be forbidden, and the man who has fallen only into moderate sins, should be tortured to the same amount in the judgment upon their vicious habit; but according to the quantity of material will be the longer or shorter time that that agonizing flame will be burning; that is, as long as there is fuel to feed it. In the case of the man who has acquired a heavy weight of material, the consuming fire must necessarily be very searching; but where that which the fire has to feed upon has spread less far, there the penetrating fierceness of the punishment is mitigated, so far as the subject itself, in the amount of its evil, is diminished. In any and every case evil must be removed out of existence, so that, as we said above, the absolutely non-existent should cease to be at all. Since it is not in its nature that evil should exist outside the will, does it not follow that when it shall be that every will rests in God, evil will be reduced to complete annihilation, owing to no receptacle being left for it?"

(St. Gregory of Nyssa, *On the Soul and the Resurrection*, p. 450)

"The church knows three restorations (*apokatastasis*): the first, that of each [person] according to the *logos* of virtue, in which one is restored fulfilling the *logos* of virtue in him; second, that of the entire nature in the resurrection, the restoration to incorruption and immortality; and third, which Gregory of Nyssa, above all, made use of in his own writings, is this, the restoration of the powers of the soul that fell into sin, returning to that for which they were created. Just as it is necessary for the entire nature in the resurrection to recover again the incorruption of the flesh at the hoped-for time, so also must the distorted powers of the soul in the duration of the ages again throw off the memories of evil lodged within it and passing through all ages and, not finding a resting place, return to God, who is without limit; and, thus, by full understanding (*epignosis*), not by sharing in the good things, it must recover again its powers and be restored to its original [form], such that the Creator may also be revealed as not being responsible for sin."

(Maximus the Confessor's, *Questions and Doubts*, Qu. 19, pp. 53-54)

If in antiquity the idea of Universal Salvation had to be concealed (and thus be even condemned) so more people can be drawn through fear in the bosoms of christianity, in our days applies the exact opposite. The concealment of this Idea doesn't attract people anymore but repels them!

So we can understand that it's now time for this Teaching to (re)emerge and be revived, if we want the present slightly more matured humanity to return to christianity. The Bishop of Diokleia, Kallistos Ware, refers precisely to this reality in his essay, *Dare we Hope for the Salvation of All?*

"In any case, it is only too obvious, especially in our day, that the threat of hell-fire is almost totally inefective as a detterent. If in our preaching of the Christian faith we hope to have any significant influence on others, then what we need is not a negative but a positive strategy: let us abandon ugly threats, and attempt rather to evoke people's sense of wonder and their capacity for love."

(Kallistos Ware, *The Inner Kingdom*, Volume 1 of the Collected Works, St Vladimir's Seminary Press, p. 204)

"But can the dogma be modified?" our mind will hasten to ask, "Doesn't this mean losing its credibility?" Of course, not; the opposite is that will happen. Nevertheless, this kind of doubt is reasonable and Kallistos Ware obviously bares it in mind; that is why in the aforementioned essay he formulates wisely the Truth in the form of a *hope*:

"On the first page of the Bible it is written, "God saw everything that he had mad, and behold, it was altogether good and beautiful (Gen. 1:31, LXX). In the beginning, that is to say, there was unity; all created things participated fully in the goodness, truth and beauty of the Creator. Are we, then, to assert that at the end there will be not unity but duality? Is there to be a continuing opposition between good and evil, between heaven and hell, between joy and torment, that remains forever unsolved? If we start by affirming that God created a world which was wholly good, and if we then maintain that a significant part of His rational creation will end up in intolerable anguish, separated from Him for all eternity, surely this implies that God has failed in His creative work and has been defeated by the forces of evil. Are we to rest satisfied with such a conclusion? Or dare we look, however tentatively, beyond this duality to an ultimate restoration of unity when "all shall be well"?".

(Kallistos Ware, *The Inner Kingdom*, Volume 1 of the Collected Works, St Vladimir's Seminary Press, pp. 194-195)

Christianity is Alive: since Jesus Christ is Alive, then His Teaching is Alive as well, and so it is possible to be interpreted and revealed deeper. If Jesus is Alive and amongst us (cf. Matthew 18:20), He can still teach us His Word; explain or develop it.

Now, christianity on the other hand is asleep. It is in hibernation, it is as petrified, so any hint of change, complement or correction, is like threatening his whole existence. Yet, in reality it threatens only its sleep or its oblivion.

And finally "christianity" is deadened and it's true that whatever changes will mean for sure its extinction; that is why it fights them with deadly fury.

The idea of the Restoration of All which was either concealed (was put to hibernation until the *winter* of humanity would pass) by christianity or murdered by "christianity", can only be awakened or resurrected by Christianity, if and when humanity shall be able to accept it and so make a *worthy use* of it.

Because for the time being it's true that fear and threat are still moving us or restraining us. If we want to be honest we will easily ascertain that we constantly seek for "alibis" in order to extend our ego-centric life and we constantly postpone our effort of changing. And it's also true that the *disease of postponent* holds the danger of *perpetuating* our egoism. So the *infinite* mercy of God can easily be a cause for our *endless self*-condemnation. That is why it is concealed from us, so we won't misuse it.

Yet, it's time now, both personally but especially collectively, to come to our Self and realize our essential missing of the Mark (sin). What does it consist of and what are its fruits? And we ought to do this, not because we will be "punished" nor to be rewarded, but simply to fulfill… the Aim of our Creation.

Missing the Mark

Sin means missing the Mark.

But why does sin is connected with the serpent and the *cunning* (evil)?

We defined the serpent as a symbol of our materialistic mind. It's well known that the serpent is a clever and flexible being and as a reptile is destined to crawl on the ground. These are also the properties of our materialistic mind. The mind of the senses can indeed be very clever and flexible but is destined to crawl on the ground, *"upon thy belly shalt thou go, and dust [earth, DRC] shalt thou eat all the days of thy life"* (Genesis 3:14). It cannot be raised to the Heavens and understand them. It perceives them only in terms of the senses and thus lowers them inevitably to its level. Nevertheless, it is not dispensable; on the contrary it is requisite in its field of action, that is, for our physical survival. So according to its use, it constitutes either a positive or a negative symbol. If we rule over it, it is an advantage, *"Be ye therefore wise as serpents and simple as doves"* (Matthew 10:16, DRC). If it rules over us, it constitutes a symbol of the cunning (evil) one, *"But I fear, lest by any means, as the serpent beguiled Eve through his subtilty, so your minds should be corrupted from the simplicity that is in Christ"* (2 Corinthians 11:3).

But what exactly is the *cunning* (evil)?

As an internal symbol it signifies, as we've already seen, the duality. Or even better, the lack of *integrity* and *simplicity*. That is why it is the father of *lies*, because it *believes* in *multiplicity*; in division; in the tree of knowledge of good and evil, which perceives it as *divine, "Ye shall be as gods, knowing good and evil"* (Genesis 3:5).

> "If the falsehood is multifarious, whilst the truth is one, therefore the nous which is elevated by the Spirit's grace to the One—the superworldly, the eminent of all, of which the many originated—is elevated to the truth itself."
>
> (Callistus Katafygiotis, *On Union with God, and Life of Theoria*, Chapter 10, p. 222, Vol. 5, Philokalia)

So the *cunning*, that is, the *divided mind*, cannot hear the Truth, the Word of God:

> *"Jesus said unto them, "If God were your Father, ye would love me: for I proceeded forth and came from God; neither came I of myself, but he sent me. Why do ye not understand my speech? Even because ye cannot hear my word. Ye are of your father the devil, and the lusts of your father ye will do. He was a murderer from the beginning, and abode not in the truth, because there is no truth in him. When he speaketh a lie, he speaketh of his own: for he is a liar, and the father of it. And because I tell you the truth, ye believe me not. Which of you convinceth me of sin? And if I say the truth, why do ye not believe me? He that is of God heareth God's words: ye therefore hear them not, because ye are not of God"* (John 8:42-47).

The materialistic mind (the cunning serpent) is not from God when it doesn't believe in the Truth which is Love, Unity. Being incapable of understanding the Unity, it sins, that is, *misses the Mark*, with the unavoidable consequence of *distorting* the Truth, falsifying and negating it, *"He that committeth sin is of the devil; for the devil sinneth from the beginning"* (1 John 3:8).

Jesus Christ, as an internal symbol, represents our spirit, the Son of God inside us, our Real Divine Self; thus our materialistic mind is none other than *the anti-christ (the son of perdition*, cf. 2

Thessalonians 2:3-4) when it denies the spirit (and its Creator) and claims in us its Divine Place, "*Who is a liar but he that denieth that Jesus is the Christ? He is antichrist, that denieth the Father and the Son*" (1 John 2:22).

So the *simple (single) eye* symbolizes the incorruptible, the One, which cannot be divided in parts—two or more—and unites everything in Love. In this case, our eye, that is, our inner perception is not distracted and not divided; it is orientated to the One, to God, to the One Source and One Cause.

The *cunning eye* is the one that is distracted; that *misses its Mark*; that *sins*; for sometimes it sees the depth and sometimes it sees the surface. Its depth might say *Yes* whilst its surface might say *No*, or the reverse.

The *simple eye* unites its various parts and its Being exclaims in *unanimity* Yes, Yes or No, No. Therefore it is undivided; *One which turns to the One.*

> "When the *nous* reaches to Him, it becomes one, because God is one. And so the *nous* is united with itself and is restored and becomes undivided. For when we contemplate the One, It becomes the cause of unity and of godlike simplicity, as it is incompatible for the *nous* to contemplate the One without becoming itself a simple one. But when the *nous* contemplates things divided and composite, unavoidably it becomes divided and diverse."

> (Callistus Katafygiotis, *On Union with God, and Life of Theoria*, Chapter 18, p. 226, Vol. 5, Philokalia)

Whilst the *cunning*; the evil; the sin; constitutes the division of our Being and our resulting disorientation.

> "If by nature the good unifies and holds together what has been separated, evil clearly divides and corrupts what has been unified. For evil is by nature dispersive, unstable, multiform and divisive."

(St Maximos the Confessor, *Various Texts on Theology, the Divine Economy, and Virtue and Vice*, First Century, 49, p. 174, Vol. 2, Philokalia)

In this point we should bear in mind that the Good unifies everything without equating them, allowing to each member to perform its own proper function to its highest degree. When the evil—which its "nature" is to divide—desires to *imitate* the Good and so tries to create unity, it equates everything, rendering them facsimiles, thinking that in this way it will lead them to unity. It is incapable of grasping that everything performs its own function and that this enforced equation will lead to the degeneration or death of the various parts and therefore to the degeneration or the death of the whole.

Now, the human Being constitutes an *undivided triad* of spirit, soul and body, in which the spirit must have the primacy and direct the activities of the other two inseparable parts of our overall Being.

But we have died to our spirit; we have fallen from its height (or depth) and therefore the division of our Being has resulted. Our soul is disorientated and hangs in mid-air between our deadened spirit and our uncontrollable body, which holds the reins of our Being for the most part and leads us to thousands desires, except from the One Desire.

This is our *sin*; our missing of the Mark: our fragmentation and our consequent disorientation. So we taste the life of the changeable, contradictory and fragmented surface; the life of the foam; instead of the Life of stability, consistency and integrity; the Life of the Depth.

"Since the *nous* becomes, according to his energies, similar to what it contemplates, inevitably then when it contemplates composite things, it becomes diverse as well, and when it falls from simplicity, it cannot be undivided. But the divided *nous* is not clean at all from sin, so the division itself is considered as sin by those who can go deep into these matters."

(Callistus Katafygiotis, *On Union with God, and Life of Theoria*, Chapter 25, p. 230, Vol. 5, Philokalia)

Stability and purity are achieved when we are *simple (single)* and not *cunning*, that is, whole and not divided; and thus orientated to the One instead to the many, seeking the *"one needful thing"* (cf. Luke 10:40-41) which is the Kingdom of God. And then the many are added, that is, derive from the One, from Love.

When we eat from the tree of good and evil, that is, when we taste the division, we die to the Tree of Life, for Real Life is One and springs from One Source.

"The beyond the intellect One is unique (one) and is declared by everyone as the prime cause of everything, as beginning, as end, as cohesion of all."

(Callistus Katafygiotis, *On Union with God, and Life of Theoria*, Chapter 24, p. 229, Vol. 5, Philokalia)

So the notion of sin refers in essence to a wrong attitude and results in the outward turning of our soul, that is, to her outward disorientation to the *things of the world*, instead of being inward directed to the things of the Spirit, of God.

Sin means for our soul to lose the *inner Mark* for which she was created, which is God, and turn *outside* to the *creation of God*, forgetting thus the Creator. Instead of turning within, to the one Cause, that is, to Love, and through Her connect with the external creation, so she can also be a channel of this Love, she forgets the inner Source and turns outside. She loses her Divine connection and is deprived of her Divine nourishment and therefore she *sins*, that is, she seeks her incessant outer nourishment from the creation; exalting thus both the creation and her own self to the highest ideals. Despite whether she claims that she believes in God or not, as long as she is outwardly turned, the result is the same.

That is why it's being said that "no one is without sin", for it is a fact that as long as we live on this earth, we will keep losing the correct focus of our attention, and one or the other aspect of life and of creation will pull us, makings thus forgetting the inner Life. And then we will inevitably serve *the "god" of external wealth, the mammon.* The mammon, is another esoteric symbol that Jesus uses, which points clearly to the need of integrity, simplicity, and is directly connected with the notion of the *cunning (evil)* and of the *darkness.*

> *"The light of the body is the eye: if therefore thine eye be single, thy whole body shall be full of light. But if thine eye be cunning [evil], thy whole body shall be full of darkness. If therefore the light that is in thee be darkness, how great is that darkness. No man can serve two masters: for either he will hate the one, and love the other; or else he will hold to the one, and despise the other. Ye cannot serve God and mammon"* (Matthew 6:22-23).

When we are led *out* of our Self and are estranged from the *inner* Source of Light, we are gradually darkened and end up in "living" in the *outer darkness* (cf. Matthew 8:12, 22:13, 25:30). When our life doesn't derive its Meaning from the inner Truth, that is, from Love, it ends up being without Meaning or with *many "meanings".* If this world is not lightened by Love, then it darkens. And we begin to *take thought of many things,* that is, to search for Meaning to everything *around us,* and not where we should, *inside us.* The result is finding the "meanings" we seek and thus feeling rich; but in reality, the more rich we feel, the more empty we are, *"The rich man seemeth to himself wise: but the poor man that is prudent shall search him out"* (Proverbs 28:11, DRC). If we are cut off from the One Source of Real Wealth, our inner perception becomes cunning, that means that it's distracted, and seeks to become rich by accumulating perishable treasures, that is, subjective "meanings" that can be lost at any time (cf. Matthew 6:19-21).

> *"He that hasteth to be rich hath an evil [cunning] eye, and considereth not that poverty shall come upon him"* (Proverbs 28:22).

The rich man has many *possessions*, *"But when the young man heard that saying, he went away sorrowful: for he had great possessions"* (Matthew 19:22), therefore a lot of "interests" and so he is *fragmented*, whilst one thing is needful. Jesus invites the young rich man to abandon all his possessions and be dedicated to one thing, to following Him. Accordingly, He says to Martha that she is troubled for many things; that she is distracted; when only one thing is needful, *"Martha, Martha, thou art careful and troubled about many things: but one thing is needful"* (Luke 10:41-42). So that is why they are *blessed those who are poor in spirit*, that is, *simple (single)*, seeking only one thing, the Kingdom of Heaven (cf. Matthew 5:3).

The rich man thinks himself wise; Martha believes that she is right; but in the end they are both lost because they have so many things and yet nothing.

The *cunning (evil) eye* is the *rich eye*, the divided one; it is the rich soul which accumulates, which takes thought for many things and loses the essence (the Mark).

The *simple (single) eye* is the *poor eye*, the plain one; it is the clean and undivided soul which cares only for one thing, for the *pearl hidden in her depths*, *"The kingdom of heaven is like unto a merchant man, seeking goodly pearls: who, when he had found one pearl of great price, went and sold all that he had, and bought it"* (Matthew 13:45-46).

So this missing of the Mark (sin) of ours, is directly connected to certain much discussed terms that have been variously misinterpreted in the past from "christianity" leading thus to all kinds of deviations. Terms such as, *idolatry, fornication, adultery*, have been perceived only literally with their deeper inner interpretation being demoted. The result of this was the sentence even unto death of men who were supposed to have committed one of these sins. So here we will attempt a brief inner interpretation of these terms, starting with idolatry.

Idolatry essentially indicates the *superficial perception*. It means seeing the result without understanding the cause. It means ignoring the existence of the cause and perceiving only the result, mistaken it thus for the *cause*.

For example, we see an orange and we consider it as a source of vital energy. This is the view of the senses which sees only the surface. It's true that the orange provides energy but it's not in itself *The* source of energy, it is only a means, a channel, which is used by the *real* Source. If in some way we remove its energy then it will rot immediately; it will decompose.

The perspective of the essence or of the depth is simple and subtle, and that is why it keeps slipping us away. The perspective of the surface, that is, idolatry, is coarser and that is why it's seizing us so easily and enters into our relations with everything; in the sense that we worship the idol, the reflection, and not the Source. So we honor the creation, which is the result, and we forget the Creator, which is the cause. That is why, sooner or later, we end up in doubting His existence, since we see the result as the cause.

We acquire relationships with the channels but not with the Source, with the creation but not with the Creator. For this reason all our human relationships are in essence idolatrous, since we relate only to the idol, the reflection and not with the Source. We worship man but we forget his cause and so we put him in the place of God. We erect idols in our heart, forgetting our first Love, *"Thou hast left thy first love. Remember therefore from whence thou art fallen, and repent [metanoise, from metanoia], and do the first works"* (Apocalypse 2:4-5).

Yet, the abolishment of idolatry, of the view of the surface, doesn't mean of course the abolishment of our relations with all the existent channels, with the various results. It is not possible to stop being related, interact, feed and be fed, in one word, *live*, for we will simply die. But our existence is very different when we are related only to the channels, forgetting or rejecting the very Source, than being related first and foremost to the Source and through Her with all Her legitimate channels. It's obvious then that our existence will be much more fulfilled and abundant, *"I am come that they might have life, and that they might have it more abundantly"* (John 10:10).

When we see the channels as sources and the results as causes, we tend to be depended from them and so become possessive. When we are related to the Source, we are free from all the channels (in the human possible degree) and so we can develop essential and healthy relationships with them. We don't captivate them nor are captivated by them. We don't have relationships of "love and hatred" with them, that is, relationships of jealously, greediness and covetousness, "*Mortify therefore your members which are upon the earth; fornication, uncleanness, inordinate affection, evil concupiscence, and* covetousness, *which is* idolatry" (Colossians 3:5), but natural and healthy relationships.

Now, the relationships we develop with anything and are based on the superficial view, are characterized by the term *fornication (whoring)*, "*Thou hast gone a whoring after the heathen, and [...] thou art polluted with their idols*" (Ezekiel 23:30). Fornication (whoring) is born from idolatry, that is, from the superficial perspective which conceives the energetic result as the energetic cause and so develops a bad (evil) relationship with it. Fornication means a relationship of *degeneration*, of *downgrading*, with any object.

All creation is Holy and should be honored as such, without however taking within us the place of its Creator. When it takes its place, we are led to idolatry which brings forth the relationship of *fornication* with it.

This seems to be a paradox and indeed it is. Even though we exalt creation unto the place of the Creator, that is, higher than it deserves, at the same time we develop a relationship of degeneration with it; we make a bad use of it. Creation becomes everything for us, our idol, and thus we develop with it a relationship of dependence and abuse.

For example, the body becomes our god and so we are led to its abuse which results in its degradation and humiliation. We end up making it an object of trade, sensation and manipulation. We *alter* it in our obsession with it; we "beautify" it, stripping it off from its natural beauty, and therefore we end up disfiguring it. We intervene to it in all kinds of unnatural and inadmissible ways, simply because it has become our god and so we cannot stop being occupied with it!

This is what *fornication (whoring)* means: a bad relation with and (mis)use of any kind of energetic phenomenon, of any kind of created thing; whether this means human beings, animals, plants, objects or ideas, religions, sciences, etc. And of course fornication is closely related to the notion of *adultery*.

The term *adultery* suggests the *illegitimate* character of our relationship of fornication with the creation. When the soul sees the *world* superficially and erect idols in her (of people, objects, ideologies, "religions") she develop a degenerative relation with them which results in her inevitable *separation* from her Cause, *"Ye adulterers and adulteresses, know ye not that the friendship of the world is enmity with God? Whosoever therefore will be a friend of the world is the enemy of God"* (James 4:4). Our soul, through our spirit and united with it, should turn inside her towards her Cause. When she finds and relates with her Cause, she is gradually united with the Holy Bond of Marriage with Love (the Source). When on the other hand she abandons her one and only legitimate Love for other "loves", then she commits adultery. So the adultery of our soul is far more harmful than any adultery of the body (and is usually the reason for the physical adultery as well) and this is because it goes unnoticed through all of our life, resulting in the loss... of Life!

We go through, or rather, we *spend* are whole life in foreign and false loves without realizing the main Source of Love which knocks day and night the door of our soul, *"Behold, I stand at the door, and knock: if any man hear my voice, and open the door, I will come in to him, and will sup with him, and he with me"* (Apocalypse 3:20).

So all this procedure: idolatry of creation – a relationship of fornication with it – spiritual adultery towards the Creator; needs to be reversed: If our soul worships God as her God, that is, if she worships the One Source of all energy, the Love, then she won't erect idols inside her but she will perceive everything as manifestations of Love and thus will honor and worship them as they deserve; developing healthy relationships with them, that is to say, relations of love and not of (mis)use. She will stop losing herself into them, which results in not being able to truly enjoy them, since she has lost her very self! On the contrary, by remaining stable in herself, in her Centre, in her heights and depths, that is, in the core of her Being, and thus in Love, in God, she will be able to be united deeply and practically with Him, but also enjoy all His manifestations. And here becomes clear the meaning of *metanoia*.

The term *meta-noia* (usually rendered as repentance) indicates a *constant* conversion of our mind (*nous*), of our attention, *inwards*; towards the *One Mark*. It means to return continually and daily to the *remembrance of God* and all else will follow, "*Seek ye first the kingdom of God, and his righteousness; and all these things shall be added unto you*" (Matthew 6:33).

There is nothing which constitutes by itself a sin and at the same time everything constitutes a sin (missing of the Mark) when it's not based on the Love of God.

"And whatever the *nous* uses—either one or many, natural or created— doesn't use it for the One, neither to concentrate itself to the initial One nor to gaze It through holy participation and the help of the illuminating Spirit in a simple, unified and single way, this is counted as sin, even if its use seems to be something good. For all that has been created by the One, leads to the One when we treat them as we should."

(Callistus Katafygiotis, *On Union with God, and Life of Theoria*, Chapter 17, p. 225, Vol. 5, Philokalia)

So sin is the oblivion of Love (Unity), and *meta-noia* the return to Her. But in what exactly does this return consist of?

"If you are healed of the breach caused by the fall, you are severed first from the passions and then from impassioned thoughts. Next you are severed from nature and the inner principles of nature, then from conceptual images and the knowledge relating to them. Lastly, when you have passed through the manifold principles relating to divine providence, you attain through unknowing the very principle of divine unity. Then the intellect [*nous*] contemplates only its own immutability, and rejoices with an unspeakable joy because it has received the peace of God which transcends all intellect and which ceaselessly keeps him who has been granted it from falling (cf. Phil. 4:7)."

(St Maximos the Confessor, *On Theology and the Incarnate Dispensation of the Son of God*, Second Century, Text 8, p. 139, Vol. 2, Philokalia)

In this point we could probably say that the Divine part inside us (the Son of God within us) is in a certain way *sinless*, in the sense that it doesn't sin directly but only indirectly, that is, through our soul (through our *human* side). Our spirit cannot perform the sin-missing of the Mark by nature, but it can be *carried away* by it; that is why Adam (spirit) is carried away by Eve (soul).

It is true that all our human agony and pain are due to the fact that we sin (miss the Mark). So Jesus, by assuming our human nature in order to elevate it, he assumed also its agony and pain. That is why He experienced its temptations and potential sin, *"Therefore He was obligated to become like His brothers in all respects, in order that He might become a merciful and faithful High Priest in things pertaining to God, in order that He might make propitiation for the sins of the people. For in that which He Himself has suffered, being tempted, He is able to help those who are tempted. [...] For we do not have a High Priest who cannot sympathize with our weaknesses, but having been tempted in all respects in quite the same way as we are, yet without sin"* (Hebrews 2:17-18, 4:15, EMTV). And of course the outcome of His struggle couldn't have been given, otherwise what would be its value? In that case, it would be a false-struggle and a mockery of the human agony.

"This notion of salvation as sharing implies – although many have been reluctant to say this openly – that Christ assumed not just unfallen but *fallen* human nature. [...] Christ lives out his life on earth under the conditions of the fall. He is not himself a sinful person, but in his solidarity with fallen man he accepts to the full the consequences of

Adam's sin. [...] If Christ had merely assumed *un*fallen human nature, living out his earthly life in the situation of Adam in Paradise, then he would not have been touched with the feeling of *our* infirmities, nor would he have been tempted in everything exactly as *we* are. And in that case he would not be *our* Saviour."

(Bishop Kallistos Ware, *The Orthodox Way*, pp. 75-76)

Jesus is essentially without sin due to the fact that His Divine Part, His Divine Nature, is not carried away by his human nature (soul) and even though He is tempted, He doesn't give in to the temptation and elevates man inside Him. So He becomes the New Adam, the new model of humanity and its new path. The first Adam had the possibility of sin (*missing the Mark*); the second Adam has the ability of transcending sin (*being the Mark*), "*The first man Adam was made a living soul; the last Adam was made a quickening (life-giving) spirit*" (1 Corinthians 15:45).

And since the first Adam (spirit) fell through the prompting of Eve (soul); the process of return (raising) is precisely the reverse.

The first Eve (soul) turns her attention outwards and misses the Mark; the second Eve, Virgin Mary, turns away from sin (extroversion) and remains a virgin (pure, single, simple), that is, she keeps her attention inwards and begets Christ (the spirit), who soon claims His initial, rightful place—the restoration of balance—and that is why in the Marriage of Cana, in the Union of the spirit (man) and the soul (woman), He exclaims, "*What—to me and to thee, woman?*" (John 2:4, YLT). And then we see that the soul rules over, *through the spirit*, the senses (servants), "*His mother saith unto the servants, Whatsoever he saith unto you, do it*" (John 2:5); she doesn't tell them, "*Whatsoever I say*", for the Lord of all our (The)anthropic hypostasis is the spirit; Jesus Christ; the Son of God.

All Is

"Who then can be saved?"
But Jesus beheld them, and said unto them,
"With men this is impossible;
    but with God all things are possible" (Matthew 19:25-26)

One of the most painful consequences of the Fall, which is also one of our biggest illusions, is our endless worry to *make it*. All of us strive constantly to make it: to survive first of all, but mostly to be related, to work, to create, to evolve, *to love and be loved*, in one word, to *Live*. Yet, the Truth is that there is nothing at all that we can make; that can be done; for already *All Is*.

In Reality, man *cannot create* (make) anything *by himself* (*Love*, life, beauty, strength, *Meaning*); he can only *participate* in the Creation and that is why he *was created* for.

The *seeming inaction* of Adam in Paradise indicates precisely this participation. Adam is not called to create anything. Everything has *already* been created. He is called to *participate* in the Creation; to be a *channel* (carrier) of Light, Strength, Beauty, Harmony, Meaning, Love. But when he becomes deluded and starts thinking that he can be himself "as god" (Genesis 3:5) and a creator by himself, then he falls in the *trap* of *worry* (of taking thought of), of sweat and labor, *"In the sweat of thy face shalt thou eat bread"* (Genesis 3:19). And here, as we have already seen, the bread doesn't refer only to the material bread, but mainly to the *psychological* and the *spiritual* ones.

Jesus is teaching the great secret of *not worrying* (*hesychia*), that is, of *participation*, through all of His Teaching. Through Martha who tries to *make it* and so is *"distracted with much serving"*, He tells us, *"Man, man, you are worried and troubled about many things"* whilst one thing is needed: what Mary "does" who is simply sitting at His feet and *doesn't do anything*, she just *participates* (cf. Luke 10:38-42, EMTV). Through His disciples, He tells us emphatically:

"Do not worry about your life [soul], what you shall eat, or what you shall drink, nor about your body, what you shall put on. Is not life [the soul] more than food and the body more than clothing? Look at the birds of the air, for they neither sow nor reap, nor do they gather into barns; yet your heavenly Father feeds them. Are you not worth more than they? Which of you by worrying is able to add one cubit to his stature? So why do you worry about clothes? Consider the lilies of the field, how they grow; they neither labor, nor spin; and yet I say to you, that not even Solomon in all his glory was arrayed like one of these. But if God thus clothes the grass of the field, which exists today, and tomorrow is cast into the oven, will He not much more clothe you, O you of little faith? Therefore do not worry, saying, 'What shall we eat?' or 'What shall we drink?' or 'What shall we put on?' For after all these things the Gentiles seek. For your heavenly Father knows that you need all these things. But seek first the kingdom of God and His righteousness, and all these things shall be added to you" (Matthew 6:25-33).

Jesus is making clear that the only thing we need is to seek the Kingdom of God, which means participate in the Infinite Wonder.

Yet, here our *pride* will claim its place within us and it will assert that what we have to *do* after all is to enter in the Kingdom of God. So for not maintaining any illusions that we can *make it* in any way to enter into the Kingdom of God, we are being given that wonderful parable of the rich man who thinks that he is capable of *doing (creating) good*, gaining thus eternal life, *"Good Master, what good thing shall I do, that I may have eternal life?"* (Matthew 19:16). But he hears that strange answer, *"Why callest thou me good? There is none good but one, that is, God"* (Matthew 19:17) which indicates exactly this *inability* to *do* (create) Good, since One is the Creator of Good. And next when he hears that if he wants to enter into Life, he must keep the commandments, which doesn't mean to *do* (create) something but to *preserve* what *already is,* he misunderstands the words of Jesus and claims that he has almost made it; he has *done* what he should; and asks whether he needs to *do* anything else in order to enter into the Kingdom of God, "*All these things have I kept from my youth up: what lack I yet?*". But Jesus tells him that he must renounce his (imaginary) achievements (because they are an impediment) and simply follow Him, that is, *participate*. So he goes away sorrowful because he feels that he has managed it so wonderfully up to now.

And here is revealed the reason why we cannot renounce our worry to make it; and this is our *egoism* (our *fallen delusory perception*).

All our *worry* to make it, is based on being "as gods" and all our egoism is built on this illusion; which results of course in all our violence: competition, anxiety, comparison and conflict.

Mary who is not worrying and remains in stillness (in *hesychia*), is not bothered by what goes on around her, whilst Martha who is worrying, compares herself with Mary and ends up feeling superior, "*Lord, don't You care that my sister has left me to serve alone? Therefore tell her to help me*" (Luke 10:40).

Jesus is teaching us in the prayer He gave us (cf. Matthew 6:9-13) precisely this *hesychia* (stillness). The *Lord's Prayer* in its essence doesn't contain some requests but the *experiential conditions* for this Divine Communion.

God puts man in Paradise (internally and externally), that is, in the abundance of Love, to cultivate and take care of it, "*And the Lord God took the man, and put him into the garden of Eden to dress it and to keep it*" (Genesis 2:15), that means to *participate respectfully* in it. Nothing else. But man becomes deluded, exalts himself and wants to be an independent creator, so he gains the labor and agony of the unceasing worry to make it; a futile effort since there is nothing to make (create). Everything *already* is.

All Is.

> "The highway dragged like a snake endlessly
>
> – as if eternally – in the fields.
>
> The stubbles were swishing; it was cold.
>
> And he walked.

He was *surrendered* to his path. [...]

The world moves slowly; things are left in their course. [...]

Eternity stares at you and ponders;

the latitudes, the distances, are devoted to your walk;

the earth exhales devoutly under your footsteps."

(Yiannis Skaribas, *The Divine Goat*, pp. 15-16, translated from Greek, publ. by Nefeli, Athens, Greece)

Nevertheless, since man *was created* free, he is left to his fate… and when he gets tired enough from his fruitless efforts to make it, he returns *humbled* (that is, *receptive*) to his Father's House where he doesn't need to worry about *anything*, since *all exists in abundance*, physically, psychologically and spiritually, *"And when he came to himself, he said, How many hired servants of my father's have bread enough and to spare, and I perish with hunger. I will arise and go to my father"* (Luke 15:17-18). And contrary to any "human" perception that thinks that this return (metanoia) might entail any kind of punishment, Jesus is teaching us that our Father runs to us, *"When he was yet a great way off, his father saw him, and had compassion, and ran, and fell on his neck, and kissed him"* (Luke 15:20), and offers us even more than before, *"Bring forth the best robe, and put it on him; and put a ring on his hand, and shoes on his feet: And bring hither the fatted calf, and kill it ; and let us eat, and be merry: For this my son was dead, and is alive again; he was lost, and is found. And they began to be merry"* (Luke 15:22-24). Yet, this illustration reveals in effect that *we* can *accept* (receive) more than before. The deeper is our humbleness, the bigger is our receptivity and so the less worried is our life.

For as we have seen one of the biggest, *joyful* secrets that Jesus Christ came to reveal us, is that we *cannot make it* in relation to anything, for there is nothing that can be done, since already *All Is*.

We can simply participate gratefully in the Sublime All, "*I am come that they might have life, and that they might have it more abundantly*" (John 10:10).

That means that all our real effort rests simply in *(self-)surrendering*, "*Thy Will be Done*" (Matthew 6:10); in being tired from our "self" so we can come to our Self and thus return to the abundance of Love, of the One.

> "*Casting all your worries on Him,*
> *because He cares for you*" (1 Peter 5:7, WEB)

Joyful News

The joyful news (Ev-angelia) that Jesus not only brought in humanity but mostly *experienced* for her sake, were spread out of necessity, as we have seen, through difficult to understand symbolisms. So the New Testament might now seem to us (and indeed is) a seven-sealed book which is chary of revealing its treasures. Yet, this shouldn't discourage us but on the contrary should urge us in developing finally a living relationship with it; knowing with certainty that if we begin penetrating even a little in its mysteries, they will constitute for us invigorating waters which will quench our spirit's thirst.

Let us sacrifice our intellectual curiosity and that egoistic mind which wants easily and effortlessly to "know everything" and let us realize that if we allow even to one of the seeds of the Scriptures to fall in the garden of our heart, it will soon grow roots and will develop into a flower or a tree of inestimable value and beauty.

Yet, we should understand that for this to happen, the ground of our heart needs to be adequately prepared. Otherwise, the Divine seeds will either be rejected or mutated.

Some of the joyful news (seeds) that Jesus brought and *planted* in the heart of humanity, were that *We Are All One*, that *All will Finally be Restored in the Initial Unity* and that *already All Is*. But these gospels were covered into parables and allegories because they can be easily distorted by our carnal and egoistic mind, thus bringing forth genetically modified fruits.

For example, the Reality of our Oneness, is distorted when we interpret it as a flattening of everything according to which "all are same" (since all are one), refusing thus individuality, uniqueness, harmony and order. And this misinterpretation is highly dangerous because it only leads to a chaos where no one can perform his right part and find his correct place in the common Whole, since everything is mixed and disorientated: relationships, personal talents, destination. In Reality, Unity doesn't indicate an unrealistic and deformed "equality" but an unbreakable interconnection of diversity:

"For as we have many members in one body, and all members have not the same office: So we, being many, are one body in Christ, and every one members one of another" (Romans 12:4-5).

"For as the body is one, and hath many members, and all the members of that one body, being many, are one body: so also is Christ. For by one Spirit are we all baptized into one body, whether we be Jews or Gentiles, whether we be bond or free; and have been all made to drink into one Spirit. For the body is not one member, but many. If the foot shall say, Because I am not the hand, I am not of the body; is it therefore not of the body? And if the ear shall say, Because I am not the eye, I am not of the body; is it therefore not of the body? If the whole body were an eye, where were the hearing? If the whole were hearing, where were the smelling? But now hath God set the members every one of them in the body, as it hath pleased him. And if they were all one member, where were the body? But now are they many members, yet but one body. And the eye cannot say unto the hand, I have no need of thee: nor again the head to the feet, I have no need of you. Nay, much more those members of the body, which seem to be more feeble, are necessary: And those members of the body, which we think to be less honourable, upon these we bestow more abundant honour; and our uncomely parts have more abundant comeliness. For our comely parts have no need: but God hath tempered the body together, having given more abundant honour to that part which lacked: That there should be no schism in the body; but that the members should have the same care one for another. And whether one member suffer, all the members suffer with it; or one member be honoured, all the members rejoice with it. Now ye are the body of Christ, and members in particular" (1 Corinthians 12:12-27).

Accordingly, the idea of the final Restoration of All in the Initial Unity, when it is misinterpreted, leads inevitably to a state of irresponsibility, lawlessness and lack of restraint. And then appears the danger of the perpetuation of this egoistic state which can only have unpleasant consequences for whosoever falls in the distortion of this incomparably joyful Reality.

And of course, it's not hard to understand what could imply the misinterpretation of the prompting of "Not worrying for" ("Not taking thought of") anything since *All Is*. Our egoistic mind hastens to consider, "So I don't *have to* do anything", distorting the Reality, *"Without me ye can do nothing"* (John 15:5); and certainly overlooks the urging, *"Seek first the Kingdom of God"* and doesn't understand that it is not easy, or rather, *it is impossible*, not to worry about anything, *outside* of the Kingdom of God. And we all know that to be in the Kingdom of Heaven is not so easy; it demands a full self-surrendering, which demands in its turn a great struggle, as paradoxical as this may seem. So the distortion of this Reality leads us to a self-destructive resignation instead to our soul-saving surrendering.

So we see that the Good News (Gospels) of Jesus Christ are covered until we are ready to receive them. Nevertheless, one of the greatest Joyful News was the Birth of Christ in humanity, *"Fear not, for lo, I bring you good news of great joy, that shall be to all the people, because there was born to you today a Saviour, who is Christ the Lord"* (Luke 2:10-11, YLT), which means that all these Realities we just mentioned, were planted in humanity's heart and constitute our potential overall and personal present and future.

So let us not hesitate and let us not postpone any more this inner journey into the world of the Scriptures, so we can start discovering ourselves these Divine Realities which are calling us and wait patiently until they can become flesh and bone within us; so that they can consist of our *Joyful Reality* as well.

Epilogue

Love

We do not all breathe in the same atmosphere. Some breathe freely only in materialism; others in spirituality; and others in false-spirituality. The freedom of one man, is the prison of another. But that doesn't mean that there is no Truth.

There is Objective Truth.

Subjective is only the relationship we develop with Her. And the only relationship some of us can have with the Truth, is through falsehood (*untruth*). And that is because falsehood is also related to Truth but in a distorted way; since *nothing* can exist outside of the Truth, outside of Love.

The driving force behind everything that happens can be perceived in a way as a struggle between egoism and Love. Or, in other words, between Love and Her negation, or better still, Her *ab-sence* (lack of essence). And since the negation or absence of Love, cannot really have any essential power over Her, it would be more correct to say that the driving force behind everything there is or happens, *is* Love.

Nevertheless, in our level, when we experience the struggle between Love and Her absence, that is, the struggle between egoism and Love, we often think that egoism is stronger than Love and that is possible to prevail in the end.

Yet, this perception is due exclusively to our limited, reversed, materialistic (earthly), and therefore *quantitative*, view. In quantity, egoism might often win but in quality it's by definition lost, since it doesn't have a substantive hypostasis; there is only as a lack (absence) of something else.

That is why it has only *quantity* and *not quality*, since it hasn't been *created*. And that is why a real moment of Love can overbalance a whole "life" of egoism, "*But the other answering rebuked him, saying, "Dost not thou fear God, seeing thou art in the same condemnation? And we indeed justly; for we receive the due reward of our deeds: but this man hath done nothing amiss."*

277

And he said unto Jesus, "Lord, remember me when thou comest into thy kingdom." And Jesus said unto him, "Verily I say unto thee, Today shalt thou be with me in paradise" (Luke 23:40-43).

It's true that the root of evil in the world is the delusion of egoism. And egoism means, as we have seen, lack of Love. Yet, lack of love means *in essence, distortion* of Love.

The word *quality* indicates what *Is*; what *has been created*. And since the Creator of All is Love, *"God is Love"* (1 John 4:8, 16) and the only thing He creates is Love, that means that the real *Quality* of all is One. So Quality can be defined also as Unity (Love-Life), which when *divided* becomes *quantity* (good-life and evil-"life").

The word *quantity* signifies essentially what *is not*; what *has not been created*; that is why it's always more than Quality. The Quality is Unique, the quantity multiple. For example, our True Love is One; false loves are many.

So we can understand that the existence of Love contains also the possibility of Her "non-existence", that is, the "existence" of hatred. And since Love means Unity and Wholeness, hatred means disunity and incompleteness.

And now we can better realize why did Jesus preach the *Gospel of Love (Unity)* and in what path He is constantly asking us to follow Him, *"If any man will come after me, let him deny himself"* (Matthew 16:24), in order to be *complete*, to become One, *"So that they all may be one, just as You, Father, are in Me, and I in You; that they also may be one in Us"* (John 17:21).

We could say that the "eternal" questions of humanity are related to the following issues:

Evil (egoism).

Pain.

Eros.

Death.

The soul (and the spirit).

The meaning of life.

God.

These seven issues have been the main questions that are troubling man since the beginning of his existence and constitute the main objects of all his essential activities: of religion, philosophy, psychology, art, medicine, science, anthropology, sociology, etc. And all these issues are interconnected by one single thread:

Evil (egoism) is the lack (absence) of Love.

Pain is the means, or path, to Love.

Eros should be based on Love and then begets Human Eros and Divine Eros.

Death is defeated, or more correctly, transcended by Love.

The soul is the human manifestation of Divine Love (and the spirit is Her Theanthropic manifestation).

The meaning of Life is Love.

God is Love.

We could say that Love is one of the aspects of God (even the word *God* is one of the aspects of the *One*). Other words which could express some of His aspects are: Life, Truth, Beauty, Consciousness, Creativeness, Goodness. All these words could very well substitute the word Love. It's just that the word Love seems to contain and summarize, as best as possible for the human standards, Reality, Unity, God. And so *Love* should be the *Mark* of all our meaningful pursuits, for the answer to all our human problems and questions is in essence *One*:

"God is Love".

Bibliography

Abba Cronios & **Abba Poemen**, from John Wortley's *The Book of the Elders: Sayings of the Desert Fathers: The Systematic Collection Translated*, A Cistercian Publications title publ. by Liturgical Press

Abba Dorotheos, *Practical Teaching on the Christian Life*, translated by Constantine Scouteris, Athens, 2000 (see also, Dorotheos of Gaza, *Discourses and Sayings*, publ. by Cistercian Publications)

Abba Isaiah of Scetis, *Ascetic Discources*, translated by John Chryssavgis and Pachomios (Robert) Penkett, A Cistercian Publications title publ. by Liturgical Press

Athanasius the Great, *Works*, Vol. 5, publ. by "Gregory Palamas", Thessaloniki, Greece (translated from Greek)

Callistus (Kallistos) Angelikoudis, *Chapters on Prayer* & **Callistus (Kallistos) Katafygiotis** (presumed the same as Callistus Angelikoudis), *On Union with God, and Life of Theoria*, from the Greek text of Philokalia, Vol. 5, publ. by To Perivoli tis Panaghias, 3rd edition, Thessaloniki, 2002 (translated from Greek)

Callistus and Ignatius of Xanthopoulos, *Directions to Hesychasts* & **Callistus Patriach**, *Texts on Prayer*, from the *Writings from the Philokalia: On Prayer of the Heart*, translated by E. Kadloubovsky and G.E.H. Palmer, publ. by Faber & Faber

Clement of Alexandria, *The Stromata*, from *The Ante-Nicene Fathers, Vol. 2, Fathers of the Second Century: Hermas, Tatian, Athenagoras, Theophilus and Clement of Alexandria* (can be found posted on the website of Christian Classics Ethereal Library)
Evagrius of Pontus, *The Greek Ascetic Corpus*, Robert E. Sinkewicz, publ. by Oxford University Press

Hermas, *The Pastor of Hermas*, from *The Ante-Nicene Fathers, Vol. 2, Fathers of the Second Century: Hermas, Tatian, Athenagoras, Theophilus and Clement of Alexandria* (can be found posted on the website of Christian Classics Ethereal Library)
Gregory of Nazianzus, *Epistle 87 to Philagrius*, p. 264 from Dr. Carl Ullmann's *Gregory of Nazianzum, The Divine*, translated by G.V. Cox, publ. by J.W. Parker (can be found posted on the website Internet Archive) & *Epistle 130 to Procopius*, can be found on the website Early Church Texts

Gregory of Nyssa, *On Virginity, On the Soul and the Resurrection*, from *Nicene and Post-Nicene Fathers, Second Series*, Vol. 5, translated by W. Moore and H. A. Wilson, published by T&T CLARK (can be found posted on the website of Christian Classics Ethereal Library)
Gregory of Nyssa, *The Life of Moses*, translated by Abraham J. Malherbe and Everett Ferguson, publ. by HarperCollins Publishers

John Cassian, *Conferences*, from *Nicene and Post-Nicene Fathers, Second Series, Vol. 11*, translated by C.S. Gibson, published by T&T CLARK (can be found posted on the website of Christian Classics Ethereal Library)
John Cassian, *On Chastity, Twelfth Conference*, from John Cassian's *The Conferences* translated by Boniface Ramsey, publ. by Paulist Press

Isaac of Nineveh (Isaac the Syrian), *Mystic Treatises*, translated by A. J. Wensinck, Amsterdam 1923 (can be found posted on the website Internet Archive; a more up to date translation is published as, St. Isaac the Syrian, *Ascetical Homilies*, by Holy Transfiguration Monastery, 2011)

Isaac of Nineveh (Isaac the Syrian), *The Second Part, Chapters IV-XLI*, translated by Sebastian Brock, Corpus Scriptorum Christianorum Orientalium, 555, publ. by Peeters

Isaac of Syria, from *Early Fathers from the Philokalia*, translated by E. Kadloubovsky and G.E.H. Palmer, publ. by Faber & Faber

Isaac the Syrian, *Ascetical Writings*, Second Part, Vol. 2b, translated into Greek from Syrian by Nestor Kavvadas, publ. by Thesvitis, Thira, Greece, 2006 (translated from Greek)

Kallistos Ware, *The Orthodox Way*, publ. by St. Vladimir's Seminary Press
Kallistos Ware, *The Inner Kingdom*, Vol. 1 of the Collected Works, St Vladimir's Seminary Press

Kallistos Ware, *The Mystery of the Human Person*, Sobornost incorporating Eastern Churches Review, Volume 3, Issue 1, 1981

Macarius the Great (Pseudo-Macarius), *The Fifty Spritual Homilies and the Great Letter*, translated by George A. Maloney, publ. by Paulist Press, 1992 (for a different translation, Macarius the Great, *Fifty Spritual Homilies of St. Macarius the Egyptian*, translated by Arthur James Mason (1921) publ. by Society for Promoting Christian Knowledge, posted on the website Internet Archive)

Maximus the Confessor, *On the Cosmic Mystery of Jesus Christ: Selected Writings from St. Maximus the Confessor*, translated by Paul M. Blowers and Robert Louis Wilken, publ. by St. Vladimir's Seminary Press

Maximus the Confessor's, *Questions and Doubts*, translated by Despina D. Prassas, publ. by Northern Illinois University Press

Maximus the Confessor, *To Thalassius on Various Questions of the Divine Scripture (Ad Thallasium)*, Vols 14B-14C, & **Maximus the Confessor**, *On Various Questions of St. Denys and St. Gregory (Ambigua ad Ioannem)*, Vols 14D-14E, from the series of Philokalia, publ. by "Gregory Palamas", Thessaloniki, Greece (translated from

Greek – for further study see, Andrew Louth, *Maximus the Confessor*, publ. by Routledge)

Nilus of Sinai, *Peristeria – To Monk Agathios,* Vol. 11A, Philokalia, publ. by "Gregory Palamas", Thessaloniki, Greece (translated from Greek), P.G. 79:811-968

On the Necessity of Constant Prayer for all Christians in General, From The Life of St. Gregory Palamas, by St. Nikodemos of the Holy Mountain, translation by St Gregory Palamas Monastery (can be found posted on the website of Orthodox Christian Information Center)

Origen, *The Philocalia of Origen*, translated by George Lewis (1911), publ. by T&T CLARK (can be found posted on the website The Tertullian Project)

Philokalia: The Complete Text, Four Volumes, publ. by Faber & Faber

Symeon the New Theologian, *The Epistles of St Symeon the New Theologian*, edited and translated by H.J.M. Turner, publ. by Oxford University Press

The Exegesis on the Soul, *The Nag Hammadi Library*, edited by James M. Robinson, publ. by HarperCollins, San Francisco, 1990

Vladimir Lossky, *The Mystical Theology of the Eastern Church*, publ. by St. Vladimir's Seminary Press

www.ingramcontent.com/pod-product-compliance
Lightning Source LLC
Chambersburg PA
CBHW070316260626
47160CB00003B/856